Dear M

by

Linda Jones

Copyright © 2024 Linda Jones

ISBN: 978-1-916981-80-5

Acknowledgements

My thanks as always to the many historians who have documented this period. Any inconsistencies are entirely my errors or tweaks to fit the narrative.

Other books by Linda Jones

The Angel

Authorhouse March 2007

ISBN:978-1-4259-9772-9

Witch Hunt

Xlibris 2011

ISBN:978-1-4628-9650-9

The Lost Heiress

Diadem Books 2015

ISBN:978-1-3264-5735-8

The Mysterious Miss Hawthorne

Diadem Books 2017

ISBN:978-1-3264-4939-1

Tenuous Connections

Diadem Books 2017

ISBN:978-0-244-95360-7

Heartsong

Diadem Books 2018

ISBN:978-0-244-71718-6

Children of Eden

Diadem Books 2019

ISBN:978-0-244-80410-7

Claiming Samantha

Diadem Books 2020

ISBN-13:9798581385104

Once and or Always

Publish Nation 2023

ISBN-978-1-916820-42-5

Chapter 1

Joanna and her father arrived on the quay just as the *Veronica*'s gangplank was lowered. They had watched the ship approach from the headland and were eager to know how she had handled on her maiden voyage.

Captain Fogarty came forward to greet them, his whiskered face split by a huge smile.

'I have no need to ask how it went,' Mr Pennicott said, giving the captain a hearty slap on the back.

'As sweet as a bird, sir. She'll break records. There are just a few details I'd like to discuss with you.'

'Get someone to show Joanna round, and we will go below.'

Captain Fogarty threw back his head and bellowed, 'Maxwell! To me!'

A dark-haired youth broke away from the group high in the rigging and swung onto a rope. Joanna watched in awe as he slid down, trod nimbly along the ship's rail and dropped to the deck in front of them.

'This is Maxwell,' the captain said, looking down at Joanna with an avuncular smile. Then to Maxwell, with a much sterner expression, 'This is Miss Pennicott, the owner's daughter. Take care of her until Mr Pennicott is ready to leave.'

Angus Maxwell said, 'Aye, captain,' and slanted a look at the girl. She could not have been more than ten years old. He felt a sudden resentment at being turned into a nursemaid but, after nearly two years at sea, he had learned to obey orders without question. He stepped to the side and said, 'This way, miss. We will start at the bow – that's the front end.'

'I know that,' Joanna replied sharply and marched ahead of him along the deck. Angus heard her father and Captain Fogarty laugh as they turned away.

He caught up with the dumpy little figure in time to hear her muttering, 'I know everything about the *Veronica*, from the first

1

drawings to what cargo she will carry. She has an engine as well as sails but will not use them all the time. Refuelling is difficult.'

Although she barely reached his chest, Angus had the impression he had just been talked down to.

They reached the foremost part of the deck and Joanna turned to look back along its length. Her pride in the vessel was evident in the way her eyes scanned every detail. Her hand lightly caressed the rail and she murmured, 'I wish I was coming with you.'

Angus realised the words were directed at the ship, not him. The thought made him grin and he took the opportunity to study her.

She was not a pretty child. Bundled up in her bulky clothes, she looked like a walking cushion. The brim of her black bonnet framed a round, pale face with a sprinkling of freckles across a snub nose. Her eyebrows and lashes were so pale as to be almost invisible, and the same applied to her lips.

As the breeze tossed wisps of frizzy ginger hair across her forehead, she pushed them back with an impatient hand. She glanced up at him and he was struck by the sadness in her wide green eyes. 'I am sorry I was rude,' she said quietly. 'It is just so hard to think of her and Papa going away without me.'

'You love this ship, don't you?'

'Yes. She is named for my mother.'

Angus did not know what to say. It was common knowledge that Mrs Pennicott had died recently. The poor child was mourning her mother and saddened by the imminent departure of her father for the far side of the world. Moved by pity, he asked, 'Who is going to look after you?'

'I am going away to school.' She suddenly smiled, mischief sparkling in her eyes. 'At least that will be better than living with Aunt Louisa.'

'Don't you like your aunt?'

Joanna laughed, a harsh, cynical sound from one so young. 'She said horrid things about Mama.' She huffed a breath through her nose. 'Although how she could know anything about Mama when she never visited, I don't know. And she is only nice to me if there are other people about. Then she acts fond and keeps

2

saying "poor child",' she mimicked the last words in a simpering tone. 'And I can leave the school when Papa comes home.'

Angus had an absurd desire to comfort the child; she sounded so lonely but determined to be brave. 'You will make friends at school and the time will pass quickly,' he said. Compassion softened his voice and made his Scottish accent more noticeable.

She shook her head sadly. 'Time has an odd way of dragging its feet when you are waiting on something.'

'That's a very wise observation for a child.'

Joanna gave him a scathing look to let him know she did not appreciate being patronised. 'Aunt Louisa says I am precocious. She says it is Papa's fault for talking to me like an adult.'

Angus stifled a laugh. She was the oddest child he had ever met. 'What does your papa talk to you about?'

Animation transformed Joanna's homely face as she launched into a recital of her lessons on navigation, ship building, trade and finance. 'He knows everything,' she finished with pride.

Angus was impressed. 'Then my future is assured. I am apprenticed to Mr Pennicott to learn all he has taught you.'

Joanna was caught by his eager tone and gave him her full attention. He was tall and very thin, with long arms and legs. She liked the way his dark, overly-long hair was tied back and stray curls half-covered his ears. He had a rather long face with sharply defined cheekbones and a determined chin. His nose was straight above a wide mouth, and his dark eyes returned her stare.

'How old are you?' she asked.

'Sixteen. Almost,' Angus replied, ignoring the four months until his birthday.

'Then you have some catching up to do.'

'I already have two years' sea experience,' Angus replied hotly, again ignoring several months.

'Where?'

'Mostly coastal, and twice to the Baltic.'

'The Baltic,' Joanna scoffed. 'You won't make your fortune that way.'

'That is why I'm going to India.'

Joanna sagged, reminded once again that she was to be left behind. 'I wish I was a boy.'

Angus was spared finding an answer as Mr Pennicott was coming along the deck towards them. He could see from whom Miss Pennicott had inherited her stocky build, although her father's complexion was much ruddier. They both had an air of command.

Mr Pennicott nodded to Angus and asked Joanna, 'What do you think of my new apprentice?'

Joanna looked Angus up and down before smiling up at her father. 'He seems keen. At least, he knows bow from stern,' she said with a mischievous grin.

'Well, that is a start,' Mr Pennicott laughed. He turned his attention to Angus. 'Captain Fogarty has given his permission for you to visit your family before we sail. You have five days. Don't be late back.' With a nod he dismissed the boy and urged Joanna towards the gangway. 'Time to go home, Jo.'

In the carriage, Joanna pressed her nose to the window until the *Veronica* was hidden by the warehouses, then she settled back in her seat and turned to her father. 'Please, Papa, let me come with you.'

Mr Pennicott sighed. 'Ah, Jo, we have been through this all before. I cannot expose you to the climate. It is too harsh for ladies.'

Joanna thought he was referring to the recurrent bouts of the fever her mother had suffered in India. They had gradually sapped her strength until she had just faded away before their eyes. 'Then why do *you* have to go?' she asked fiercely.

Mr Pennicott shook his head. How could he explain to a child something he did not fully understand himself? The truth was, George Pennicott did not like women. A decade earlier he had had been a relatively successful merchant who had grown tired of seeing middle men cream off most of the profits from his goods. He needed direct access to the rich aristocrats who craved the exotic Eastern artefacts he was so good at procuring.

He had struck a deal with an impoverished earl with five daughters. The price of Lord Stanley's sponsorship was marriage to one of his older daughters and regular offerings of gratitude – nothing as sordid as money, of course, just expensive artefacts that could be sold in time of need.

4

The eldest daughter, Louisa, had quite frankly terrified George with her blatant sexuality so he had accepted Veronica, the timid younger sister. Consummating the marriage had been a disaster. As virgin as his bride, half-drunk and clumsy, he had left his new wife sobbing into her pillow and rushed to his dressing room to be violently sick. Fate had blessed his one and only coupling with a child – and cursed him by making that child female.

Life with Veronica had been bearable in India, where he could abandon her for long periods as he travelled the country, but her health had broken down and he had been forced to bring her and the child back to England. Here he again ignored his wife for long periods as he went about his business, but Veronica's deteriorating health made him feel guilty enough to remain in England.

During Joanna's infant years it had been easy to overlook the fact that she was a girl. She was sturdy and had a bright, enquiring mind, and he treated and taught her as he would a son. But of late he had been forced to recognise that she was growing up and he found her company increasingly disturbing. His wife's death had given him an escape route.

In an effort to change the subject, he said, 'You seemed to be getting along very well with young Maxwell.'

Joanna shrugged and started to question her father about his apprentice. Where had he come from and why had he been taken on?

Mr Pennicott welcomed her interest. She had been so subdued since he told her of his intention to return to India that it played on his conscience. The tropical climate was just an excuse; it was the thought of her approaching womanhood that made him desperate for escape. If only she had been a boy, everything would have been different. She had a mind any man would be proud of in a son.

He replied to her questions as though he were speaking to a colleague. 'He was recommended by a Lady Leith. I believe his family have fallen on hard times. Fogarty speaks well of him.'

'Will you let me know how he gets on?'

'I'll do better than that. I will make it part of his training to send you regular reports. After all, he could become your agent one day.'

***

Angus walked into his grandmother's elegant drawing room looking very different from the young sailor who had shinned down the *Veronica*'s stays. His coat of fine dark-grey cloth had been cut by an expert, and narrow trousers accentuated the length of his legs. A stiff collar and neatly tied neckcloth lifted his chin proudly. Only the dark, untamed hair marked him as not quite a gentleman of fashion.

'Angus!' Lady Leith rose from the couch and held out both hands in welcome.

Angus crossed the room, swept her tiny figure into his arms and whirled her around until she laughed like a child. 'Put me down, you rogue,' she gasped, hiding her love and pride behind a frown.

He set her gently back onto her feet and bent to kiss her cheek. 'It's all arranged, Nana.'

'That is wonderful. Now sit down and tell me all about it. What did Mr Pennicott have to say?'

Angus flipped up his coat tails and perched on the edge of a chair facing her. 'He hardly spoke to me. I expect Captain Fogarty told him all he needed to know.' He smiled and added, 'Or, perhaps, it was your glowing testimonial. What did you write?'

'That I had known you all your life. That you had received a good education until your family circumstances changed and you decided to make a new life for yourself.'

She watched a shadow darken his face. 'That certainly sounds better than saying my mother drowned herself and my sister was married off to an old man so my father could drink himself into oblivion.' The bitterness in his tone seemed to chill the room. Tension sharpened the angles of his face and his eyes were like chips of jet.

He got quickly to his feet and went to stand by the window. He did not see the busy street; in his mind's eye was the picture of a grey stone tower that seemed to float in the mist rolling in

6

from the sea. He raised his eyes and stared hard until the blue sky burned the image from his brain.

Lady Leith came to stand beside him. She laid a hand on his arm and gently urged him back to sit with her on the couch. 'Don't let bitterness cloud your senses, Angus. Megan is quite happy with her marriage. Lord Rencombe dotes on her. And your father was not really to blame for Clara's death.'

She put a finger against his lips when Angus started to protest. 'No, let me finish. I loved my daughter but I was not blind to her faults. I do not believe she intended to kill herself. It was just another attempt to get her own way.'

Honesty forced Angus to accept her words. His mother had hated living in the old castle overlooking the Firth of Forth. She had missed the hectic gaiety of society and often filled the house with friends who would amuse and flatter her. As a child, Angus had failed to realise how fundamentally incompatible his parents were, only seeing his beautiful mother as a victim of his father's ill temper.

Their last, fatal quarrel had been over his father's refusal to let his wife go to London alone. Angus's mother had run from the room, threatening to kill herself. She had done that before, but this time his father did not follow her. Instead he had shouted, 'The devil take you then!', and poured himself a large whisky. Angus and his elder sister had reached the shore just as a huge wave swept their mother to her death.

Lady Leith took hold of his hand and asked gently, 'Will you go to see your father?' Although she had little time for her son-in-law, she did not like the thought of his estrangement from his only son. Angus, for all his bravado, was too young to be adrift in the world.

'There is no time,' he replied gruffly. 'We sail in five days.'

'So soon!'

'The sooner the better. But, if it pleases you, I will write to Father. I shall be away for a long time.'

7

Chapter 2

It was a cold, grey day when Joanna came to see her father off on his voyage to India. She threw her arms around his waist and hugged him tightly, knowing it was too late for yet another request to be taken with him.

Mr Pennicott reluctantly returned the squeeze before moving her back a pace. He patted her shoulder and said, with barely concealed impatience, 'No fuss, now. Keep your chin up,' before turning to stride towards the ship.

As soon as he reached the deck, sailors rushed forward to pull up the gangplank and secure the rail. Mr Pennicott had already disappeared without a backward glance. Ropes were tossed and, with a hiss of steam, the *Veronica* edged slowly into the channel.

Behind her, Joanna could hear her Aunt Louisa complaining about the cold and demanding they leave. Uncle Horace Fulton made soothing noises but for once ignored his wife's demands.

Joanna watched as the ship turned towards the sea. *I won't cry,* she resolved and swallowed hard. A hand descended roughly on her shoulder and her aunt said, 'Come along, now. There is nothing left to see.' Joanna wanted to stay until the ship was out of sight but was already being half-dragged towards the waiting carriage.

Uncle Horace was more gentle as he helped her inside and took his place beside her, leaving his wife in sole possession of the forward-facing seat. Louisa spread her skirts and stared at Joanna with an expression of distaste. 'I hope you are not going to start snivelling. Your complexion is bad enough already.'

Joanna firmed her lips to hold back a retort. Aunt Louisa had beautiful features but they were always distorted by bad temper. Joanna wondered if she ever laughed and she felt sorry for Uncle Horace. 'Henpecked,' Papa had said when the couple came to Mama's funeral and she had asked why Uncle Horace tolerated his wife's bad manners. 'It pays him to do as he is told,' he had muttered then refused to discuss it further.

Horace took Joanna's hand in a comforting clasp. 'You have been very brave. Pamela would be crying her eyes out if I were to go off and leave her.'

'Nonsense, Fulton! Pamela is much too well-bred to display vulgar emotion!' his wife retorted.

Joanna had never met her cousin and wondered if she was as disagreeable as her mother.

'That has cut me down to size,' Horace whispered, smiling at Joanna and earning a withering glare from his wife.

Fortunately, before Aunt Louisa could think of any more scathing remarks, they arrived at Mr Pennicott's house. When the carriage stopped, Joanna jumped out and ran up the steps. Marshall, the butler, was holding open the door. Aunt Louisa puffed in behind her complaining, 'Don't you know it is bad manners to enter before your elders?'

'It is my house,' Joanna replied.

'Go to your room, you impertinent child.' But Louisa's order was wasted as Joanna was already halfway up the stairs.

Marshall relieved Lord Fulton of his hat and coat while the housekeeper came forward to help his wife. Louisa ordered tea 'Immediately!', then followed her niece upstairs, but only as far as the drawing room where she settled herself on the couch by the fire.

'Did you hear the way she spoke to me?' she demanded as Lord Fulton came into the room.

'No, my dear,' he replied mildly. 'I was speaking to the coachman.' Avoiding his wife's eye, he picked up a newspaper and became conveniently deaf to the rest of her complaints.

Down in the hallway the housekeeper, Mrs Clark, sniffed. She had taken umbrage at Lady Fulton's haughty attitude. It had been the same when the Fultons came to Mrs Pennicott's funeral. That had been their first visit; hopefully this would be their last.

'Acts like she's the mistress here,' Mrs Clark grumbled as she and Marshall made their way back to the lower regions of the house. 'I am glad Miss Joanna will not be going to live with her.'

Marshall was too dignified to agree out loud but secretly echoed the sentiment. It had taken all of his training not to intervene on the child's behalf when Lady Fulton's carefully phrased insults were made to sound like commiserations. And there would be more to come at dinner: Lady Fulton did not approve of Miss Joanna dining with adults.

Joanna had taken all of her meals in the dining room since her mama had become too ill to leave her room. Mr Pennicott had not liked to dine alone and he had held forth on topics the child could not have been expected to understand. At first, that was; now she was likely to offer and defend her own opinions. That was unusual, but not against any law Marshall had ever heard of. He shook his head in anticipation of the fireworks at dinner if Lady Fulton tried to lord it over Miss Joanna.

Alone in her room, Joanna thought how bare it looked. Like the rest of the house, it had been stripped of everything but basic furniture. All the pictures, ornaments and personal possessions had been packed away for storage because the house was to be leased out. The trunk with the things Joanna would take to school with her stood at the foot of the bed; only her toilet items, nightdress and change of clothes for the morrow remained.

After removing her outdoor clothes, Joanna was tempted to stay in her room out of Aunt Louisa's way but she would not behave as though she were deserving of punishment. This was *her* house. Papa had placed it in trust, along with all the things in storage. She could not stay here at present, but it was something to look forward to.

When Papa came home, he would be her guest and that novel thought cheered her. He would be more welcome than the disagreeable woman making herself at home in the drawing room. Joanna was in no hurry to join her there, so she decided to go down to the kitchen to say goodbye to the staff. A small thrill of rebellion lifted her lips; Aunt Louisa disapproved of familiarity.

As she left her room, Joanna heard a noise from a room that ought to have been silent. The door to her mother's bedroom was slight ajar and through the gap Joanna saw her Aunt opening and closing drawers. She pushed open the door and demanded, 'What are you doing?'

Louisa swung round, her face red with either guilt or annoyance. 'I was … was…' she stammered, then remembered she was being questioned by a pudding-faced child. Her anger overcame her discretion. 'How dare you question me? I hope that school beats some manners into you. I have had to give up an extra day to see you delivered after you insisted on going to the docks. I could have been rid of you and on my way home by now.'

Joanna had had enough. She turned her back while her aunt was still speaking and walked from the room – straight into the solid bulk of her uncle. He reached past her and closed the door. He did not speak, just put his arm around Joanna's shoulders and guided her down the stairs to the drawing room.

When they were seated side by side on a sofa, he said, 'They will not beat you at school. I have seen the prospectus and physical punishment is not allowed.' He had been present when schools were discussed with Mr Ebstone, Pennicott's lawyer. Mr Pennicott had approved it because Mr Ebstone recommended it. Louisa had seconded the choice because it was too far from London for regular visits.

'Why does she hate me?' Joanna asked quietly.

'Now, now.' Horace took hold of her hand. 'You know better than to expect me to criticise my wife.'

Joanna noticed that he had not insulted her by denying it. She had often wondered why her aunt never visited. Her grandfather came occasionally to discuss business with Papa, and once, for her mother's funeral, he was accompanied by his son, her uncle. But they had not spoken to her beyond a vague greeting. Only Uncle Horace, who was not really related to her at all, had shown her any kindness.

She sighed and slipped her hand free. 'If you will excuse me, I want to see Mrs Clark.'

Horace did not try to detain her and watched sadly as she left the room. He knew full well the reason for his wife's animosity but explaining it would have placed him in a poor light.

Although he was a viscount, he was not wealthy and he was not a wise investor. Several times Mr Pennicott had bailed him out of difficult situations. Louisa knew this but could not show her disdain directly to a mere trader from whom they might need help in the future. And so, she vented her spleen on an innocent child. But that was going to stop.

***

11

Mrs Clark and Miss Watson, the late Mrs Pennicott's maid, were sharing a pot of tea in the housekeeper's room when Joanna knocked on the door. 'Come in, chick,' Mrs Clark said with a smile. 'You must be in need of a warm drink after being out in that nasty wind.'

The warm welcome was Joanna's undoing, and the emotions she had been holding back erupted in a sob and a torrent of tears. Mrs Clark folded the child in her arms and exchanged a knowing look with Miss Watson.

Both women, middle-aged and childless, had taken the strange little girl to their hearts. They had been appalled at the way she was brought up. Instead of hiring a governess, Mr Pennicott had taken over her education when her nanny was killed in a road accident. Joanna had learned to read from ships' manifests and auction catalogues, and she had learned to count and calculate from balance sheets. She knew more about India than England, and more about exotic spices than good English flowers.

'There, there,' Mrs Clark crooned, patting her back. It was inadequate, but what else could she say? The poor child had not yet got over the death of her mother and now her father was leaving her to the mercy of that harridan upstairs.

Miss Watson's thoughts ran along the same lines. She had been with the family since their return to England and been hired more for her nursing skills than experience as a lady's maid. It had been obvious from the start that Mrs Pennicott faced an early demise. The gentle lady had adored her daughter and worried about what would become of her. She had confided her fears to Miss Watson. It was not right to take a little girl to warehouses, dockyards and meetings in public houses, but Mrs Pennicott lacked both the emotional and physical strength to prevent her dynamic husband from treating the child like his son and heir.

When she had calmed down, Joanna sat primly on a stool by the fire and accepted a cup of tea. It broke the older women's hearts to hear her launch into remarks about the weather as though she were an adult visitor. It was behaviour she had learned from watching the ladies who had called on her mother.

Joanna finished her drink. 'I really came to say goodbye and thank you. Aunt says we will be leaving very early tomorrow.'

'As I have been informed,' Mrs Clark said stiffly. Miss Watson's raised eyebrow made her moderate her tone and she added cheerfully, 'Well, it's not a very long journey to Gloucester. You will have most of the day to get to know your new school friends.'

The novel idea of having children for friends took Joanna by surprise. The youngest person she knew was Winnie, the kitchen maid, who was always too busy to chat. Joanna had given very little thought to the reality of school. Everything had been arranged so quickly; it was only a few weeks since her mother's death and most of the intervening time had been spent with Papa as he supervised the packing of their household contents.

Miss Watson got to her feet and held out her hand. 'Come along, Miss Joanna. Let us go upstairs and make you tidy for dinner.'

Mrs Clark picked up the tea tray and returned to the kitchen. Lady High-and-Mighty Fulton was going to be livid when Joanna turned up in the dining room. She had made it known to Mr Pennicott that children did not dine with adults.

'Do they not?' he had returned, seeming surprised. But he had not sent Joanna from the room.

***

As Joanna and Miss Watson reached the top of the stairs, they heard Lady Fulton's voice from a room further along the corridor. The words were thankfully unclear but when a deep, masculine voice interrupted her she shrieked, 'Never! I will not…' Again, she was interrupted.

Miss Watson hurried Joanna into her bedroom and closed the door. Joanna had been moved down from the nursery when her nanny was killed to make it easier for Miss Watson to take over her physical care. Now she lingered by the door as Miss Watson poured water from the jug into the washbowl.

'Miss Watson,' she said quietly. 'I don't think I want any dinner.'

Watson looked at Joanna's woebegone face and understood it was not lack of appetite. She made a swift decision and smiled. 'As it is your last evening, how would you like to dine with us below stairs? We could make a party of it.'

'Oh yes, please! I am going to miss you all.'

'Then that is settled. No need to change. Just wash your face and hands.'

Joanna's party below stairs was forestalled when Uncle Horace came to take her down to dinner. 'Your aunt has a headache and is lying down,' he told her. 'I shall be very glad of your company.' He offered his arm as though she were a grand lady and escorted her down the stairs.

Throughout the meal he kept up a stream of inconsequential remarks until Joanna relaxed and started to enjoy herself. It was not quite the same as dining with Papa, who usually dominated the conversation, because Uncle Horace asked questions. He also told funny stories about his own school days, adding that he did not expect Joanna to get up to such mischief.

Marshall returned to the kitchen to deliver the verdict that Lord Fulton was a fine gentleman and deeper than one would have suspected.

Chapter 3

Next morning Miss Watson came to help Joanna dress and pack her last few items before ringing for Sam, the gardener-handyman, to take down the trunk. Mrs Clark brought up breakfast on a tray and advised Joanna to stay in her room until the coach arrived. Then she hugged her, kissed her cheek, told her to be a good girl and rushed from the room before giving way to tears.

It was not long before Miss Watson returned to say the coach was at the door. She waited with Joanna until they heard Lord and Lady Fulton pass the door before they left the room. Marshall had all the staff, including Sam, lined up in the hall. Lady Fulton sailed past them without a glance but Lord Fulton stopped to speak to Marshall and slipped something into his hand.

The servants all smiled at Joanna as Miss Watson escorted her to the door and waited on the step until the coachman had helped her into the coach and shut the door.

It was a chilly morning and the temperature in the coach seemed even lower, despite knee rugs and hot bricks. Joanna, who did not usually mind the cold, felt as though a lump of ice was lodged in her chest. Every time she glanced at her aunt on the opposite seat, the block of ice grew larger.

Louisa Fulton's expression was enough to freeze palm trees in the desert. She stared at Joanna with eyes that never blinked; Joanna tried to stare back but was forced to look away first. Lady Fulton did not speak for the whole of the journey, even when they changed from the carriage to a railway train. Uncle Horace sat beside Joanna, ignored his wife as she ignored him and went to sleep.

Joanna had never felt so alone. She had left the only home and people she had ever known; any memories of babyhood in India were long forgotten. Mama was dead, and Papa was sailing to the other side of the world. Joanna would have given anything to jump off the train and run back to the comfort of Mrs Clark and Miss Watson. Even Marshall would have welcomed her with a smile. But that was just wishful thinking; she was just a child, subject to the whims of adults.

It would not always be so. One day she would take charge of her own life. That resolve kept the tears at bay but brought little warmth to her spirit.

After they left the train at Gloucester station, a hired carriage took them out of the city. Joanna could tell from the way the vehicle tilted that they were making for higher ground. They passed through a couple of villages surrounded by bare fields and pastures where sheep huddled against the stone walls.

From her seat Joanna could not see where they were going, only where they had come from. She had been given very little information about the school other than its situation 'near Gloucester'. From travels with her papa, Joanna knew that could mean two miles or ten. She hoped it was less; the sooner she got away from Aunt Louisa, the better.

Even before she finished that thought, the carriage turned sharply between stone gateposts and a sign appeared bearing the legend: *MISS WARING'S SCHOOL FOR THE DAUGHTERS OF GENTLEMEN.*

They had arrived. Joanna's stomach gave a lurch of mingled excitement and apprehension. Would the other girls be friendly? Would the teachers be as critical as Aunt Louisa? She would soon find out.

The carriage stopped in front of a large, grey-stone house. Uncle Horace got out and turned to help his wife. Before he could offer Joanna the same service, Aunt Louisa took his arm and almost dragged him up the three steps to a huge front door. The coachman had gone to remove her trunk from the boot so Joanna was left to jump down unaided. She had no time to look around because the door had been opened and her relatives had already gone inside.

Joanna hurried up the steps and into a low-ceilinged, flagstone-floored hall. She heard Uncle Horace telling a girl in a blue dress that they were expected as he handed her a card. 'Please come in,' she said. 'I will tell Miss Waring you are here.'

Before the girl could do so, a door on the left opened and a tall, angular woman stepped out. She was dressed in a very plain, dark-grey gown. Her light-brown hair was confined in a knot at the back of her head and wire-rimmed spectacles perched halfway down her pointed nose.

She took the card but did not glance at it before saying, 'Lord Fulton, Lady Fulton, I am Miss Waring. Please come into my office. You too, Joanna,' she added when Joanna hesitated to follow them.

It was a very masculine room. A large desk stood at right angles to a window overlooking the forecourt, with one straight-backed chair behind it and two similar chairs in front. Book and display cases lined two walls. Four leather armchairs were grouped either side of a roaring fire in a carved stone surround. A low table between them held a tray with cups and saucers.

Miss Waring helped Lady Fulton to remove her coat, murmuring something about not feeling the benefit when she left, but Joanna was too engrossed in the surroundings to take much notice. Her eyes widened when she spotted a large globe, a telescope on a tripod and, of all things, a skeleton hanging by a hook on the top of its skull.

'Take off your coat and come closer to the fire, Joanna,' Miss Waring called.

Joanna looked around and saw her aunt and uncle were already settled in the chairs closest to the blaze. She did as she was told and had to take the seat next to her uncle. It meant she was still subject to Aunt Louisa's scrutiny, but it was better than sitting beside her.

The warmth of the fire did little to melt the ice in her chest. Her aunt was regaling the teacher with a list of Joanna's shortcomings, punctuated by frowns in her direction. 'It is to be hoped that you do not regret taking her on.' Aunt Louisa sounded, and even managed to look, sorrowful. 'She is sorely in need of being taught that children should be seen and not heard. She has been over-indulged and is prone to voice her own opinions. Her wilful insistence on going to the docks yesterday made us delay our return to London and our own dear daughter.'

Joanna risked a glance at Miss Waring, who was sitting at an angle in her chair as she listened to Lady Fulton, to see how she was receiving the report. She was nodding from time to time but not actually saying much. Joanna had the impression that Miss Waring liked Aunt Louisa as little as she did.

It was only quite recently that Joanna had begun to consciously assess ladies. From the ladies who had visited her mama, she had absorbed the knowledge that appearance mattered. They brought fashion journals and discussed in detail the clothes pictured in them. Newspaper accounts of society events were dissected, with particular attention to who had worn what. But appearance did not always reflect character. How a person had behaved was another all-important topic, and the ladies could be quite scathing at times.

The visitors were kind to Mama, telling gentle lies that she was looking better and would soon be out and about again. Away from her hearing they spoke of how Veronica's looks had suffered with remarks such as, 'She used to be so pretty.'

At their first meeting, Joanna had seen that her aunt was quite beautiful. She had blonde hair like Mama, but it was more abundant and dressed in a more elaborate style. Joanna had innocently expected her to have the same kind and gentle manner. Aunt Louisa opening statement – 'Good heavens, how did *Veronica* produce such a pudding-faced child' – had disabused her of that idea!

Lady Fulton's monologue was interrupted by a light knock on the door and the entry of another blue-clad girl bearing a teapot and milk jug on a tray, which she placed on the table in front of Miss Waring.

Miss Waring took over the conversation as she poured the drinks and passed the cups. 'You must be in need of this on such a cold day. May I offer you a biscuit? They were made just yesterday in the cookery class.'

Lady Fulton's hand hovered over the plate as she eyed them dubiously. 'You say these were made by the pupils?' She decided not to take one. 'I suppose, coming from the lower classes, they need to learn such things. My daughter would not dream of stepping into a kitchen.'

Uncle Horace took a biscuit, tasted it and gave his verdict: 'Delicious.'

Miss Waring offered the plate to Joanna who took one and said thank you.

18

'She should not be allowed sweet treats,' Lady Fulton said, still in her caressing voice. 'She is sadly overly plump already. Takes after her father.'

Joanna knew she was being goaded into behaving in the way Aunt Louise had recently described, but she refused to give her aunt the satisfaction.

As soon as Lady Fulton returned her cup and saucer to the tray, Miss Waring stood up. 'Thank you for bringing Joanna. As you have a long journey ahead of you, we will not detain you any longer.' She picked up Lady Fulton's coat and held it out for her to put on.

After a startled glance, the Fultons had no option but to take their leave. Joanna stood up but made no attempt to follow when Miss Waring accompanied them into the hall. Aunt Louisa left without a single glance at Joanna but Uncle Horace patted her shoulder and slipped a small card into her hand. 'You can write to me here if you have any worries,' he said quietly. 'But I am sure you will have a splendid time.'

It was a kind gesture but Joanna realised it was as flimsy as the card in her hand. Uncle would not do anything against his wife's wishes.

Miss Waring returned to the room and shut the door. 'Now, Joanna, would you like more tea or another biscuit? I shall certainly have one.' She took the seat recently vacated by Aunt Louisa and poured more tea. And she was smiling, a real smile, not the faint movement of the lips bestowed by Aunt Louisa!

Still smiling, she said, 'Welcome to my school, Joanna. First, I would like to say how sorry I am that you have been so suddenly bereft of both parents. I had a long letter from my old friend Mr Ebstone about your family background. He speaks very highly of you but I prefer to make my own assessments.'

That puts Aunt Louisa in her place, Joanna thought gleefully.

Miss Waring continued, 'We will get to know each other slowly. I demand good conduct but I am not a dragon. If you do wrong, I shall tell you privately. When you do well, my praise will be heard by all. Now, to practical matters. I would prefer you to wear a uniform like the other girls but you may retain your mourning for a short time if you wish.'

19

'I don't look good in black,' Joanna said, echoing another of her aunt's pronouncements.

'Looks are not everything,' replied Miss Waring with a sweep of her hand to indicate her own appearance. 'Perhaps just a black armband? My girls are all separated from their parents for one reason or another, and they will understand that you are missing yours. As today is Saturday, there are no lessons. I will take you now to Miss Fielding, our matron, who will see you settled and introduce you to some of the other girls. I am sure you will soon make friends.'

That ended Joanna's interview. She was taken upstairs and handed over to a comfortably plump lady who reminded her of Mrs Clark. Her trunk was unpacked in a room with four beds and side cabinets. The two wardrobes and dressing tables were shared.

Then it was off to the linen room, where Joanna was measured for her school uniform. Miss Fielding talked all the time, mostly to herself, answering her own questions and applauding her choice of garments.

Several ready-made dresses were deemed suitable with a little adjustment and carried out immediately. Enveloping aprons and mob caps were added to the pile, together with the information that household duties were part of the curriculum. A brown, hooded cloak completed the uniform. The instruction that outdoor shoes were to be removed in the hall and placed on the wooden rack completed Miss Fielding's introductory lecture.

They took the clothes back to the bedroom where another girl was sitting at one of the dressing tables. As she turned, Joanna thought she was seeing a fairy! The girl was so dainty, with silvery-white hair and the sweetest face Joanna had ever seen.

'Hello,' she said, coming forward. 'My name is Iris Armitage. I have the bed next to yours.'

'You have saved me a task, Iris,' Miss Fielding said with a smile. 'I was just about to take Joanna to meet some of the other girls.'

'I will do that,' Iris replied cheerfully. 'I expect they are in the day room as it is so cold outside.'

The rest of the day passed in a whirl of new faces and experiences. If there had not been such a disparity in size, it could have been said that Iris took Joanna under her wing. She made introductions, showed Joanna the classrooms and other amenities, sat beside her at meals and generally acted like a mother hen with one chick. Joanna instantly loved her.

Chapter 4

Eight years later

Puberty was kind to Joanna. As she grew taller than all her friends, her childhood chubbiness transformed into womanly curves. Her hair darkened to a deep red, saved from garishness by a hint of chestnut; it was thick, with a natural wave, and hung past her shoulders when not confined. Her brows and eyelashes were darker too, and they drew attention to eyes that were a mixture of green and gold and away from the freckles which no amount of cucumber cream could banish. Her mouth was generous and usually smiling. But nothing could be done about the shape of her face. Stripped of its rolls of fat, it appeared square with a jaw too wide for beauty.

Joanna seldom thought about her looks. Aunt Louisa's comments had been spiteful but accurate. Now, when she caught sight of herself in a mirror, she saw a tall girl with an embarrassing amount of bosom, a plain face, too much garish hair and a critical expression. She was as she was and accepted that this ugly duckling would never be a swan.

Or so Joanna thought. When she smiled or was animated, she became truly attractive in a unique way. But, of course, she never saw herself from other people's perspective.

None of those fine attributes were in evidence on a cold February day as Joanna sat huddled over a bowl of steaming water. A thick towel was tented over her head to trap the camphor fumes that were making her eyes sting. She raised the edge of the towel and took a breath of cooler air.

'Put that towel back, Joanna,' Miss Fielding, the matron, called from the far side of the room.

'I can't breathe.'

'That is why you need the inhalation.'

Joanna retreated like a tortoise into its shell and silently cursed the heavy infection that had swept through the school just after the start of term. Most of the pupils and some of the staff had been laid low by high temperatures, streaming noses and aching bones. Joanna had fared better than some but still suffered from a blocked nose and wheezy chest. These twice-daily inhalations were torture.

By the time Miss Fielding released her, Joanna's hair was sticking to her head and her face looked like a boiled beetroot. She went up to her bedroom to lie down and cool off. She had just settled under the eiderdown when Iris entered the room carrying a tray, which she placed on the bedside table. 'I have brought you some lemonade,' Iris whispered. 'Are you feeling any better?'

'Do I look it?'

Iris studied her with gentle sympathy. She did not comment but her silence confirmed Joanna's fears. 'That bad?' she said ruefully.

Iris poured a glass of lemonade and handed it to Joanna, who took several refreshing gulps. 'Thank you, Fairy. That was just what I needed.'

Iris laughed quietly. Joanna had named her Fairy on the day they first met. It was an apt description: with silvery-white hair and a dainty figure, Iris seemed to float through life, spreading happiness. Strangely, despite her fragile appearance, she was one of the few who had escaped the infection. She had helped those staff who were still on their feet to look after the other girls.

She said now, 'I can't stay. I'm taking drinks to Maureen and Sara.' She topped up Joanna's glass and went out as quietly as she had entered.

Joanna drank her lemonade and wondered what her life would have been like without Iris. From the first day, when she was feeling so sad and lonely, Iris had been her best friend. Nothing seemed to ruffle her calm demeanour but that was deceptive: like a swan, Iris sailed serenely through life, paddling like mad beneath the surface. She was never still – not fidgety, just busy making sure everyone else had all they needed.

It was a trait Iris had inherited from her father, Reverend Armitage, the son of a viscount. He had married a mill-owner's daughter and turned his back on high society. He gave the appearance of a slightly vague scholar but he was aware of the smallest needs of others. He worked tirelessly for his parishioners, and Joanna was just one of the lost and lonely he

23

had gathered into the fold. As soon as it became known that she was virtually without family, she had been almost adopted. She spent most of the school holidays with the Armitage family; she was welcomed, although Miss Waring had quietly advised her to decline the invitations to visit other branches of the Armitage family. Those were the times when Joanna realised that being a welcome guest was not the same as truly belonging.

She finished her drink thinking how lucky she was to have such friends. And there were always Max's letters to look forward to.

On that happy thought, Joanna got out of bed and went to the cupboard to get her writing box. It had come as a gift for her thirteenth birthday, ostensibly from her father, but after three years of exchanging letters with Max she knew who had chosen it. She ran her fingers over the shiny, striped coromandel wood and smiled as they traced the delicate mother-of-pearl inset in the lid. In it she kept every letter Max had ever written, that she had treasured and re-read many times.

She picked up the one that had arrived earlier in the week and read it through again. Max's letters were always welcome, but this one contained the happy news that he was planning to come to England. He did not say when but Joanna began her reply anyway. Hopefully he would receive it before he left India. If not, they would be able to catch up on their news face to face. What bliss it would be not having to wait months for a reply .

Joanna picked up her pen and wrote swiftly. She didn't have to consider her words; she could just pour out her thoughts in the knowledge that Max liked to hear what she had been doing. Just thinking about him made her feel better.

Dear Max,

What a time we have been through…

Chapter 5

Angus Maxwell stepped down from his hired carriage and surveyed the building with a feeling of familiarity. Joanna had added sketches to her very accurate descriptions of her life at school. The grey stone house with its steep gables and uneven roof levels was exactly as she had depicted in one of her early letters.

He walked to the end of the carriage drive knowing that he would see planted terraces descending the side of the hill. There they were, drab at this time of year but his mind's eye clothed them in the summer colours of rhododendrons, hydrangeas and buddleias in full bloom. Joanna's favourite retreat, the grotto, was out of sight but he could see the roof of the dovecote above a yew hedge. He retraced his steps to take in the opposite view and pictured her sitting on the seat beneath the old oak tree.

He smiled. Joanna had such a way with words and drawings that he knew he would recognise her friends and members of staff. He had tried to return the compliment in his letters to her but did not feel he had done justice to the sights and sounds of India. At first his letters had been bald accounts, lists almost, of what he had seen and done. But over the years they had become more relaxed. Mr Maxwell and Miss Pennicott were dropped in favour of Max and Joanna, and their letters included personal opinions and aspirations. Although they lived thousands of miles apart, they had become close friends and he was looking forward to renewing their acquaintance.

Still smiling, he climbed the three steps to the front door and pulled the bell chain.

Miss Waring had watched the young man's arrival from the window of her office. Male visitors were a rare occurrence and this one was not acting like a stranger. She frowned at his leisurely inspection of her property and, when he approached the steps, she shot out into the hall like a watchdog from its kennel. She had the door open before the bell chimes had faded away.

Max took an involuntary step back from the ferocious woman who was glaring at him from behind wire-rimmed spectacles.

'Miss Waring?' he said with a smile. 'I am Angus Maxwell. I have come to see Joanna Pennicott.'

'Have you indeed?' Miss Waring replied, coldly. 'Come into my office.' She marched towards an open door to the left, leaving him on the doorstep. *Miss Waring on the warpath,* Max thought with a grin before stepping into the hall and closing the front door.

Three sickly-looking young girls in mob caps and aprons had converged on the hall and stared at him until Miss Waring barked, 'Back to work, girls.' Max felt a frisson of concern. Joanna had told him household chores were part of the curriculum, but those waifs looked worked to death.

He followed Miss Waring into the office and she closed the door before taking a seat behind the desk. She did not invite him to sit. 'Now, Mr Maxwell, why are you visiting Joanna Pennicott?'

'I have a letter from her father.' He reached into his pocket and drew out a slim, plain envelope.

His name had finally registered in Miss Waring's memory. She usually read all correspondence from non-relatives but had given up reading Mr Maxwell's dry reports years ago. It was unusual that Joanna's father wanted her kept informed of business transactions but not something she could forbid. She wondered now if she had been remiss.

She held out her hand for the letter but he did not hand it across. 'I am instructed to see Joanna read this and discuss its contents,' Max said firmly. The dragon behind the desk glared at him. He stared back.

Miss Waring's expression darkened at the stand off. With a nostril-pinching sniff, she rose and went to the door. He heard her tell someone to fetch Joanna; at least she prefaced it with 'please'.

They waited in tense silence, each deep in their own thoughts. Miss Waring did not keep her girls in purdah and they socialised regularly with boys from her brother's school. She had seen first-hand how secluded girls could be overwhelmed when suddenly exposed to the male of the species – and this specimen was handsome enough to turn the heads of even the most experienced debutantes. *If she were twenty years younger?* Miss Waring quashed the thought and tried to focus on the effect Mr Maxwell would have on Joanna.

Max had taken a stand to the side of the window, trying to reconcile the teacher's hostile attitude with the warm, caring woman that Joanna admired. Miss Waring was reported to be very advanced in her teaching methods. Like Joanna, most of her pupils were from professional or business families and she trained them to be helpmates rather than social butterflies. The thought of Joanna as a butterfly made him smile. The impression he had gained from her letters and caricatures suggested a much more robust and forceful creature.

Joanna was in the junior common room helping a younger girl with her knitting when she received the message to go to the office. 'You've got a visitor! A man!' the girl added with unconcealed curiosity. Visitors were always the source of much speculation and gossip.

Joanna thanked the messenger without showing any signs of excitement and went up to her room for a notebook. Mr Ebstone, her only visitor, was early this month; perhaps he had news of the investments he had made on her behalf. She tucked her bedraggled hair into a mob cap and wrapped a warm shawl around her shoulders. There was unlikely to be a fire in the small room where she always saw the lawyer.

She went down and tapped on the office door before entering. The severe expression on Miss Waring's face made her pause. Miss Waring was usually smiling after taking a glass of sherry with Mr Ebstone, an old acquaintance, before sending for Joanna. Perhaps he had brought bad news.

'Close the door, Joanna. Mr Maxwell has brought you a letter from your father.'

Joanna's eyes swivelled to the man who stepped into the light from the window. Surprise robbed her of her wits for a moment and she stood, open mouthed, trying to see a tousle-headed, lanky youth beneath the fine tailoring of this broad-shouldered stranger.

'Max?' she croaked. Part of her brain knew he must have changed over the years, but not to this extent. His hair was shorter and clung to his head in gentle waves. His face had filled out and was framed by a closely trimmed beard. His dark eyes, which she had noticed at their first meeting, were fixed on her face. She looked away quickly.

Her second thought was, *Oh, why must he come now when I am looking such a fright?* She had no illusions about her looks and accepted that she would never be beautiful, but today she looked worse than usual.

Max was equally startled. He had not expected Joanna to turn into a raving beauty but he was shocked by her appearance. Joanna on paper was confident and witty, not this nervous creature clutching the folds of her shawl with shaking hands. She looked ill. After that first, startled glance, she had lowered her eyes but not before he had seen that they were red-rimmed. Had she been crying? Was she being ill-treated? And she was dressed like a servant.

Miss Waring's fears had gone through the roof at Joanna's familiar address. Now the pair were staring at the floor like naughty children. Indicating the chairs facing the desk, she said, 'Sit down, Joanna,' and then belatedly to Max, 'you too. The letter,' she reminded him for he seemed to have forgotten why he was there.

Joanna took the letter from Max's hand without looking at him. To the schoolmistress she explained, 'Max... Mr Maxell is my father's apprentice. Perhaps Papa is planning to come home.'

'Not that I know of, Joanna,' he said, ignoring the older woman's frown. 'And I am no longer an apprentice. Your father has made me a partner. I have come to register the partnership and check the progress of our new ship.'

It was the first time he had spoken since Joanna had entered the room and the sound of his voice did funny things to her insides. He still had a soft Scottish burr, but now it seemed to rumble from the depths of his broad chest.

The partnership was no great surprise. Over the last several years, Max had taken a large part in expanding the business, travelling to other countries in search of new markets.

'Read your letter, Joanna,' Miss Waring instructed, when the girl sat staring at the envelope, lost in her thoughts.

With trembling fingers Joanna opened the envelope and drew out the single sheet covered in her father's badly formed handwriting. The individual letters looked as though they had been sprinkled from a pepper pot and the spelling was atrocious. With a sigh, she concentrated on deciphering the words.

Max moved back to the window as she started to read.

Dear Jo

Miss Warin has writen to ask were you go when you leave the skool. I don't know. To your Ant but I know will not agree to that. I am at a loss. Better ask Miss Warin to range something.

I hav taken Maxwell into partnership and he will delever this letter. Discuss any worrys with him.

Keep your chin up.

George Pennicott

Joanna did not know whether to laugh or cry. It was so typical of Papa to forget she would have grown up – or even to remember that she was a girl. She did not doubt that he loved her in his own way, but he was not good at putting his thoughts on paper. He sent her frequent and expensive gifts, and her room was filled with ivory carvings, silver bowls and colourful wall hangings, but nothing remotely feminine. Once he had sent her a jewelled dagger!

She had never thought to ask for anything different. School life limited her needs: Miss Waring ordered her clothes; entertainment was included in the school fees, and she received a generous allowance, most of which Mr Ebstone invested on her behalf.

Joanna passed the letter to Miss Waring. Family letters were not usually read but this did concern her. Miss Waring's eyebrows rose in surprise. 'Your father wrote this?'

Joanna nodded and blushed so fiercely that Max expected the blood to seep through her skin. 'Papa has difficulty writing,' she explained humbly.

It had not taken Max long to realise that although George Pennicott was a very intelligent man, he was almost illiterate. He could converse fluently and with a wide vocabulary in several languages, but he was incapable of putting his thoughts on paper.

Miss Waring read the letter through several times. She had come across a similar condition for a former pupil and that helped her to unravel the garbled message. Her eyes widened at the suggestion that Mr Maxwell be involved in arranging Joanna's future and she looked up. 'Mr Maxwell, do you know the content of this letter?'

Max returned to his chair. 'I believe I know the gist.'

'I do not require the gist!' Miss Waring slammed the letter down on the desk and covered it with her hand. 'I asked for specific instructions and Mr Pennicott has thrown the problem back into my lap! Without the written authority for me to deal with it!' Miss Waring's voice rose with each exclamation.

'Perhaps I could just stay here,' Joanna suggested.

Miss Waring's tone softened and she smiled sadly. 'You have already stayed with me too long. Not that I am complaining, it has been a pleasure to teach you. But it is time for you to take your place in society.' She took a steadying breath. 'Joanna, you are a considerable heiress. You cannot simply step into society without a strong guardian. Your father needs to be here.'

'If she waits for George to return, Joanna will be with you into her dotage,' Max informed her. 'Nothing short of a life-threatening situation will make him leave India.'

Joanna had been thinking. 'I already have a guardian. Mr Ebstone acts *in loco parentis* while Papa is out of the country.'

Miss Waring laughed out loud. 'Gerald Ebstone! I cannot see him taking you to dances and driving you in the park.' She sobered again. 'Besides, it would not do at all. He is unmarried and it would give rise to unsavoury speculation – even if he agreed to do it.'

'Then perhaps he knows someone who would.'

'Joanna! That is the most sensible thing that has been said in this room in the last half hour.' Miss Waring became quite animated. 'Gerald Ebstone is from a titled family, a younger son. He is sure to have suitable contacts. I shall write to him immediately.'

Max was heartened to detect traces of the Joanna he had come to know through her letters. He had come to England with the intention of marrying her but the teacher's words echoed his own worry. If English society was anything like the way the European contingent behaved in India, the tabbies would tear her to shreds. She was woefully lacking in grace and beauty, not that that mattered to him, and the trade connection was even more despised in England. As Miss Waring had pointed out, Joanna's

30

expected fortune would attract the kind of men who were prepared to disregard her looks and background for the sake of her money, although the teacher had worded it more tactfully.

Over the years, he had given little thought to Joanna's appearance; it was the intelligent and witty letter writer of whom he had become fond. When he had undertaken this commission, he had envisaged Joanna being placed in the temporary care of a respectable, middle-class family while he arranged their marriage. He just needed to know how she felt about the situation, though he did not think she would have any objections.

'Miss Waring,' he said. 'While you write your letter, may I have a few minutes alone with Joanna?'

The stern schoolmistress sprang back into evidence. 'That would be most irregular.' Then Miss Waring remembered the only positive statement in Mr Pennicott's letter: Mr Maxwell was to be consulted. 'Very well. You may walk outside for five minutes. Wrap up warmly, Joanna.' Her gimlet stare returned to Max and she added, 'And do not go beyond my sight.'

When Joanna came downstairs after collecting her cloak, she saw Max talking to Iris in the hall. They made a startling tableau, he so large and dark, Iris fair and dainty, and they were so wrapped up in their conversation that they did not hear her approach.

For the first time ever, Joanna felt a stab of jealousy. How could Max not be impressed by Iris's beauty? It was so unfair. Max was *her* friend! She had always accepted her lack of looks as a fact of life, but now she wanted to hide away in a dark place rather than see him compare Iris with herself.

The pair turned simultaneously and noticed her. They were both smiling; whether it was at her or an afterglow from their conversation, Joanna did not wish to know. 'I must change my shoes,' she said, her voice coming out rather sharply, and hurried to the shoe rack. As she pulled on her boots, she saw from the corner of her eye that Iris was still speaking earnestly and even had a hand on Max's arm.

She stood up and announced, 'I am ready. We only have five minutes.'

Max said goodbye to Iris and opened the front door. Joanna waited on the steps while he closed it behind him. He was still smiling. 'You described your fairy precisely,' he said, rubbing salt into Joanna's bruised ego.

'Yes. Everyone says she is the most beautiful girl they have ever seen.'

'And kind, too. She was just telling me how unwell you have been.' Max looked down at her and shook his head. 'I thought you were being ill-treated!'

Miss Waring rapped on the office window and made walking motions with her fingers. Max waved back, earning another frown. He took Joanna's hand and placed it on his arm just to annoy the schoolmistress and walked her to the edge of the carriage sweep.

Joanna suddenly felt shy. His arm was warm and strong beneath her hand, and she was conscious of his long legs brushing against her skirt as they walked. Her tongue felt as if it were sticking to the roof of her mouth, which hardly mattered as she could not think of a thing to say.

It was left to Max to open the conversation. 'I hope Mr Ebstone manages to find you a sponsor. I have to go to Glasgow to see how the new ship is progressing.' He paused to give impact to his next words. 'George wants you to launch her with your own name.' Which was not quite true; it was Max who had persuaded him.

'Oh, he does?' Joanna nearly burst with pleasure. Papa had not forgotten about her! She grabbed Max's free hand and looked up. His eyes were a very deep blue.

The surprise brought a touch of colour to her cheeks and a sparkle to her eyes. Max was taking in the transformation when she asked, 'When will that be? Will you take me to Glasgow?'

'I will let you know when, but I will not be able to take you.' He glanced back at the office window. 'Even if that were allowed, I have other business to attend to and I do not want certain people to know I am in England. A launching is bound to attract a lot of publicity.'

Joanna understood. Max had revealed little of his background but had mentioned that he was estranged from his family.

Another loud rap on the window informed them that their time was up. Max squeezed her hands and smiled. 'I hope you feel better soon and that all goes well for you in the future.'

'Will I see you again?'

'Most definitely, though I can't promise when. But we will continue to write.'

'I enjoyed reading your letters. I hope your business goes well. Thank you for coming to tell me about the launching.' Joanna was embarrassed to realise she was gabbling and still holding Max's hand. She withdrew quickly and turned back to the building, Max just a step behind her.

Miss Waring was waiting at the open door as though she had been about to come and fetch them. Joanna hurried towards her.

'Miss Waring! I am going to launch a ship!'

'How exciting,' Miss Waring replied, wondering if that was the only information that needed to be delivered in private. It was to be hoped the colour in Joanna's cheeks was due merely to the cold wind. 'Come inside now,' she instructed. 'The wind is very cold.'

As Joanna passed her, Miss Waring held out her hand to dismiss Max but he spoke first. 'If you have written your letter, I could deliver it by hand. I have other business to transact with Mr Ebstone and will be going to Bristol directly.'

Miss Waring reluctantly invited him into her office, shooing Joanna away when she made to join them. Mr Maxwell had been much too familiar. Iris was still hovering in the hall after mentioning to the schoolmistress that she had met him. The familiar address and Iris's excitement had filled Miss Waring with alarm; Iris also appeared to know more about the handsome stranger than she ought.

The sooner Mr Maxwell was on his way the better. She did not want him turning the heads of any other impressionable girls.

**

'Oh, I do like your Max!' Iris said when Joanna entered the senior girls' sitting room. 'He was so worried about you.'

Joanna had recovered from her flash of jealousy and pulled Iris to sit beside her on the couch. 'He came to tell me that I am to launch Papa's new ship. Oh, and to bring a letter about where I am to go when I leave here. Miss Waring was most upset.'

As clearly as she could remember, Joanna recounted the meeting in Miss Waring's office though she omitted her own reaction to seeing Max. She shared most things with Iris but this feeling was too confused and personal.

'Do you think Mr Ebstone will find you a sponsor?' Iris had no such fears for her own future because it had long been arranged that her Aunt Beatrice, Papa's sister-in-law, would bring her out the following year. 'Perhaps Papa could ask Aunt Bea to bring you out?'

'Oh, I could not impose. Your family have been so kind to me, but I cannot expect to move in such exalted circles.'

'I don't see why not. Your mama was a lady, even if her family looked down on your papa. And you were quite at ease last year when we visited Grandmama.'

'That was an informal visit, and we spent most of the time in the garden.'

Iris had to concede that a short visit to an elderly dowager was not quite the same as entering high society. She shrugged her shoulders. 'Oh well, I am sure Miss Waring and Mr Ebstone will arrange something between them. Now, tell me about launching the ship.'

Joanna had little to tell, apart from the fact that it was to bear her name. It seemed a bit of an anti-climax and the conversation flagged as each girl turned her thoughts to Max.

Joanna had never given Iris his letters to read but she had shared some of their contents. They both envied his freedom to travel and lived vicariously through his adventures. His character had come through loud and clear, and they had both fallen a little in love with him. Speculation as to his appearance had fallen far short of the mark: meeting him in the flesh had literally taken Joanna's breath away. It was hardly surprising if he had felt the same way on meeting Iris, but she still felt that little bit of resentment. Max was *her* friend.

She felt confused as to what that friendship actually meant. It suddenly felt a lot less than she wanted.

Chapter 6

Similar thoughts occupied Max's mind on his journey to Bristol. He had never analysed his feelings for Joanna. At first he had been sorry for the odd little girl who had recently lost her mother and then parted from the father she clearly admired. He had not been happy with the task of writing to her, but he had been prepared to do almost anything to gain Mr Pennicott's approval.

Over the years, the exchange of letters had gradually become a pleasure. Even at an early age, Joanna had relayed and commented on items of news beyond the day-to-day activities in the school. She was intelligent, clear sighted and had a wry sense of humour, and it had been easy to forget she was only a young girl. They corresponded as equals and Max had been looking forward to lively discussions on topics that did not grow stale in the inevitable gap between letters.

The thought of marriage had not entered his head until the arrival of Miss Waring's letter. That letter had thrown George into a panic. He had a blind spot where his daughter was concerned and would probably have forgotten her entirely if Max had not reminded him to send birthday and Christmas gifts accompanied by a personal note.

It was the only time George's writing problem was ever openly acknowledged. It was an odd situation; he could converse fluently in several languages and was a demon face-to-face negotiator, but dealing with an absent buyer was different. He knew to the last sovereign what his goods were worth, but he had trouble putting words on papers.

Max, on the other hand, had a talent for treading the fine line between deference and confidence and he had taken over the written transactions. He was ably assisted by Mahet Lloyd, their Anglo-Indian secretary. Between them they did what they could to guard George's secret.

George also had strategies of his own. He always carried a document case and could extract the right document at any given time; instead of reading them, he identified the papers by their subtly different paper clips. If he was handed something new, he

35

would say he had forgotten his glasses and pass it to one of his colleagues to read aloud. If he was unaccompanied, he would ask to take it away for further consideration. The system usually worked well.

In the case of Joanna's gifts, however, Max was adamant: she was aware of her father's problem and it would mean a great deal to her if he made the effort to write. He had then stood over his employer while George laboriously scratched out a few lines.

Miss Waring's letter had changed everything. George was finally forced to acknowledge that his daughter was now a young woman whose future needed to be arranged. Typically, he had off-loaded the problem onto Max.

'You should marry her,' George had declared with a nod of satisfaction. 'It will tie everything up neatly.' His grin had faded at Max's open-mouthed look of astonishment. 'What's the matter? You seem keen enough to rush down to the docks every time a ship comes in to see if there is a letter from her.'

Once over the first shock, Max discovered that he was not actually averse to the idea. He felt sure Joanna would see the advantages of their union, and the more he thought about it the more the idea of marrying her appealed to him. But he also knew her well enough to realise that she would not take kindly to being ordered into marriage.

It had seemed so simple while he was thousands of miles away. He had vaguely assumed Joanna would be placed in the care of some respectable family in a quiet town where he could visit and gradually bring her around to the subject of marriage. If Joanna were pitchforked into society, it would be very difficult for them at meet at all.

Her appearance had come as shock, only partly allayed by Iris's explanation of recent illness. He did not know quite what he had expected. She would obviously have matured but he but he had subconsciously superimposed George's robust and ruddy features onto a young woman. In reality, Joanna displayed a feminine vulnerability that confused him.

Thoughts of femininity immediately turned his mind to Iris. She really was the most beautiful girl he had ever seen, and looking into her blue eyes he had barely taken in her words. When Joanna had joined them, the contrast was cruel and must have been remarked upon many times. He had been amazed that they were such close friends, but on second thoughts it was not surprising at all. Iris and the rest of the Armitage family had all-but adopted Joanna when she was at her lowest ebb, and Joanna's affection for them had somehow comforted Max. He knew what it was to be far from home and without friends.

Apart from his grandmother, Max had no other personal contacts in England. Joanna's letters had been a link to a life he would have lived if he had not run away to sea when he was fourteen. He had often hankered for the misty hills of his homeland but pride forbade him to crawl back to his father. He had buried his homesickness and applied himself to carving out a new future.

That future had now taken on an entirely new aspect.

***

Max arrived at the lawyer's office without an appointment, but as soon as his card was taken in Mr Ebstone came out to greet him.

'Mr Maxwell! We meet at last. Please come in.' They went through the ritual of exchanging news and the pouring of drinks before they settled down to business.

'What has Mr Pennicott sent me this time?' Mr Ebstone asked. He had handled the British side of George's business for many years and was well paid to see to the transfer of goods without the necessity of talking money.

'One simple and one – well, perhaps difficult task.' At the lawyer's look of enquiry, Max took the partnership deed from his case and handed it across the desk.

Mr Ebstone read it through, not betraying his thoughts on the content by a single twitch. He had a round, placid face and a comfortably plump body, which made him appear somewhat indolent. A bald head and thin, reedy voice made him seem older than his forty-four years. Anyone who assumed that these added up to weakness, however, soon discovered their mistake if they tried to get the better of him. He had a razor-sharp mind that could have carried him to the heights of his profession, but he preferred the everyday business of wills, deeds and small disputes that, with his tactful handling, seldom reached the courts.

When Mr Ebstone finished reading the document, he sat back and regarded Max, thoughtfully. 'Well, my lord, you have decided to come out of hiding at last.'

Max grinned. 'How long have you known?'

'Many years. George is no fool. I was ordered to investigate your background before you set off for India. You did not make it easy to trace you.' He gave a quiet laugh. 'And Lady Leith spun me a story that was too heart-breaking to be believed.'

'I thank you for your discretion. I trust I can continue to be Angus Maxwell as far as the world is concerned?'

'The world will not learn of it from me. But,' Ebstone tapped the document before him, 'registering this cannot be kept entirely private. George Pennicott is well known and so too is Angus Maxwell. Someone at some time is going to put the two together when they hear Lord Robert Angus Maxwell Urquhart of Strathcairn has taken a partnership in George's company.'

'Let us hope it is later rather than sooner.' Max shook his head. 'My father will have an apoplexy and I don't wish to be the cause of his early demise.' That had not always been true: at one time Max could have cheerfully killed the Earl of Strathcairn himself. But years and distance had blunted his bitterness, although he still had no wish to be reacquainted with his father.

Mr Ebstone broke into Max's wandering thoughts. 'You mention another potentially difficult matter.'

'Yes.' Max took out Miss Waring's letter. 'It is about Joanna.' He handed the letter across.

Mr Ebstone read it through twice. Only a slight tension around his eyes betrayed surprise, or maybe humour, before he looked up at his visitor. 'Do you know the content of this letter? Miss Waring has not expressed herself as clearly as usual.'

'The gist,' Max replied, finding it hard not to laugh. 'The lady was rather agitated.'

'As one might expect. My guardianship of Miss Pennicott was only ever a legal safeguard. Miss Waring is far more suited than I to decide on a young lady's future. Here, you had best read it for yourself as your name is also mentioned.'

Max took and read the letter. Miss Waring had written of Mr Pennicott's letter and his abdication of all involvement in Joanna's future. Mr Maxwell was to be consulted, which she considered highly improper. So too was Joanna's suggestion that Mr Ebstone undertake her debut. The letter ended with the heartfelt appeal: *What am I to do?*

'I echo the dear lady's sentiments. What am I to do?' Mr Ebstone said with feeling. 'Has Mr Pennicott given you any indication of what he expects?'

Max laughed. 'George expects...' He paused for thought. George's expectations were set out in another document that was still in Max's briefcase. He ought to hand it over but was reluctant to do so.

Coming to a silent decision, he spoke again. 'George hopes he will not be drawn into the matter.' He considered for a moment. 'Mr Ebstone, I have no wish to sound critical but George is totally at sea in all matters feminine. He does not socialise in mixed company. He has no idea how a young lady should be introduced. To be brutally honest, I think he actually resents the fact that Joanna is a girl, a young lady.'

Mr Ebstone nodded. 'George Pennicott has been my friend for many years but he only once visited my home whilst my wife was alive. It was a difficult evening. He behaved as though Mariah carried some infectious disease and could hardly bring himself to exchange a civil word.'

The lawyer huffed an exasperated breath. 'None of which helps us resolve this matter. It is a great pity Joanna will have nothing to do with her aunt – not that Lady Fulton would welcome the task of bringing Joanna out. We need a lady of impeccable character and enough standing to overcome Joanna's background.' He shook his head. 'I am very much afraid certain gentlemen will only see her inheritance and not a fine, intelligent young lady.'

That was very much what Max had been thinking on the train. One name came to his mind. 'Joanna has mentioned an acquaintance with Lady Ridgeworth, a relative of her closest school friend. I remember her writing about a visit she made to her home and how kindly Lady Ridgeworth treated her. Could she be appealed to?'

Mr Ebstone frowned in concentration. 'I do not know the lady, but Viscount Ridgeworth is very much involved in political affairs. His wife would have entrance to all the most select gatherings. I could make a tentative approach on the basis that she has already met Joanna, but it is a very great favour to ask.'

That was where the matter rested. Before they left the office, Max asked, 'Please may I leave some papers with you for safe keeping? There are a couple of matters I am not ready to implement yet, but I do not want to carry them around with me.'

The lawyer was agreeable and found a large envelope. Max begged paper and wrote a letter which he attached to the outside of the envelope. 'When – or if – I am ready to proceed, I will write to you. This letter explains my reasons for the delay. Thank you for your assistance. Please will you let me know how things are arranged for Joanna? I have corresponded with her for the past eight years and I believe we have become friends. In George's absence I feel some responsibility for her happiness.'

Mr Ebstone agreed, but Max was left to wonder how he could ensure Joanna's happiness if he never got to see her.

The lawyer shook his head. 'I wish George Pennicott felt an equal responsibility. Joanna is an exceptional young lady, not one of your empty-headed females with no thoughts beyond what to wear. I have been making investments on her behalf and at her suggestion. I worry that marriage to the wrong man will stifle her.'

The thought of Joanna marrying anyone but himself filled Max with sudden horror. Had he made a mistake in urging Ebstone to arrange a London season for her? What if she formed an attachment? No! The sooner he spoke to her and explained everything, the better.

The thought of her refusing him sat like a stone in his chest and he was tempted to tell the lawyer not to go ahead with finding a sponsor. But that would be selfish: Joanna had been incarcerated in a girls' school for eight years and deserved a chance to sample the kind of life she was entitled to.

Max silently cursed the urgent business that would take him out of the country for the next few weeks. He would have to hope for the best until he saw Joanna in Glasgow for the launch.

He pushed the other problem to the back of his mind until he heard from George.

Chapter 7

Joanna recovered from her cold and life almost returned to normal. But not quite.

She had detected a subtle shift in her relationship with Iris. From their very first meeting the two girls had confided in each other, so the very fact that Iris did not refer to Max's visit caused Joanna some disquiet. It was quite clear that her friend had been very taken with Max and he with her. It was not surprising, but it made Joanna wish she was small and beautiful instead of a great lump with too much bosom, freckles and red hair.

Several years ago, Miss Waring had given Joanna a detailed biology lecture. The schoolmistress knew from personal experience how terrifying the onset of bodily development and menstruation could be for an ignorant girl. Children growing up in a rural environment absorbed sexual knowledge without realising it, but girls from a more sheltered background like Joanna needed to know why their bodies were changing. Without undue drama, Miss Waring had also outlined what happened between a man and his wife. She had been adamant on that last point: it was not to be indulged in outside the sanctity of marriage!

Joanna had been fascinated and disgusted in equal parts. Disregarding the edict that the subject should not be discussed with the other girls, she had fled straight to Iris. Iris's reaction had been nonchalant. She had seen her mother pregnant with her younger brothers, she had witnessed animals mating in the fields. It did not take a huge leap of intelligence to transfer the act to humans.

'How can you even look at your papa knowing what he...?'

Iris had cut her off with a laugh. 'Well, Mother does not seem to mind – there *are* four of us!'

Now Joanna's mind was applying those facts to Max and herself. Since meeting him in the flesh she had been experiencing graphic dreams that left her feeling ... what? She did not know the right words to describe it, not that she could tell anyone, even Iris. They did not actually do *that* in her dreams, but she had

41

definitely wanted to. The very thought made her blush. It would be too embarrassing if Iris were having similar dreams.

Joanna had just realised that she loved Max.

Several years ago, when the other girls were discussing their dream husbands, Joanna had accepted that no one was likely to fall hopelessly in love with her. She had laughingly informed Iris that it would suit everyone if she married Max. It would be a step up for a penniless boy with no known background. Now he was halfway there with a partnership and he had turned into a rather magnificent man who could pick and choose his mate. It was a very depressing thought.

Two weeks passed without any word from Max or Mr Ebstone. Joanna did not like to ask Miss Waring if she had any news in case it sounded as though she were eager to leave the school. Which she was, not because she was unhappy but she because she felt as if a door to the adult world had been opened only to be slammed shut in her face.

She tried to stifle her longing to see Max again. He obviously did not feel the same way and had even stopped writing to her. But there was no point in worrying; at least she would see him when she went to launch the ship.

Even the thought of entering society had lost much of its appeal. It had been a novel suggestion but had not really made much of an impact. If Mr Ebstone was unable to find her a sponsor, she would just have to stay where she was and make herself useful as a trainee teacher.

Teaching was something she had talked about with Iris while the other girls were conjuring images of an ideal husband. Iris did not want to marry and had set her heart on becoming a teacher. Joanna liked the idea of a home and family, but with her poor self-image she thought men would only find her attractive for her inheritance. If that was the case, she would just as soon remain single and occupy herself teaching until she reached an age where she could concentrate on managing her own affairs. She had long ago given up any hope of joining her father in India. Her life would have to be whatever she could make of it herself.

That discussion had been before she met Max again. Now she did not know what to think.

***

Spring was definitely in the air on the day that Iris received a surprise visit from her parents. A little later Joanna was called to join them in the office. Reverend and Mrs Armitage greeted her with smiles and Iris was almost bouncing in her chair with excitement.

Miss Waring told Joanna to sit down beside Iris, who grabbed her hand and squeezed it, and Reverend Armitage started to explain the plans that had been made on Joanna's behalf.

He was a very handsome man with classical features and only the faintest touch of grey to dim his golden-blond hair. He had the tall, spare figure of an athlete and was totally unaware of the impact he made on women. By contrast, his wife was as round as a dumpling with a homely face that hid an awareness that her working-class background was viewed with disfavour by some.

Mr Ebstone had been busy and Joanna listened intently to the arrangements. The delay had been caused by confusion as to which Lady Ridgeworth Joanna had visited. A reply to his letter to Viscountess Ridgeworth came from Lord Ridgeworth, Iris's uncle. He said his wife had never met Miss Pennicott and he could only assume the meeting had been with his mother, the Dowager Viscountess. However, his wife was not averse to the idea and he would be in touch after he had made some enquiries.

'My sister-in-law, Iris's Aunt Beatrice, is very willing to introduce you to society,' Reverend Armitage said, smiling gently. 'We have been in correspondence, and it is decided that Iris will join you in London for her come-out this year rather than next.'

'It will be so exciting doing it together,' Iris said breathlessly. 'And John is…'

'Iris!' Miss Waring interrupted. 'Please allow your father to continue.'

It transpired that although Lady Beatrice Ridgeworth had never met Joanna, she did know of her. Joanna had been almost part of the Armitage family for so long that she had been mentioned many times as Iris's closest friend. Iris's parents were happy to endorse her character and parentage, and on that basis Lady Beatrice was looking forward to launching both girls at the same time.

Joanna was lost for words until Miss Waring prompted her with a frown. 'Oh, thank you, thank you,' she said. 'I don't know what else to say. How kind of Lady Ridgeworth to go to so much trouble.'

Reverend Armitage laughed. 'Bea will not find it a trouble – she is the most sociable lady imaginable. It is you who will be wilting from all the activities she has planned!'

There being little else to discuss, Reverend and Mrs Armitage rose to leave. Mrs Armitage hugged Joanna and told her she deserved all the efforts made on her behalf. The reverend smiled gently and told her that, whatever happened, she would always be welcome in his home.

Joanna accompanied them out to their carriage with Iris hanging onto her arm. As soon as the vehicle moved away, Iris threw her arms around her friend's waist. 'We are going to have such fun! You will love Aunt Bea. She is Uncle Simon's second wife and much younger. She is very beautiful and wears the most divine clothes. I can hardly wait for next week.'

Joanna felt too emotional for words. She had all but forgotten that her mother had been the daughter of an earl. If Mama had lived, she would have been the one to introduce Joanna. It was a long time since she had really missed her mama but this change of circumstances brought back the loss like a sharp blow. Every girl needed her mama at this crucial point in her life.

That thought made Joanna return her friend's hug. How must it be for Iris to be presented by an aunt because her mother would not be accepted by the highest sticklers?

The mention Iris had made of her brother, John, was almost as exciting. Until quite recently, Reverend Armitage had been the viscount's heir, followed by John. The family had happily ignored the situation; Reverend Armitage was unsuited to life in high society and John hoped to take over his maternal grandfather's woollen mill. When they did think about it, they pinned their hopes on the widowed viscount remarrying and producing an heir of his own. Those hopes had been realised when Lady Beatrice had presented him with a healthy baby boy.

John still needed to know how to manage the estates because the viscount was already in his fifties and might die before his son was old enough to assume control. To that end, John had attended university and was now ready to learn about society so he would be capable of mentoring his young cousin if the need arose.

'Is John really willing to give up the mill?' Joanna asked. 'He has worked so hard on improving the workers' conditions.'

'He has not given it up, just delayed his full involvement for the time being. We were all so delighted when Bea had a son. Although he never mentioned it, Papa was dreading the thought of assuming the title and compelling John to deputise for him.'

Iris grinned. 'Can you imagine him getting dressed up and going to parties?'

'I can see him giving a blistering speech in the House of Lords!' Both girls laughed as they pictured it. Reverend Armitage was a mild man, and his stern sermons were listened to for their rarity. He usually advocated tolerance and forgiveness but, when aroused, he could rain hellfire down on the heads of the truly evil.

Iris's thoughts had returned to her brother. 'I can imagine the sensation John will create when he's dressed up and going to parties!' she giggled. 'It is just as well we will be there to protect him from all the debutantes and mamas. Poor boy, he will regret ever going to Town.'

'And what about the sensation you will create? All the men will be tripping over themselves to dance with you.'

Iris shook her head. Modesty was a family trait; neither John nor Iris had ever traded on their looks though they were not blind to the effect they had on other people. Both took after their father and from him they had learned that beauty was only skin deep. He had taught all of his children to look beyond a person's face and appreciate the character within. It made Joanna feel at ease in their family instead of sticking out like a brown hen in a flock of exotic birds.

The sound of a bell reminded the girls that, however excited they felt, the school routine continued on its normal course. As they made their way to the classroom, Joanna thought it was going to be difficult to concentrate on French verbs!

Chapter 8

It had been arranged that John would escort the girls to London, but the day before they were due to leave a carriage drew up outside the school. A group of girls, enjoying their free time in the unusually warm sunshine, watched as a footman in smart livery jumped down from beside the driver and opened the carriage door. He helped down two ladies. They both wore brown travelling costumes but the style and quality of the younger woman's dress marked her as a lady of quality. Her companion was older, larger and not so openly friendly.

Lady Ridgeworth smiled at the watching girls and asked, 'Please could one of you tell Miss Waring that Lady Ridgeworth would like to see her?'

There was a little pushing and shoving until the youngest girl sped away to the front door. The others trailed behind the two visitors, agog to see what was about to happen.

Miss Waring met them as they entered the hall. Lady Ridgeworth held out her hand. 'Miss Waring? Please forgive my intrusion.'

Miss Waring shook the proffered hand. 'Lady Ridgeworth, welcome. Please come to my office.'

'I could not wait for Iris and Miss Pennicott to arrive in London,' Lady Ridgeworth began as soon as they were alone.

Without staring, Miss Waring had assessed the elegant clothes and small velvet hat that exactly matched the lady's light-brown hair and wondered if Lady Ridgeworth had come to assess Joanna for herself.

'Neither could my mother-in-law,' Lady Ridgeworth continued with a wry grimace. 'Upon her orders, I have been sent to convey the girls to Bath for a preliminary kitting out.' She laughed, an action that lit her unremarkable face to something approaching beauty. 'Mother-in-law will not have them arriving in town in their school uniforms.'

Miss Waring did not know whether to be charmed or insulted. Her pupils did have other clothes for when they left the school premises, and mostly they were supplied with new outfits when they went home for their holidays. Miss Waring attended to those girls like Joanna who had no accessible family. The clothes might not be very fashionable but they were the best Miss Waring could find.

'They do have other clothes.' She looked again at her visitor. 'Perhaps not up to your standard.'

'Oh, it does not worry me,' Lady Ridgeworth assured her quickly. 'But my mother-in-law would consign anything less than the highest couture to the charity basket! I do believe she owns more clothes than I do!'

Having met the dowager, Miss Waring had to agree. The expression 'mutton dressed as lamb' came to mind and was squashed as unkind.

'Will it cause you much trouble?' Lady Ridgeworth asked.

Miss Waring's wandering thoughts were jerked back to the present. 'I beg your pardon? Do you mean to take the girls today?'

Lady Ridgeworth looked at her intently. That was definitely dismay on the teacher's face. 'Oh, I see that it would. How thoughtless of me. Do they have much to pack?'

'It is not that.' Miss Waring pulled herself together. 'It is just that we usually give a party for the girls when they leave us.'

'Then we must not disappoint them.' Lady Ridgeworth pursed her lips before saying, brightly, 'Could you possible find me a bed for the night? I would love to join in the celebration and then we can leave tomorrow!'

Her winsome smile completely disarmed Miss Waring. She thought of the plain bedrooms, the narrow beds and shared washing facilities. 'It will seem very spartan,' she warned, 'but of course you are welcome.'

'There, I knew it! Iris has told us how good you are!' Lady Ridgeworth turned to her maid who was waiting patiently just inside the door. 'Vera! Take the carriage into Gloucester and purchase whatever I will need for the night. Oh, and some treats for the girls who will be staying on. You don't mind?' She addressed the last remark to Miss Waring.

'Not at all.' Miss Waring felt a little out of breath. She was used to being in charge but this lady was rather like a whirlwind carrying all before her.

After the maid had left on her errand, Miss Waring sent one girl to fetch Iris and Joanna and another to order a tray of tea.

Lady Ridgeworth removed her hat and outer jacket and made herself comfortable in one of the large armchairs. She looked around, 'What a very interesting room.' She jumped to her feet. 'May I look through your telescope?' Unused to being denied, she was already skipping across the room. 'How does it work?'

Miss Waring showed her how to adjust the focus and stood back. 'It is better at night when the stars are out. I use it to teach the girls just how insignificant we are on our tiny planet.'

Lady Ridgeworth was not listening. With a series of 'Ohs' and 'Ahs', she swung the telescope from side to side. 'Oh, it makes the gravel look like huge boulders. And I can see houses on that hill!' Only the arrival of Iris and Joanna dragged her away from the new toy.

Iris was enveloped in a hug and Joanna held at arm's length while Lady Ridgeworth looked her over. 'Mother-in-law was right. With that hair you will stand out.'

Joanna was not sure if that was good or bad, but Lady Ridgeworth was rattling on about someone called Monsieur Claude who was a magician with hair. Joanna did not think he had used his skill on Lady Ridgeworth whose hair was styled in a simple knot at the back of her head.

Iris moved closer to Joanna and whispered, 'Don't worry. She stops for breath at least once a week!'

The tea tray arrived. As she poured the drinks, Miss Waring wondered what she was going to do with her volatile visitor for the rest of the day. It was impossible to guess her age; one moment she was very much a grand lady and the next as impulsive as a young girl. She would have to rely on Iris to entertain her aunt.

She passed her visitor a cup of tea and said, 'I will have to leave you soon to take a class. Iris and Joanna will be excused lessons for the rest of the day. I am sure they will be glad to show you around.'

'Oh, it is choir practice,' Joanna said, sounding disappointed.

'Singing!' chirped Lady Ridgeworth and clapped her hands. 'I adore singing.! Please may I join you?'

Miss Waring had no choice but to agree, so they finished their tea and trooped off to the music room.

Fortunately, Lady Ridgeworth had a reasonably good voice; the disruption came from her request to teach the girls a new song. It was phrased as a request but Miss Waring had come to accept that, coming from Lady Ridgeworth, it was tantamount to an order. The song was sung in overlapping parts, causing much hilarity when different sections of the choir forgot which phrase they were meant to be singing. The girls loved it, but Miss Waring heaved a sigh of relief when a bell rang to announce the end of the lesson.

The next hurdle was lunch. Food at the school was nutritious and plentiful but Miss Waring knew it would not be like the meals usually served to a titled lady. She briefly considered having a daintier meal prepared and served in her office-cum-sitting room but Lady Ridgeworth had embraced a day as a schoolgirl and had assumed she would eat in the dining room with the girls.

She politely declined a place at the teachers' table. 'Please may I sit with the girls?' she pleaded. 'I have not had this much fun for I don't know how long.'

She queued at the counter and carried her own plate of cottage pie and carrots to one of the long tables, where she sat on a backless stool. Plain water was the only beverage on offer but she accepted it as though it were the finest wine. She appeared a little confused when their empty plates were passed along to the girl at the end of the table who carried them away.

'This is such fun,' she laughed when the rest of them got up to collect their puddings.

From her place at the teachers' table, Miss Waring wondered how the occupants of Lady Ridgeworth's table had managed to eat anything while keeping up a stream of conversation. She did not insist on silence at mealtimes but would normally have censured the volume of laughter. Lady Ridgeworth had not dominated the conversation, just acted like a hostess making sure everyone had a chance to speak. Everyone having a wonderful time and receiving envious glances from the girls at the other tables.

At the end of the meal Lady Ridgeworth thanked Miss Waring. 'I never went to school. I did not know it was such fun.'

'You would not say that if it was your turn for washing up or cleaning the grates,' Iris assured her with a laugh. Then she added, 'But I expect you would make a game of it!'

Joanna had been very reticent about joining in the banter at the table. She liked Iris's aunt but did not want to put herself forward; so much depended upon Lady Ridgeworth liking her. On the other hand, she did not wish to be thought dull.

As the teachers and other girls dispersed for the half-hour recess before afternoon lessons, she suggested, 'Would you like to see around the grounds? The plants are not at their best, but I think you will enjoy the view from the grotto.'

They did not need coats and, although the sun was shining, it was not powerful enough for them to need parasols. Joanna led the way to her favourite part of the garden, reached by steps descending the terraces. At every level there were signs of new growth and the smell of damp earth. The grotto faced out towards the city of Gloucester, which seemed to float in a light haze.

'Oh, this in enchanting!' Lady Ridgeworth exclaimed. 'I feel like one of the gods looking down on my realm. Is that the cathedral?' she asked, pointing.

Iris and Joanna identified some of the other churches and away in the distance the line of the Malvern Hills. 'I do not know how you can bear to leave this lovely place,' Lady Ridgeworth remarked as they sat on the stone bench and gazed at the view. 'I spent the early part of my life in East Anglia, which is very flat. This is much more interesting.'

Joanna added to the conversation by describing the scenery around Bristol and the Severn Estuary, and that led to the subject of her father sailing to India. 'I so wanted to go with him at the time,' she said wistfully. 'I was very nervous about coming to school.' She smiled at her friend. 'But Iris has been my friend from the very first day. Her family have been so good, and now you are going to take that kindness even further. I do thank you, Lady Ridgeworth,' she finished sincerely. She had to blink hard to hold back the threatening tears.

'Now, now,' Lady Ridgeworth replied. 'I am really looking forward to seeing you take the town by storm.'

'Me?' Joanna gasped.

'Well, both of you. The contrast will have everyone's attention.' She caught the look of dismay on Joanna's face and took her hand. 'That was a compliment! With the right clothes and your beautiful hair styled properly, you will look quite stunning.'

'Even with freckles?'

'Even with freckles. You will wear them with pride, as our grandmothers wore beauty patches.'

They continued to chat about the activities awaiting them in London until a chill wind sprang up to remind them that is was still early March. Iris led the way saying, 'It must be time for lesson break. I wonder if we will still get biscuits with our tea, what with it being party time in a few hours.'

Iris drew further ahead when Lady Ridgeworth stopped to examine the leaf buds just breaking open on a bush. Without looking up, she asked, 'What do you hope to achieve from this season?'

'I'm sorry. I don't understand,' Joanna replied.

'Are you hoping for a marriage proposal? Iris's parents feel she is too young to make any commitments this year. In the absence of your father, I need to know who has the authority to sanction any proposal you receive.'

Joanna ignored the image of Max that immediately came to mind. 'I have not really given much thought to marriage.' She intercepted Lady Ridgeworth's sceptical glance and added, 'Truly. Until a few weeks ago I was resigned to staying with Miss Waring until I reach my majority.'

'Is there really no chance of your father returning? Or perhaps sending for you to join him in India?'

Joanna laughed. 'It is a firm no to your first question. I do not believe he ever had any intention of returning. And as for the second, I can only say – I hope not!'

Lady Ridgeworth frowned. 'I am sure you said you wanted to go to India.'

'I did – when I was ten years old! I have since discovered that the only thing I inherited from my mama is an intolerance of very hot weather.'

'That would make life difficult.'

They had reached the school and the subject was dropped in favour of examining the parcels the maid had stacked on the common-room table. As Joanna and Lady Ridgeworth entered, Vera was fending off the inquisitive fingers of the girls who clustered around.

'There you are, my lady!' she said with feeling. 'What am I to do with all this? The food items have gone straight to the kitchen but,' she actually grinned at her mistress, 'I thought a few other bits would not go amiss.'

'No, indeed! What have we here?'

Vera had obviously taken the instruction 'a few treats' liberally. She had raided the stalls in Gloucester market for ribbons, combs, beads and other knick-knacks. At a glance Joanna decided there were enough items for every girl to receive a gift, plus a few extra. How they were to be distributed without starting a war was another problem.

The arrival of Miss Waring restored order and solved the problem. 'With your permission, Lady Ridgeworth, we will let the girls take turns to select a gift. The rest can be given as prizes in the party games.' Leaving Vera to oversee the selections, Miss Waring took their guest to her office where they could drink their afternoon tea in peace.

It was a very productive half-hour. Lady Ridgeworth asked pertinent questions and received candid answers. By the time the teapot was empty, they had reached agreement on Mr Pennicott's unsatisfactory behaviour, Joanna's good character and intelligence, and a promise that whatever happened during the season, Joanna would always be assured of a home at the school.

Lady Ridgeworth did not share Miss Waring's unease about Mr Maxwell's involvement. If he was well set-up physically and financially, he would be a prime husband candidate for Joanna, and they shared a common background and a long correspondence. She would worry about Joanna's aversion to the heat as and when the occasion arose.

***

The party was a great success. The austere dining room had been transformed with colourful balloons and streamers. Excited girls in their best dresses danced reels, played games and generally had a wonderful time, even before the food was laid out on the tables that had been pushed back against the walls.

The teachers had relaxed their dress code and either supervised the games or watched indulgently from the side lines. Lady Ridgeworth, wearing a pretty pink blouse Vera had bought to brighten up her travelling costume, joined in the fun and handed out the prizes.

At eight o'clock, Miss Waring reluctantly drew the revels to an end. She presented Iris and Joanna with photographs of the school contained in a leather wallet that could be folded back to form a standing frame. Opposite the photographs were personal messages of good luck and encouragement from the teachers. Then it was evening prayers and the girls were sent off to bed.

Iris and Joanna were the last to leave. One on each side, they kissed Miss Waring's cheeks and whispered thank you before they ran off giggling.

Miss Waring, a little pink in the cheeks, spoke to her guest. 'Thank you for your contributions to the party and especially for joining in the games. The girls enjoyed it immensely. I am sure it is not the kind of party you are accustomed to.'

Lady Ridgeworth laughed. 'Indeed! In London I would not even be ready to go out. But I have enjoyed myself so much. May I thank *you* for making this a day I shall never forget?' She turned away suddenly as though taking one last look at the room, but not before Miss Waring had noticed her quivering lips.

'My lady?' Miss Waring said softly.

'Please forgive me. It is just that I never went to parties when I was a girl. This,' she waved a hand to indicate the room, 'is all so innocent. They tried hard to win the games, but it was all friendly and several times I noticed the older girls giving way to the young ones. At Ton parties one always has to be the best dressed, the best dancer, the most successful.' She laughed ruefully. 'And when success is achieved, there is always someone to find a fault. I feel it would be kinder to leave Iris and Joanna with you than to subject them to society.'

'I had a season many years ago and know exactly what you mean,' Miss Waring confided. 'I was not a success, but I have found great satisfaction in teaching my girls to see through the artificiality. I am confident they will find the path they are meant to tread.' She shrugged her shoulders. 'Oh, my, we are getting maudlin. Would you care to pursue a more cheerful conversation in my office, which is also my sitting room?'

'Thank you, no. I think I will end my one and only school day on the right note and retire to my bed. Thank you again.' With a wave and a smile Lady Ridgeworth went up to the plain bedroom where Vera Martin had laid out a cotton nightdress and the essential toiletries. For the first time in many years, Bea washed her face and hands in cold water and put herself to bed.

Chapter 9

Next morning the whole school turned out to wave goodbye to Iris and Joanna. There were a few moments of chaos as everyone hugged or shook hands before the girls were helped into the carriage by the footman.

Joanna had a fleeting thought as to where he, the driver and the carriage had been since yesterday. The school only had a small trap and an ancient pony housed in a shed behind the vegetable garden; it was not large enough for a carriage, and there was nowhere for the driver and footman to sleep. Next moment her thoughts swung back to the present. *This was it. The start of a whole new life!*

As the carriage pulled away, Iris asked with a huge grin, 'Did you sleep well, Aunt Bea?' It was the first opportunity she'd had to ask because Miss Waring had wisely sent a light breakfast up to Lady Ridgeworth in her room. She did not want to strain the lady's good nature by serving her porridge and warm milk in the dining room.

'Yes, thank you, Iris,' she replied. 'But I do not understand why you are laughing.'

'Well, it was not like your room at home!'

Lady Ridgeworth pictured her spacious bedroom in London, with its wide bed and soft pillows and usually a large warm husband. Just the thought of it made her want to return to it very soon. Her smile was reminiscent as she said, 'It was a bit lonely.' She waited for the giggles to subside. 'And I do not usually go to bed quite so early.'

She caught sight of her maid's raised eyebrow and quickly changed the subject. 'That green costume suits you very well, Joanna.'

Joanna was rather proud of her outfit. She knew it was not the height of fashion but Miss Waring had approved the slightly dipped waist and the way most of the skirt material flattened the front and bunched at the back. She would have liked to return the compliment – Lady Ridgeworth's costume had a definite bustle and the pink blouse added a touch of lightness to the sombre brown – but it seemed too personal so she simply replied, 'Thank you, Lady Ridgeworth. Miss Waring chose the costume but I made the hat myself.'

'Very nice, too. You are not a frilly person. You must resist the modiste's efforts to cover you in bows and ruffles. You must go for understated elegance.'

Joanna replied dutifully, 'If you say so, Lady Ridgeworth.'

'Hmm,' Lady Ridgeworth murmured. 'I think we can dispense with the Lady Ridgeworth. As we will be spending some time with my mother-in-law, it will cause confusion. Iris calls me Aunt Bea, so you may call me Lady Bea. That still has a slight tinge of formality and will not upset too many people.'

There was a pause in conversation while they transferred from carriage to train. The footman saw them settled in a first-class carriage before taking himself off to join the lesser mortals in third class.

Lady Bea took up the conversation where she had left off. 'As I was saying, manners in London can be formal to the point of stuffiness. It annoys me, but I will try not to show you up in public.'

She said that so seriously that it took Joanna a moment to realise that Lady Bea was promising to mind her own manners for the sake of her young charges. She exchanged a puzzled look with Iris who was trying hard not to laugh. A soft snort from Vera left Joanna more confused than ever. Iris touched her hand and whispered, 'You'll see.'

'My mother-in-law is a stickler for convention,' Lady Bea continued, ignoring the suppressed giggles. 'But you will know that already, having visited her before.'

'It was a very short visit,' Joanna explained. 'Miss Waring took a small group of us to Bath on a sketching trip. As Iris was one of the party, Lady Ridgeworth invited us all to afternoon tea.'

'And Grandmama was in a very mellow mood that day,' Iris added. 'After greeting us and admiring our sketchbooks, she sent us girls into the garden so she could talk to Miss Waring. Tea was taken ceremoniously in the dining room – the full menu and maids to serve. I don't think a word was spoken the whole time.'

Joanna recalled the meeting. If that was an example of Lady Ridgeworth in a mellow mood, she was dreading the coming days.

'Simon says she gets that from the Queen. Mother-in-law was a personal friend of Her Majesty,' Lady Bea added for Joanna's benefit. 'Meal times are for eating, not gossiping. I am still working on getting her to change her mind.'

'Best of luck!' Iris laughed.

The rest of the short journey to Bath was spent reminiscing about meals past and in particular last evening's party.

The cab from the station stopped half way along a terrace of tall white houses. The footman helped them alight and then they crossed three wide steps that bridged a sunken area protected by delicate iron railings.

The door was opened by an elderly man who smiled at Lady Bea before whispering, 'Her ladyship is in the drawing room.' His voice held a warning note and Bea touched his arm. 'We will see ourselves up,' she said and beckoned the girls to follow her up the curved staircase to the first floor.

Joanna's second meeting with the Dowager Viscountess Ridgeworth was a far cry from the welcome she had received when they first met. Dressed in a highly elaborate gown of purple silk, and with a frivolous lace cap perched on top of her tightly curled grey hair, Lady Ridgeworth sat regally in a wing chair facing the door of the drawing room. She was on the small side and rather thin, but still managed to look imposing.

Lady Bea sailed into the room unannounced, Iris and Joanna trailing in her wake.

'Where is Pontin? Why is he not here to announce you?' the Dowager demanded.

'I told him not to, Mother-in-law. You were expecting us and I knew my way up the stairs. Why subject the poor man to an unnecessary climb?'

'It is what I pay him for! And I expected you yesterday.'

'I was delayed.'

The Dowager sniffed. 'Your luggage managed to make it on time.'

'It was on a different train.'

The Dowager sniffed again and muttered something about lack of organisation. Ignoring the outburst, Lady Bea bent down and kissed her wrinkled cheek. 'Well, we are here now. Iris come and kiss your grandmama.'

Joanna took the opportunity to refresh her memory of the cluttered room. If anything, there were even more knick-knacks, cushions and fringes than she remembered. Dark-green wallpaper and curtains added to the claustrophobic atmosphere.

After Iris had greeted her grandmother and received a grudging pat on the shoulder, Lady Bea drew Joanna forward. 'Miss Joanna Pennicott, Mother-in-law. I understand you already know her.'

Eyes like chips of coal focused on Joanna's face. She forced herself not to cringe and converted the urge into a curtsey. 'How do you do, Lady Ridgeworth?'

'Hmm.' Lady Ridgeworth's eyes travelled down Joanna's length and back up to her face. 'Hmm,' she muttered again. 'No looks to speak of, but her figure will have the men drooling. A pity the money comes from trade.'

Joanna was appalled by such rudeness and longed to answer back, but she was a guest in the lady's house and bit her tongue.

'Don't just stand there! Have you nothing to say for yourself?'

Joanna summoned up a smile. Returning the straight glance, she said demurely, 'Thank you for inviting me into your home, Lady Ridgeworth.'

The old lady snorted and actually smiled. 'Spirit! I like that. I am not deceived by that innocent smile, miss. You want to give me my own back!' Joanna simply inclined her head. 'Take them away, Beatrice. The sooner you have them looking fit for company the better. And where did you get that blouse?'

Lady Bea fluffed the pink frill at her neck. 'Gloucester. Don't you just love the colour?'

'Go away. You never had a dot of dress sense. I will come to London with you and supervise their wardrobes.'

Iris gasped and said, 'Really, Grandmama, there is no need to exert yourself. We will mana—'

'I will exert myself how and when I wish! And if your late arrival is your idea of managing… Oh, take yourselves off, all of you, and don't keep me waiting for my lunch!'

Once they were out of earshot, Lady Bea heaved a sigh of relief. As she led the way up the second staircase she said, 'Sometimes, Iris, I wish your papa was not such a dutiful son. I deliberately kept our plans to the smallest circle possible, but in his weekly epistle he told of your trip to London and Mother-in-law took the matter into her own hands.'

Vera met them at the door of Lady Bea's bedroom. 'The young ladies are upstairs. They will have to share because Mr John Armitage is expected today.'

'John is coming here?' Iris echoed. 'Is that another example of Grandmama taking over the arrangements?'

'The first of many,' Lady Bea replied morosely. She pulled back her shoulders and firmed her lips. 'There will be trouble ahead. Mother-in-law's ideas do not match well with my own.'

'I am sorry to cause you problems,' Joanna said and was quickly reassured that it was not personal.

'Well, it is personal in that I am not considered a suitable wife for a viscount, let alone a chaperone for Lady Ridgeworth's granddaughter. It is an ongoing struggle that I am determined to win!' Lady Bea finished with a cheeky grin.

Vera led the way up a narrower staircase, saying over her shoulder, 'I have unpacked for the young ladies and laid out the most suitable gowns. What Lady Ridgeworth will have to say about them, I can well imagine.' She stood aside to allow Lady Bea and the girls to enter a sparsely furnished room.

Lady Bea looked around and frowned. 'I am sorry about this.' Her hand indicated the two iron beds with mismatched quilts, the plain chest of drawers and a meagre square of carpet between the beds. 'You ought to have the room next to mine. Still sharing, of course, but this is the servants' floor.'

'John will have the other room,' Iris informed Joanna. 'Grandmother would not dream of relegating him to the top floor. And it is only for a night or two.'

'Rather like being back at school,' Joanna added.

Lady Bea had to admit the similarity to her last night's accommodation. She left them to change with a final warning not to take too long.

Chapter 10

The dowager was already seated at the head of the table in what Iris referred to as the breakfast room when the others entered. She did not greet them and waited only until they were seated before signalling to the butler and maid to begin serving. Joanna thought it was a lot of fuss for a meal that consisted of cold cuts, bread and fruit; it looked set to be as formal as the tea she had eaten in the main dining room the previous year.

'I thought we might take a walk this afternoon,' Lady Bea remarked.

'I do not approve of talking during a meal,' Lady Ridgeworth said firmly.

'As you wish, Mother-in-law. We will be careful not to address any questions to you directly.' That was said with a smile, but Joanna noted the challenging tilt of Lady Bea's chin before she turned slightly in her seat to face Joanna and Iris on the opposite side of the table. 'We are very fortunate to have two such fine spring days in succession. I cannot promise views as spectacular as those you showed me yesterday, but Sidney Gardens has some very interesting plants.'

Iris seemed to shrink down inside her dress, but Joanna could not ignore such a pointed remark. 'I have been in the gardens before. Miss Waring included them in our sketching trip.'

They were all surprised when Lady Ridgeworth said, 'Your drawings were far superior to Iris's. Her picture of the Royal Crescent made it look fit for demolition.'

Lady Bea continued to ignore her mother-in-law and answered Joanna. 'I rather liked your Miss Waring. I shall ask Simon to buy me a telescope.'

'I don't approve of too much learning for girls,' Lady Ridgeworth muttered.

It seemed to Joanna that Lady Ridgeworth did not approve of very much at all. Lady Bea ceased baiting the old lady and lunch continued in silence; fortunately, it was a very short meal.

Lady Ridgeworth rose from her seat as soon as she had eaten her fill and the others had perforce to do the same, even though they had not quite finished. As they followed her back to the sitting room, they exchanged smiles behind her back.

Lady Ridgeworth sat in her favourite chair and arranged her skirts fussily. 'A walk is out of the question. A seamstress has been summoned to take measurements for some decent clothes. I will not have you parading around Bath looking like maids on their day off.'

'Oh, bravo!' Lady Bea said wryly. 'I knew you could be relied upon to have everything in hand.' The apparent compliment hit the old lady like a verbal blow against which she had no defence. Her lips tightened, but before she could think of a cutting remark Lady Bea turned to the girls. 'It was Mother-in-law's suggestion that you have a taste of genteel society before I launched you in London.'

The 'suggestion' had been a two-page letter outlining the family's reputation, Bea's unsuitability as a chaperone and Simon, Lord Ridgeworth's stupidity in allowing his wife, whom he ought not to have married in the first place, take charge of an unknown girl with a mercantile background. The real root of the dowager's interference was the fact that Iris, her granddaughter, was also involved.

They were saved from a blistering lecture by the appearance of the butler to announce that the dressmaker had arrived. Lady Ridgeworth led the way to a small reception room on the ground floor and settled herself in the only comfortable chair. A selection of fabrics and several half-finished dresses were draped across the remaining furniture, leaving nowhere for the rest of them to sit down. The dressmaker smiled and suggested the young ladies might like to look at some fashion plates, but Lady Ridgeworth told her to just get on with the measurements.

Joanna found it rather embarrassing to stand in her plain cotton shift while she was turned this way and that and discussed as though she were a dummy. Miss Waring had taught her girls that there was a fine line between pride and modesty. She had allowed no silly coyness; bodies grew and functioned, and although the functions were not discussed neither were they anything to be ashamed of.

The same went for their shape. Joanna had well-developed breasts and hips whereas some girls were as flat as boards.

Hearing her body discussed in detail by strangers was hard to bear. She had ventured only one comment when Lady Ridgeworth decried the absence of a corset: 'Miss Waring believes good posture is more important than artificial constrictions.'

'What does she know of fashion?' the dowager snorted.

Joanna was tempted to reply but a slight shake of Lady Bea's head made her hold her tongue.

The next couple of hours were a masterly display of verbal fencing. Lady Ridgeworth issued orders, which Lady Bea nodded and then ignored. Joanna had to avoid eye contact with Iris in case she gave way to outright laughter. At least it took her mind off her own embarrassment when it was Iris's turn to be measured.

Lady Ridgeworth gave in first, not acknowledging defeat as much as boredom. 'I have had enough of this,' she declared. 'The clothes will all have to be discarded once we have you dressed by a London modiste. You may join me for tea. And don't be late!' she ended as she marched out of the room.

Joanna looked at the crestfallen woman gathering up her tape, pins and samples. 'Thank you, Mrs Down. I particularly like your design for the afternoon gown. I am sure it will remain one of my favourites.'

'Well done, Joanna,' Lady Bea said when the dressmaker had left the room. 'You took the words out of my mouth. Politeness always overcomes rudeness.'

'Papa says all workers are worthy of respect,' Iris said, speaking for the first time since they had entered the room.

Joanna thought she should take a leaf out of her aunt's book when it came to dealing with her grandmother. Her friend was always slow to put forward her own point of view and people tended to think she was weak, but Iris was like her father, always looking for the smoothest path on minor matters. She had nerves of steel when something was important.

'Quite right too,' Lady Bea agreed. 'My mother-in-law tends to think her title and her age give her leave to look down upon others.' She gave a small laugh. 'She is quite impartial. I have seen her be equally – shall we say brusque? – with people of higher rank.'

Joanna cast her mind back to their visit the previous year. Closer acquaintance with Lady Ridgeworth explained why Miss Waring had been in such a bad mood for the rest of the day. She suspected the schoolmistress's tactic had been similar to Lady Bea's: she would not have returned rudeness with rudeness, but neither would she have forgiven the insult.

The thought of being constantly under the eye of such a martinet put a blight on Joanna's spirits.

To her relief, afternoon tea was taken in the drawing room. The butler poured and a maid passed the cups and offered a plate of very small biscuits. Joanna barely had time to nibble on one before Lady Ridgeworth started her interrogation. She wanted to know why Lady Bea was arranging for her to come out. 'I can understand playing down your father's background, but don't you have any female relatives on your mother's side?'

Joanna explained that her aunt, Lady Fulton, had ignored her from the day she was delivered to the school. 'Fulton?' Lady Ridgeworth repeated. 'Is she the daughter of Lord Stanley?'

'Yes. So was my mother.'

'I do not appreciate pertness! But it gives us something to work with. I shall make a point of speaking to Stanley. His acknowledgement will be beneficial.'

'I have not seen any of my relatives for eight years, my lady. I hardly think they will take an interest in me now.'

Lady Ridgeworth gave one of her signature snorts. 'But now you are marriageable, with a fortune at your back! Stanley will want a hand in any negotiations.'

Joanna was almost bursting with denial, but Lady Bea stepped in to divert the dowager's attention and she was allowed to finish her – now cold – tea in peace.

They escaped from the drawing room as soon as the tea tray was removed. Joanna leaned back against the wall in the hall. 'Phew! I think I have changed my mind about going to London. Please send me back to Miss Waring.'

Lady Bea laughed softly and drew her further away from the drawing-room door. 'Fresh air is what we all need.' She led the way down the stairs and through a rear door into the garden. It had grown quite chilly, so they sheltered in the lee of the tall hedge.

Joanna suddenly started to laugh. 'I thought we were to be treated to another mostly silent meal in the dining room. On reflection, that would have been preferable to that inquisition!'

'Mother-in-law does not take her afternoon tea in the dining room.'

'She did last year.'

Iris joined in the laughter. 'Oh, Joanna. That was different. We were *invited to tea!*' She emphasised the words for effect.

Lady Bea shivered. 'It really is too cold to be standing out here.'

'Where else can we go? I don't want to go back to the drawing room,' Iris said as they made their way back indoors. 'Perhaps we could just take a long time changing for dinner.'

That led the conversation onto the tricky subject of what the girls were to wear. Neither had brought a proper dinner gown, Joanna because she did not possess one and Iris because she only dressed for dinner when she visited with her parents. At school, the main meal of the day was taken at midday with a high tea-cum-supper in the early evening. No-one changed their clothes during the day unless it was for a sporting activity or an outing.

Lady Bea studied the few clothes the girls had brought with them and decided it would have to be their Sunday best. 'Prepare yourselves for another lecture,' she warned. 'Mother-in-law will use this to stress how right she was to bring you here for *proper clothing!*'

Joanna could not see what all the fuss was about. Her Sunday dress was of good quality cotton, printed in a tartan of green, gold and black on a white background. It was well made, even if it lacked any claim to fashion. It was a schoolgirl's dress with a round neckline and elbow-length sleeves; the skirt fell from a natural waistline and ended at Joanna's ankles as she had continued to grow since it was made last summer. It was also a bit tight across her chest. It was definitely not a dinner gown.

Iris's dress was similar but in blue with tiny white flowers. And who was going to see them anyway? One elderly lady who would likely find fault if they stepped straight off the pages of a fashion journal!

The maid who brought up their washing water offered to stay and help the girls to dress but they refused. For years they had helped each other and saw no reason to change the habit now. Joanna was just finishing arranging Iris's hair, another long-time and enjoyable habit, when they heard the sound of approaching footsteps and male voices.

Iris leapt to her feet. 'It's John!' she cried and rushed out of the room and down the stairs to greet her brother. Joanna stayed where she was. She had not seen John recently, but she did not want to intrude on the family reunion. He had spent the last two years at university and most of his holidays were taken up by the woollen mill. She could hear Iris's excited voice and his deeper tones, and just for a moment it made her feel rather lonely.

Iris returned to the bedroom still bubbling with excitement. 'I am so glad he arrived before dinner. He is a great favourite of Grandmama's and should put her in a good humour.'

Chapter 11

When they entered the drawing room a little later, it seemed that Iris's prediction was correct. Lady Ridgeworth, resplendent in a gown of yellow silk that did nothing for her aged complexion, was smiling at John and holding his hand. The smile disappeared when John left her to greet Joanna.

'My word, Jo, aren't you looking grown up?' He took hold of both her hands and bent down to kiss her cheek. Iris moved up beside them and he placed an arm around their shoulders and turned them back towards his grandmother. 'It is as well I am going to London to watch over these two. They were both scruffy schoolgirls when I last saw them.'

Lady Bea entered the room and was greeted in the same exuberant fashion. If Lady Ridgeworth had tightened her lips any further, they would have disappeared altogether. 'And it is to hoped that all of you will behave with more decorum. I shall make sure you do.'

John's face fell into an expression of dismay. 'You are not coming to London, too?' It sounded almost like a groan.

'It appears to be necessary. I knew Beatrice was not a suitable chaperone,' the dowager continued as though he had not spoken.

'I don't need a chaperone,' John protested, loud enough to capture his grandmother's attention.

'No! You need someone to teach you proper manners.' Lady Ridgeworth snorted again. 'Ridgeworth has his head too full of unnecessary reforms to do so. He is as bad as you, mixing with riff-raff!' she continued sharply. 'He is old enough to know better!'

'I am quite looking forward to discussing those reforms with him,' John said seriously. 'I have made some improvements at the mill but—'

'You will not mention that!' Lady Ridgeworth cut in. 'You have had the sense to leave it behind and it is best forgotten.'

'I have not given up the mill, Grandmama. I am proud of what I have achieved so far. For the foreseeable future I must leave it in the hands of a manager, but it is mine and I will be keeping a close eye on it.' John sounded calm, but Joanna could see his fists were clenched tightly behind his back. She admired him for taking a stand and not bowing to his grandmother's prejudices.

She was embarrassed to be a witness of such a personal argument and sought to distance herself by mentally stripping the room of all its clutter. Thankfully the argument was curtailed by the appearance of Pontin to announce dinner.

John offered his grandmother his arm, which she accepted with rigid dignity, and they led the way to the dining room. Bea, Iris and Joanna exchanged rueful glances and follow behind.

The long table was laid with white linen and an ugly silver epergne. A quick glance at the cutlery warned Joanna not to expect a feast; each place was only set with two spoons, a knife and a fork. The settings were widely spaced and the spare chairs had been moved back against the walls.

Joanna was actually grateful for Lady Ridgeworth's silence-at-meals rule. Even Lady Bea gave up the struggle for conversation. They worked their way through a thin soup, indifferent roast and a fruit tart, the only conversation a murmured word to the servers. It was not a pleasant or relaxing meal.

She was dreading their return to the drawing room and the resumption of the argument. It would be embarrassing, but at least it would divert Lady Ridgeworth's attention away from her own shortcomings.

As it turned out, John refused to argue. Much like his father, he was courteous and slow to anger but he would not be dictated to. His reply to Lady Ridgeworth's opening salvo was, 'You said the mill was not to be mentioned, Grandmother. Let us instead discuss our travel arrangements for tomorrow.'

Of course, that started up a whole new line of dissent. By the time Joanna escaped to her bedroom, it had been grudgingly decided that they would stay in Bath for two more days. John would not agree to any longer and threatened to leave next morning if there was any more argument.

As soon as the girls closed the bedroom door, Iris collapsed onto her bed in giggles. 'I did not find it funny,' Joanna said, flopping down onto the only chair in the room. 'How your grandmother can criticise our clothes when she obviously has no idea of what is suitable for an old lady… Oh, sorry. I should not be…'

'Criticise away,' Iris responded. 'You are only saying what everyone thinks and is too scared to put into words. I am just grateful Aunt Bea will have the final word on what we wear or do.'

Joanna stepped out of her shoes and Iris got off the bed to come and unfasten the buttons at the back of her dress, then they turned around so Joanna could return the service.

'Iris,' she asked tentatively. 'How much of an embarrassment will my father be? Or rather that my fortune comes from trade?'

'Not nearly as much as Grandmama makes out. It will be sniffed at behind your back and politely glossed over to your face, but everyone wants money even if they will not admit it.'

Joanna folded her dress neatly and kept her face hidden. 'That is a very depressing thought. I will be judged even before I meet people. Any indiscretion will be put down to my lack of breeding.' She turned suddenly. 'I am not looking for a husband. The very thought of being courted for my money makes me feel sick.'

They took turns at the wash basin before climbing into their beds. It was comfortingly familiar to have Iris sleeping just an arm's length away and, as usual, they settled back on the pillows and discussed the events of the day.

'I am glad John will be travelling to London with us,' Iris remarked. 'Grandmother is sure to find fault with everything from the speed of the train to the other passengers. John has a knack of diverting her.'

'It is going to be uncomfortable anyway,' Joanna added ruefully. 'Unless Mrs Down makes exceptional clothes, we will be in for another lecture.'

Iris nodded. 'Appearances are everything to my grandmother.'

Joanna hesitated before asking, 'Does your grandmother wear cosmetics?'

Iris giggled. 'Yes, but she would deny it. And a hairpiece when she goes out. She does not like being old.'

Joanna wondered if anyone enjoyed being old. She had never had much contact with elderly people, but she had observed them in church and other places. It must be awful to lose one's hair or not be able to move freely. Even so, she did not think it gave them any right to be rude.

She remembered Iris once mentioning that her grandmother did not have many visitors; having met her, Joanna could understand why.

Chapter 12

Breakfast next day was a lively – if frugal – meal. Lady Ridgeworth breakfasted in her room so her visitors were free to enjoy conversation, the first topic being food. They were served toast and boiled eggs, one each for the females and two for John.

'I shall be ready for lunch as soon as I leave the table,' he remarked, cutting the top off his second egg.

'If lunch is like yesterday's, you will be starving by dinner time,' Iris laughed. 'I am actually missing school porridge. At least it set you up for the day.'

'What are your plans?' John asked Lady Bea.

'My plans,' she said wryly, 'are likely to be disregarded as soon as Mother-in-law emerges from her room.

'Then I suggest we escape forthwith.' John grinned at his companions. 'Can you manage to sneak up to your rooms and fetch your coats? I will meet you in the hall.'

Eager to comply, the ladies hurried back to their bedrooms. Lady Bea was almost caught. She happened to let her bedroom door close more sharply than she had intended and a strident voice from the next room demanded, 'Is that you, Beatrice?'

Bea froze, fully expecting her mother-in-law's maid to come and fetch her. After a few moments she silently caught up her coat and hat and tiptoed from the room, carefully easing the door shut behind her. She almost ran down the stairs to where the others were waiting.

A startled Pontin helped her on with her coat. As she thanked him, Lady Bea whispered, 'You have not seen us leave.' The old man bowed deferentially but could not hide a smile.

Iris let out a whoop as soon as they were on the pavement. 'Shh!' Lady Bea cautioned. 'Mother-in-law's room is at the front of the house.' They moved away from the door before she asked John, 'Where do you suggest we go this early in the morning?'

'I know the exact place.' He offered Lady Bea his arm. 'This way.' He refused to give any further information. Iris followed behind with Joanna, complaining that her brother was a tease.

A gentleman was leaving a house a little further down the street and he hesitated on the step until John and Bea had passed. As he stepped onto the pavement towards the girls, Joanna gasped, 'It's Max!' Hand outstretched, she took a few quick steps forward until they were face to face. 'Max! What are you doing in Bath?'

Max tipped his head to Iris while taking Joanna's hands in a firm clasp and replying, with a broad smile, 'Joanna! I thought you were in London, or at least on your way.'

Lady Bea had noticed the girls' absence and turned back. The sight of them conversing with a strange man reminded her she was supposed to be their chaperone. She hurried back, almost towing John with her. 'Iris! Joanna! Is this man accosting you?'

Joanna and Iris spoke together, trying to explain. The name Maxwell was all Lady Bea needed to relieve her anxiety, but it also raised a lot of questions.

Joanna remembered her manners and introduced Max to Lady Bea and John. Max shook hands and asked permission to call on Joanna while she was in Bath. 'I do not think that would be a good idea,' Lady Bea said, then had to explain that they were staying with her mother-in-law and it was sure to cause trouble if an unknown man was invited into her home. She looked to John for support.

John, in turn, was taking note of how Iris seemed very familiar with Mr Maxwell and his protective instincts flared. The information he had gleaned from his parents suggested the man was a long-time acquaintance of Joanna's but had lived abroad. If this was the way Iris was going to behave with strange – and undeniably handsome – men in London ,Aunt Bea would need to keep her on a leash! He needed to know more. 'Mr Maxwell, we are just on our way to breakfast…'

'Breakfast?' his three female companions exclaimed, and Max raised a puzzled eyebrow.

'Breakfast,' John repeated. 'If you care to join us, you may visit with Joanna without my grandmother throwing a fit. We are going to Sally Lunn's bakery. I, for one, am starving!'

Max was more than happy to accept. He needed to know how Joanna felt about this young, blond Adonis.

It was an awkward grouping. Etiquette demanded Lady Bea have one of the males as escort, and John was in the position of host at the moment so it should be him. But that would leave Joanna, and more importantly Iris, clinging to Maxwell's arms. Lady Bea proved an adequate chaperone by fastening on to Mr Maxwell's arm and leading the way. There was no impropriety in John escorting his sister and Joanna.

Joanna was peeved. She had been so delighted to see Max and now he was walking ahead chatting to Lady Bea like an old friend. She was also being ignored by John, who was questioning Iris in a tone far removed from his usual banter.

'I met him when he came to see Joanna at school,' Iris protested.

'And he invited you to call him Max? Very fast work!' John scoffed.

'Oh, don't be so stuffy! We always call him Max. That is how he signs his letters.'

John nearly exploded. 'He writes to you?'

'No, of course not. Joanna shares—'

Joanna had had enough and cut in. 'Stop bickering like ten year olds! Max is perfectly respectable. He writes to me at my father's command – who else was I to share my news with? Now, if you are so hungry let us catch up with the others.' She grabbed John's arm and quickened her pace. Attached to her brother's other arm, Iris had to skip to keep up.

Max was also being questioned by Lady Bea, albeit in a more friendly manner. Lord Ridgeworth was an indulgent husband up to a point, but he had not given his consent to her chaperonage until he was satisfied with Joanna's credentials. 'Tell me how you come to know Joanna,' she asked.

Max's answers corresponded reassuringly with what she already knew from Mr Ebstone, and her match-making instincts took flight. He would make Joanna an ideal husband!

It was not far to Sally Lunn's bakery shop. Through the bay window they could see several empty tables at the rear and John ushered his party inside. The smell of fresh baking overlaid with coffee was enough to make one drool. The tables were laid for four, so John called for another chair and made sure Iris was tucked between her aunt and himself.

When they were all seated, he explained to Max the necessity for a second breakfast. Max had been fed more generously but said he could always find room for another cup of coffee. The sight of another diner tucking into one of the famous buns made him decide he had room for one of those as well.

They gave their orders. The ladies had buns with butter and honey and John recommended Max to try one with hot bacon; sweet or savoury, they were equally delicious. The atmosphere relaxed as backgrounds and relationships were discussed.

Max, being the outsider, was the main focus of attention but he did not allow it to become an inquisition. He had questions of his own: firstly, why was Joanna in Bath when Mr Ebstone had made arrangements for her to go to London?

He was relieved to see that Joanna could well hold her own in the five-sided conversation and that she treated Armitage with the relaxed friendliness of long acquaintance. In turn, Armitage seemed more intent on blocking his sister's part in the conversation than paying attention to Joanna.

Max found it hard to direct his attention to anyone other than Joanna. Her voice, to which he had never given any previous thought, was melodic, as though she were suppressing a smile. It was a far cry from the dull, nasal tone he had heard at the school. And there was a vibrancy about her that quite overshadowed her more beautiful friend.

Both girls wore their school uniforms and in the warmth of the tearoom Joanna had opened the cloak wide to partially reveal a very feminine figure. What hair he could see under her plain felt bonnet glowed almost crimson in the light of the overhead lamps, and her eyes sparkled with humour. This was the picture of Joanna he had built up in his mind over the years. She met his occasional glances with a smile that made him wish they were alone.

Eventually Lady Bea reluctantly drew their attention to the time. 'We need to return.' She smiled apologetically at Max. 'My mother-in-law does not know we have come out.'

'She will by now,' John laughed.

'Yes, so we had best make haste.' Lady Bea pulled on her gloves and started to rise. 'It was very pleasant meeting you, Mr Maxwell.'

'With your permission, I would still like to visit Joanna. I have matters to discuss with her.' He had been surprised and very pleased to encounter her in the street. He was spending a few days with his grandmother in the house from which he had emerged. They had talked late into the night, discussing his activities in the last eight years and his plans for the future. The launching of the new ship had brought Joanna into the conversation, but he had not mentioned a possible marriage.

He had told his grandmother of his meeting at the school, omitting how plain and downtrodden Joanna had looked. He mentioned the arrangements Mr Ebstone had made for Joanna's come out, and was reassured that his grandmother could give a good account of Viscountess Ridgeworth, with whom she was acquainted. 'Not a bit like her mother-in-law,' she had said with a twist of her lips. 'Your young lady will have a wonderful time.'

Not so wonderful that she forgot all about him, Max hoped. He very much wanted to get to know Joanna and wondered if it would be safe to visit her in London. He did not want to run the risk of bumping into his father, who might very well be there at this time of year.

That morning Max had breakfasted alone, looked after by Ashford, the butler. With his grandmother still in bed, he had decided to go for a walk and reacquaint himself with the town. Seeing Joanna and Iris walking towards him had seemed like a gift from heaven, but then he had been forced to share her company with a chaperone and Iris's decidedly suspicious brother.

John suggested, 'Come to the house now. I shall tell Grandmama you are a business acquaintance. Charm her a bit. She likes young men.'

'No,' Lady Bea protested. 'That will not do. Mr Maxwell is a legitimate emissary from Joanna's father. He will come to the house a few minutes after we enter and ask to see me.' She gave Max a mischievous smile. 'I will introduce you to Lady Ridgeworth and *then* you may charm her.'

'It will also soften our scold for going out,' Iris added.

Max could not see how that would allow him time with Joanna, but he would have a foot in the door and an introduction.

Chapter 13

The truants' reception was every bit as bad as they had expected. Pontin let them into the house and said apologetically, 'Lady Ridgeworth requests your immediate presence in the drawing room.'

They climbed the stairs like prisoners ascending the scaffold and had barely set foot in the room before Lady Ridgeworth demanded, 'What is the meaning of this?' She glared at each in turn. 'Just look at you. Not one of you dressed respectably for walking about town. You have brought shame upon my house.'

Joanna risked a sideways glance at her companions. Admittedly she and Iris looked like schoolgirls, but Lady Bea had on a very smart coat and hat. John, however, did not have a hat or gloves, a serious faux pas in the old lady's eyes.

Before they could offer any excuses, they heard the sound of a firm knock on the front door. Pontin must almost have run up the stairs because the delay was so brief before he entered to room to announce Mr Angus Maxwell had called to see Lady Ridgeworth.

'I don't know any Maxwells,' Lady Ridgeworth replied testily. 'And it is too early for calls. Send him away.'

Pontin looked uncomfortable but continued with his errand. 'He asks to see Lady Beatrice Ridgeworth.'

'Then why did you not say so?' the old lady huffed. 'It is an impertinence, but you may show him up.'

Max thought the tableau in the drawing room resembled a scene from a play. An old lady sat in a throne-like chair with his breakfast companions standing meekly before her. Ignoring the younger people, he stepped forward and bowed to the dowager. 'Lady Ridgeworth, forgive my early call but I wanted to see you before you left for London. I am Angus Maxwell, Mr Pennicott's partner, and have been charged with making sure you are happy with the arrangements made by Mr Ebstone.'

Joanna watched an almost coquettish smile lighten the dowager's face. All trace of her earlier anger vanished as she held out her hand. 'It is no trouble at all, Mr Maxwell. Won't you take a seat?'

Max glanced around. As though spotting the others for the first time, he looked back at Lady Ridgeworth with a puzzled frown. 'My family,' she said shortly. 'My daughter-in-law, Viscountess Ridgeworth, my grandson, Mr John Armitage, and his sister, Iris. And Miss Pennicott.'

Max gave a masterly impression of being surprised. 'Viscountess?' Max bowed to Lady Bea. 'My lady, I think it is you I need to speak to.'

'You had better speak to me,' Lady Ridgeworth barked. 'I shall be going to London with them.' She was no longer simpering.

'Begging your pardon, my lady, but I have financial details to discuss. You would not want to be involved in such sordid details, would you?' Max spoke with gentle deference and a smile that could surely have thawed icicles. It certainly worked on one vain old lady.

'You may discuss them with Mr Armitage. He will be accompanying us to London, too.'

Max smiled again but shook his head. 'Mr Pennicott's contract is with Lady Beatrice Ridgeworth as Joanna's chaperone. Joanna will also need to be present.'

The dowager gave in with forced dignity. 'You may use the breakfast room.' She dismissed them with a wave of her hand and only waited for the door to close before turning her wrath on her grandchildren.

***

Lady Bea and Joanna handed their outdoor clothes to Pontin, who was hovering at the head of the stairs, and went down to the breakfast parlour. Once inside, Lady Bea smiled at Max and said, 'I am sure we do not need to discuss the generous, indeed open-ended, allowance made for Joanna's requirements. I have already assured my mother-in-law that I will *not* be accepting a fee. It is my pleasure to take care of Joanna. Now I will gaze out at the garden and sing quietly while you talk to Joanna.' She suited her actions to her words and moved to the window.

Joanna and Max sat close together at one end of the table, both suddenly tongue tied. Max was fascinated by Joanna's hair.

Freed from her bonnet, he could see that it was not crimson. He tried to think of another suitable description. Maroon? Chestnut? Perhaps a combination of both. It put him in mind of a rich burgundy wine when the glass was lifted to the light. It was thick and glowing and the loose strands fell into natural waves. He wanted to touch it.

Joanna was having similar thoughts. Max's black hair also had a natural wave where it touched his ears and neck. Added to his tanned skin, it gave him a rather rugged and carefree appearance. From the neck down he was even more impressive.

They had not touched beyond that first exuberant greeting but she could still feel the firm clasp of his hand. It had been difficult to let go, difficult not to stare at him in the teashop, but she had been gratified that he had barely glanced at Iris.

'You are looking well,' Max managed to say.

Joanna laughed. 'I was mortified that I looked so haggard when you came to the school. I am normally very healthy. Iris was the only person who did not succumb to the infection. She looks as though a puff of wind would blow her away, but she can run us all into the ground and have energy to spare.' Joanna knew she was gabbling and could have kicked herself for bringing Iris into the conversation.

'Indeed,' Max replied. There was no denying Iris's beauty and he could appreciate it on a purely visual level, but she did not attract him in the same way as Joanna. 'You will be pleased to have her company when you step out into society. And that of her brother.' It was a leading question; their interaction over breakfast had been reassuring but he wanted to hear Joanna's opinion.

Joanna picked up on his enquiry and grinned. 'Yes, it will certainly liven things up! He is going to town to learn about the Ridgeworth estates but is bound to socialise as well. We expect John to be pursued by all the debutantes and their mamas.'

Did a title appeal to Joanna? He wanted to say 'I am heir to an earldom', but it was not the right time to reveal his origins.

George Pennicott was impressed by his heritage, which added another reason for Max to marry Joanna. Coming from a mercantile background, George had been looked down upon by his in-laws even though they had accepted his financial help.

Seeing his daughter married to a title would be some kind of kickback.

Joanna was looking at Max questioningly, obviously waiting for a comment. He groped for her last statement. Ah, yes. 'It would be a large step for him.'

'John is the owner of a woollen mill and happy to be so. I admire him for putting his own wishes aside for the time being.'

She admired him! Was it for doing his duty or for his Adonis' looks and the comfort of long acquaintance? Would the marriage-orientated atmosphere of society encourage Joanna to see the man in a different light? It was a worrying thought and Max was beginning to think he might have to risk going to London after all.

He had been quiet for too long, so Joanna tried for another topic. 'Do you remain in Bath for very long?'

'I am undecided. How long will you be here?'

'John insists we go the day after tomorrow.'

Him again! But Joanna had not finished. 'Lady Ridgeworth, the older one, insists that Iris and I have new clothes.' She laughed. 'Although she says they will have to be replaced by a London modiste. Appearances are very important to her.'

Max came to a decision. Raising his voice slightly, he called to Lady Bea, 'My lady, would you be willing to bring Joanna to dine with me before you leave for London.'

Bea turned and stepped closer to the table. 'At your hotel?'

Max stood up as she approached, which gave him a moment's respite. Ah, he had not thought it through, but he was sure that as his grandmother already knew Lady Beatrice and would forgive the liberty he was about to take. 'I am staying with a family friend, Lady Leith. I will ask her to send an invitation. For this evening, perhaps?'

Bea agreed and there seemed little else to say. Max asked if he should take formal leave of Lady Ridgeworth. 'If you can spare the time,' Bea laughed. 'Mother-in-law is a stickler for correctness but I warn you, you may not escape very soon.'

Lady Ridgeworth did try to detain him but Max pleaded an urgent appointment and made his escape. He went straight back to his grandmother's house and told her all that had happened. She agreed to his plan and the invitation was sent off.

Chapter 14

'We have been invited to dinner with Lady Leith!' Bea exclaimed a little later when she read the note.

'It is very short notice,' her mother-in-law said crossly. 'Bad manners, as though we are stopgaps when others have cancelled.'

Bea sought for words that would cause the least offence. 'The invitation is for Joanna and me. As you know, Lady Leith has been very kind to me in the past and has only just heard that I am in Bath. You will excuse us from dining with you?'

It was not really a question; Lady Ridgeworth could not actually prevent them from accepting the invitation but that did not mean she was going to consent without protest. 'It is still bad manners when she knows you are residing in my house. She could not invite you alone. It would be more appropriate for me to accompany you.' She sniffed. 'Not that I value an invitation from her.'

'Then is it just as well Joanna has also been invited.'

Lady Ridgeworth tried to protest but Bea refused to argue. Joanna was the principal guest, though there was no need for her mother-in-law to know that. 'It can do Joanna no harm to have an acquaintance with another influential lady when she gets to town.'

'Our influence is more than she could have expected!'

Bea stood up and beckoned Joanna to follow her. 'We need to see what you are to wear this evening. Hopefully Mrs Down will have sent one of your new dresses.'

Iris managed to sidle out of the room with them. She touched Joanna's arm. 'I am sorry Grandmother was so rude to you. She can be...'

'There is no need to apologise on her behalf, Iris,' Joanna said, giving her friend a hug. 'That reference was to my father being in trade. I am not ashamed of him or his efforts. I never expected a London season, and I am very grateful to Lady Bea for sponsoring me. I wish for no higher approval.'

Joanna had always been aware that many in high society looked down on people who made their own fortunes instead of inheriting them. She also knew that those same, high-nosed aristocrats were avid for the luxury goods her father imported. Their two-faced attitude annoyed her, but she was a realist. If such people thought themselves too high and mighty to associate with her – so what? The Armitage family and Lady Bea were exceptions, and she was glad of it.

Mrs Down had been busy, but she was in awe of old Lady Ridgeworth and had completed Iris's dinner dress first. Perhaps that was unfair; it was, after all, easier to alter one of the partially made dresses than to start from scratch on a garment to fit Joanna's more ample figure. Joanna would have to wear her Sunday dress again and hope it did not offend Lady Leith.

Lady Bea said it was charming and advised Joanna to wear her hair loose, just caught back from her face with two silver combs. 'You can try for more sophistication when we get to London.'

***

Bea and Joanna walked the short distance to Lady Leith's house. Architecturally it was identical to Lady Ridgeworth's, but the differences were apparent as soon as they stepped into the hall.

The butler was young and actually smiled at Bea as he took their coats. The informality continued as he said how nice it was to see Miss Beatrice again. Then he pulled a face and gave an exaggerated bow. 'I beg pardon, my lady.'

Far from taking offence, Bea returned his smile and actually touched his arm. 'Old habits die hard, Freddie. I am glad to see you are still here and,' she gave his formal attire a quick glance, 'promoted to butler!'

With another smile, he conducted them to the drawing room. It was a far cry from Lady Ridgeworth's cluttered apartment. Here everything spoke of quality and restrained elegance, and the warm atmosphere was not totally reliant on the merry fire in the marble hearth.

Lady Leith was of an age and similar build to Lady Ridgeworth, but there the similarity ended. She came forward and greeted them with a wide smile and a quick embrace for Bea. Joanna had been curious as to why Max had been so confident that his hostess would not object to entertaining strangers at a moment's notice until she remembered that Lady Bea was known to her.

When Joanna was introduced, Lady Leith took her hands. 'I am so pleased to meet you at last. Angus will join us later, but we have a little time to get to know each other.'

Joanna feared she was in for another inquisition. And what did the lady mean by *'at last'*? Lady Leith asked questions about Joanna's family, but in a friendly manner that was in no way offensive. Joanna liked her immediately and gave more details than she had in her responses to old Lady Ridgeworth's questions.

It appeared that Lady Leith was acquainted with some of Joanna's maternal relatives and did not hold them in high esteem. 'You will be much more comfortable in Beatrice's care,' she remarked. 'Louisa Fulton is not generally liked although she is received everywhere, of course.'

With gentle prompting from Lady Bea, Joanna was soon telling of her years at Miss Waring's school. Inevitably there were lots of references to Iris and holidays spent at the vicarage. 'Once Reverend Armitage hired a house at Weston Super Mare and we had a lovely week playing on the sand, swimming and watching the Punch and Judy show.'

'Did you ever stay with your aunt?' Lady Leith asked.

Joanna shook her head. 'For several years I received birthday and Christmas gifts from Uncle Herbert. He said they were from the whole family but there were never any personal notes from my aunt or cousins.' Lady Leith shook her head sadly and Joanna was quick to add, 'But I did not mind. I would rather receive nothing at all than reluctant gifts and insincere greetings.'

There was a short silence before Joanna rushed on to describe the gifts she had received from her father. 'Papa does not have much idea of what life is like at school,' she laughed. 'His first gift was a tiger-skin rug, complete with head. It terrified us, and Miss Waring arranged for it to be sent to the British Museum. He also sends things like wooden carvings, wall hangings and boxes of spices. The spices were used in the kitchen but cook did not really know what to do with them and we had some very strange meals. Once he sent me a jewelled dagger that Miss Waring placed in her curiosity cabinet for safe keeping. Oh,' she gasped, 'it must still be there.'

'I am sure you will not need it in London,' Lady Bea chuckled. 'I wondered what you had in those other trunks. I hope you will be able to display them wherever you go to live after the season.'

That was another conversation stopper. Joanna was trying not to look beyond the next few months. Nothing had been said about her long-term future, except Reverend Armitage's comment that she would always be welcome at the vicarage and Miss Waring's open invitation. Most girls had a season with the aim of attracting a husband, but Joanna's thoughts on marriage had been vague until meeting Max had made her realise that her light-hearted suggestion of marrying him had become her dearest wish.

For several years she had held on to the nebulous thought that her papa would come home, she would live with him and they would return to their previous habits, or he would send for her to join him in India. But no longer.

She had been too young when her father went away to understand the significance of him putting the Bristol house in trust for her future use. It was only when she started to take an interest in her own finances that she realised she was all-but an orphan. She would have to forge her own future. From Max's detailed reports she had a good grasp of the export and import business. In their letters they had also discussed scientific developments and investments, but that knowledge was of no use to her as a single, under-age female. She would either have to marry and hope her husband allowed her to continue to manage her affairs or remain single and wait until she was old enough to be considered responsible.

To fill the growing silence, Lady Bea started to tell the older lady about her day at the school. She had just described the lunch when Max joined them.

He paused in the doorway of his grandmother's drawing room and took in the scene. Joanna was sitting beside Lady Leith, laughing at something Lady Bea had just said. With her glorious hair loose, she looked even lovelier than she had that morning. When she noticed him, a delicate colour came into her cheeks and she looked away.

'Angus,' Lady Leith called. 'Come and sit down. I know you are outnumbered but we do not bite!' With a wave of her hand she indicated the space beside Lady Bea on one of the sofas. It placed him directly opposite Joanna, whose eyes never quite rested on his face – which was unfortunate because he could not stop looking at her.

The two older women exchanged a knowing smile. Lady Leith said, 'Beatrice was just telling me about her visit to Joanna's school.'

'Yes, I had a lovely day. I had never been to a party I enjoyed more.'

'A party?' Max queried and joined in the laughter as Bea described playing games and eating chocolate cake. 'I must persuade Simon to send my stepdaughter Cynthia to Miss Waring. She is twelve years old now and we have been considering a change of governess.'

'It is a long way from London,' Joanna remarked. 'She will surely miss being away from you and her father.' She was thinking about her own loneliness in the early days.

Lady Bea broke into her thoughts. 'It is only a few hours by train and she will come home for holidays.' The stark contrast with Joanna's situation hit Bea and she hurried to change the subject. 'Mr Maxwell, won't you tell us about your travels? I have never been further than France.'

'Oh, yes!' Joanna exclaimed. 'Did you come via the Suez Canal?' While Max described his most recent journey, she allowed herself to look at him more frequently. She had thought him handsome before, but his formal evening clothes accentuated the breadth of his shoulders and his white cravat lit up his face. His dark eyes sparkled with humour and his mouth...

Joanna whipped her thoughts away from his mouth as it made her feel quite strange. *Concentrate on his words,* her conscience demanded. *Say something sensible.* With an effort, she dredged up a comment from one of his letters. 'Papa must be very pleased he did not get rid of his early Suez shares. Mine are doing very nicely now the canal is in regular use.'

'Your shares?' Lady Leith exclaimed. 'You hold shares in the Suez Canal Company?'

'Yes. Among other things.'

'But young ladies…'

Max laughed. 'Joanna is not one of your usual young ladies. She has a grasp of business many men would envy.'

'Well I never!' Lady Leith sounded amazed but not particularly disapproving.

It gave Max an idea of how he could spend time with Joanna. 'Perhaps after dinner Joanna would like to go through the balance sheets I brought with me? They are more detailed than the reports I usually send.'

At a quick nod from Bea, Lady Leith agreed. It was not something she would ever have imagined a young couple wanting to discuss but at least they would be talking and the mention of business had certainly broken Joanna's shyness.

The change in her demeanour was dramatic: her eyes sparkled and her voice took on a more confident note. Speaking of her background, Joanna had been diffident, even sad, although she had obviously enjoyed her school years. If even a smidgeon of her present enthusiasm had gone into her letters, it was no wonder Angus was keen to get to know her better.

Dinner was a lively meal. Lady Leith kept the conversation to light, impersonal topics that encouraged the younger ones to air their likes and opinions, and the older ladies found it encouraging that they shared interests other than business. Both girls enjoyed outdoor activities, although Joanna had never learned to ride a horse; she mostly liked long walks, enjoying nature and watching the stars at night.

Max admitted he was not a great reader of literature, preferring books that taught him about other cultures, whereas Joanna said she read any book she could get her hands on. At that point she smiled at Max and said, 'And I enjoyed reading your letters and hearing about your travels.'

It was as though time stopped and her surroundings melted away. All she was aware of was Max's answering smile; it was almost tangible, like a caress. She could not look away.

'I expect you are very excited to be going to London for the first time, Joanna?' Lady Leith remarked, bringing Joanna back to the here and now.

'Oh, I have been before. Before he went away Papa often took me about with him.' Joanna laughed softly. 'I was too young to realise how unusual that was.'

'Not many fathers take time to be with their children,' Max said, thinking of his own father. 'You will enjoy revisiting all the sights.'

This time Joanna laughed out loud. 'I doubt Lady Bea will be taking me to warehouses and docks!'

The two ladies were scandalised. 'Warehouses and docks!' they echoed in unison.

'And banks and coffee houses.' Joanna was enjoying their reaction. 'I liked the coffee houses best because the men bought me cakes and biscuits.' She looked at Max and said ruefully, 'I was very fat when we first met.'

Max was too honest to deny her statement and wished he dared say that he liked the way her weight had been redistributed. Gallantly he replied, 'It was too short an acquaintance to notice. I was more taken with the way you lectured me on the superiority of your father's ship.'

That raised the topic of Joanna launching the new ship nearing completion in Glasgow. 'That sounds very exciting,' Lady Bea said. 'Simon is sure to want to come with us. He is very interested in factory workers' conditions. I don't believe he has ever turned his attention to shipyards before.'

When the meal was finished Max declined the offer of brandy and accompanied the ladies back to the drawing room. 'Would you like to see those accounts now, Joanna?' he asked.

Lady Leith threw up her hands. 'I thought we had managed to eliminate that topic.' She shook her head and sighed. 'But if that is your idea of enjoyment, you may use that table and not bore us with your facts and figures.' She indicated a table set in the window bay. 'Angus, please be careful as you move my aspidistra.'

As Max carefully lifted the heavy plant in its colourful bowl and placed it on the floor, Joanna said to Lady Leith, 'It sounds funny to hear you call him Angus. I always think if him as Max.'

'That is not really his...'

85

Max interrupted her. 'Mr Maxwell is too formal for long-time correspondents. Max suits me very well. I do not need any other names.'

Joanna was a bit surprised at the sharpness of his tone; it sounded very much like a warning. But she was given no time to ponder. 'Here, Joanna,' he called, holding out a chair. When she was seated, he moved a lampstand a little to the side and said, 'That is better.'

He certainly thought so: the soft light brought out the rich tones in Joanna's hair and outlined her figure. He allowed his hand to linger on her back as he settled her in a chair and pulled forward another so they were sitting at right angles, close enough for him to observe her face without staring.

The older ladies settled themselves on one of the sofas by the fire facing the window. They were near enough to the young couple to satisfy propriety but too far away to overhear Max and Joanna's discussion, which was just as well because Joanna ignored the papers and asked, 'Don't you like being called Angus? I know that is your name because I have seen it on documents.'

Max shrugged. 'That is what I have always been called.'

'Has Lady Leith known you for long?' Joanna did not wait for a reply before adding, 'Of course, she must have. You would not have invited us into her home if you had only met her recently.'

To distract her, Max pushed a balance sheet across the table. 'This shows the figures up to the end of last year.'

As he pointed out the various columns, Joanna let her mind wander. She had recalled her papa saying that Max had been recommended to him by a Lady Leith, and there had been something about him losing his family – or was it that the family had fallen on hard times?

In all the years of writing, Max had seldom mentioned his childhood and then only briefly. Of his family or why he had gone to sea at an early age, she knew nothing at all. It was as though he had suddenly sprung to life aged fourteen. It had never seemed to matter because she had said little about her own childhood.

At first Max's letters had been focused on the present, where he had been and what he had been doing, as though he were delivering a report. Gradually he began to reveal his feelings – sadness at the exploitation of the natives, awe at the splendours of the scenery and his aspirations for the future. Joanna had lived his adventures second hand, trying to feel the excitement of sea journeys and native festivals, trying to conjure the tastes, sounds and smells.

Now that seemed a very one-dimensional relationship, as though Max were a character in a very gripping novel. Now – well, now he was very real and she wanted to know more. She was very aware of him and that their arms were almost touching. If she leant a little to the side…

'Joanna?' Max's query jerked her back to the present. 'Is there anything I need to explain?'

'Yes,' she replied, banishing wayward thoughts. She turned the paper so they could both see it clearly. 'I have noticed for the last few years that the highest profits come from investments and shipping. Look at this.' She pointed to one column and raised her eyes to check he had followed her finger. 'Trading is not doing well at all. Papa seems to be buying much more than he sells.'

'He does,' Max agreed. 'I have no wish to sound critical – George has been very good to me – but lately he has lost interest in the business. He buys things he admires and cannot bear to sell them.' He shook his head. 'His bungalow, the furniture, even the clothes he wears, make up a museum of Indian culture. He has become more Indian than the men he spends time with.'

'That is why he does not want to come home,' Joanna said sadly. 'He loves India more than he ever loved me.'

Max covered her hand, which was closed tightly on the papers, crumpling the edges. It would be cruel to agree with her but insulting to deny it. 'It is an obsession,' he explained. 'He once told me that the years he spent in England were out of duty to your mother. And you, of course. He was – is – so proud of your achievements. But India holds his emotions. Do you understand?'

Joanna nodded. 'I think I always knew. Papa was different when he spoke of India, eager in a way that never entered his voice on any other subject.' She turned her hand so that she could clasp Max's fingers and smiled at him. 'Thank you for looking after him. I understand now why he made you a partner. You have been running the company for quite a while.'

Her admiration made Max feel like a worm. Yes, he had made the company what it was today and deserved some recognition, but George had gone way beyond. He had made Max, or rather Lord Robert Urquhart, his sole heir and handed over the daughter he had not seen for eight years like a bonus.

He thrust the memory away. There were things Joanna needed to know that could not be explained in a few words here; he needed time and privacy.

Joanna was still smiling shyly in a way that made him want to take her into his arms and propose straight away. For years she had been at the centre of his thoughts. Her letters had revealed a strong, intelligent woman he had come to respect. He had accepted George's suggestion that they marry with his head because she would make a fine partner; finding her so physically appealing was beyond anything he could have hoped for.

'What are your arrangements for tomorrow?' he asked eagerly. 'Will you have time to see me again? I have so much to say that cannot be said here.' He cast a rueful look at the ladies by the fire who were pretending not to notice their conversation. He raised his voice slightly and asked, 'Perhaps you would care to walk in the park tomorrow?'

'Oh, I would like that. But we will have to ask Lady Bea.' Joanna pulled a wry face. 'And perhaps Lady Ridgeworth has something planned. She seems very much in charge.'

Max was cheered by her enthusiasm then dismayed at the thought of the crusty dowager. He would not be allowed within arm's reach of Joanna if the old lady had her way. He smiled at the thought. He wanted Joanna in his arms; he wanted them to reach a firm understanding before Joanna was exposed to all the gallants in London. To do that, he needed to see her alone. Soon.

Joanna took the matter into her own hands and crossed the room to speak to Lady Bea. She relayed Max's invitation and asked, 'Will you allow me to walk out with him?'

Bea looked up at Max, who had followed Joanna across the room, and agreed readily. 'We may have to fight for our freedom, but I will not allow mother-in-law to dictate our activities.'

'Hear, hear!' Lady Leith applauded. 'I will help you. Angus and I will call and I will send you young ones out, perhaps not as far as the park but into the garden.'

She sat back looking very smug. Living in the same town, she met her neighbour frequently. They were not close friends but Lady Leith, as an earl's widow, held a higher title and was prepared to exert her authority. 'Our call will be to thank Lady Ridgeworth for allowing us your company this evening.' She gave a sly little laugh. 'It is always best to start with a compliment!'

'Have you finished with your figures?' Lady Bea asked.

Joanna felt guilty because she had forgotten every word of Max's explanation. He covered her hesitation by saying they still had things to discuss but they could do that tomorrow.

She moved back to the table while Max gathered up the papers and returned them to his briefcase. Soon the evening tea tray would be brought in, indicating that the visit was drawing to an end. Aware that any further conversation would be overheard by his grandmother and Lady Ridgeworth, Max kept his tone light as he discussed the merits of a walk around Bath. His comment, 'We will enjoy it together,' sounded very much like a promise.

The butler and a maid brought in the tea tray and their private time was over. As Lady Leith poured the tea, Lady Bea asked, 'Do you remain in Bath for long, Mr Maxwell?'

He replied, 'I have to travel to Europe but I will be back in time for the launch. I will see that you are informed of the details as soon as possible.'

They made polite conversation until Lady Bea said it was time leave. Joanna said a warm goodbye to Lady Leith and thanked her in advance for tomorrow's call, then Max insisted on escorting Bea and Joanna the few yards to old Lady Ridgeworth's house.

As Bea climbed the steps, Max placed a hand on Joanna's arm and whispered, 'Joanna, there are reasons I do not want it known that I am in the country.' At Joanna's look of alarm, he hastened to reassure her. 'I am not wanted for some dire crime, it is just that there are people I prefer not to meet just yet.' He looked up and saw Lady Bea waiting in the open doorway and added quickly, 'I will explain tomorrow.'

Joanna nodded in agreement if not understanding, and wished him goodnight. Max waited until they had been admitted and the door had closed before walking away. He did not return directly to his grandmother's house but paced the quiet streets, rehearsing what he would say to Joanna on the morrow.

***

'That was a very pleasant evening. I do like your Mr Maxwell,' Lady Bea remarked with a sideways glance as they climbed the stairs.

Joanna blushed at the implication but did not comment as they tiptoed past Lady Ridgeworth's bedroom. Bea opened her own door quietly and wished Joanna goodnight before going inside.

Joanna climbed the second staircase, eager to tell Iris all about her evening. She entered the bedroom and called softly, 'Iris, are you awake?'

There was no response so she undressed by the light of the street lamp to avoid disturbing her friend. When Joanna climbed into bed there was a loud creak from the ancient springs and she could not stifle a laugh. However, despite the noise Iris lay unnaturally still.

Joanna laughed softly again and said, 'You are not really asleep, are you?' She reached across the gap and touched Iris's arm. It was rigid and did not even a twitch away from Joanna's cold hand.

She shrugged and turned onto her side. 'Oh well, if you don't want to talk, I'll tell you all about it in the morning. Good night.'

Not quite all, she thought as she tried to get comfortable. Her feelings for Max were too new to share.

Chapter 15

Joanna was alone when she awoke next morning and the covers on Iris's bed were thrown back. She called, 'Will you be long behind the screen?' and was puzzled when there was no reply. She got up to poke her head around the screen. Iris was not there.

Her confusion increased when she saw Iris's flannel was dry and there was no water in the slop pail. Iris was usually so fastidious – what could have made her leave the room without washing? Why would she not talk to her last night, and why was she avoiding her today?

Joanna did not like mysteries and hurriedly washed and dressed. She was about to leave the room when she noticed Iris's brown cloak was missing from the hook on the door. This was getting stranger and stranger.

She went to the window that overlooked the rear garden and saw Iris and John sitting close together on a rustic seat. His arm was around her slumped shoulders and she was holding a handkerchief to her face. Joanna's first instinct was to rush out to join them but, whatever was wrong, she needed to speak to Iris alone.

She sat on the bed to think. She had spent such a happy evening with Max and Lady Leith and had expected to share the details with her closes friend. Some of those details had coloured her dreams, dreams more graphic than ever before. Now she knew the scent of Max's cologne, the warmth of his hand touching hers at the table, the strength of his arm when he escorted them back, all of which had intensified in her dreams. Max holding her and... Then she had woken up, frustrated at being denied whatever came next.

Now Joanna was frustrated by Iris's strange behaviour. She gave a huff of annoyance. Sitting here was not going to solve the problem and she was hungry, even for Lady Ridgeworth's meagre breakfast.

Only Lady Bea was sitting at the table when Joanna entered the dining room. 'Did you sleep well?' she asked. 'Iris has already eaten. She said she did not like to disturb you.'

Joanna poured herself a cup of tea and reached for the toast rack. Without looking at her companion she asked, 'Did Iris seem alright? She pretended to be asleep when I went to bed.'

'I do not believe her evening was as enjoyable as ours. John mentioned that Iris had gone to bed early after a lecture from her grandmother.'

That woman! Joanna managed not to say the thought out loud. Why had she lectured Iris, who had barely said a word in her grandmother's presence since they arrived?

That woman, who usually stayed in her room until after ten o'clock, swept into the dining room and glared at them. Without any greeting she demanded, 'Where are Iris and John?'

'They had finished eating just as I arrived. I think they went out to the garden,' Lady Bea replied calmly.

Joanna could have confirmed the fact but kept her eyes on her plate and said nothing. She felt uncomfortable in the strained atmosphere but did not want to draw attention to herself.

'Pontin!' Lady Ridgeworth yelled. 'Fetch my grandchildren in from the garden. You two come with me.' The old lady turned and stomped off towards the stairs.

Bea sighed. 'We had best go and find out what has upset her this morning.'

Joanna gulped down her tea and pushed a slice of toast into her pocket. She doubted they would be allowed to return to their breakfasts.

The drawing-room door was open so there was no chance of them sneaking past without Lady Ridgeworth seeing them. 'Beatrice! Come in here!' Bea tried to wave Joanna away but the old lady called, 'And Miss Pennicott.'

Lady Ridgeworth was seated in her favourite chair facing the door. She began her interrogation by demanding to know every detail of their visit to Lady Leith, from the dinner menu to what their hostess had been wearing. Bea answered as briefly as she was allowed, and Joanna tried to make herself as inconspicuous as possible.

'Did she tell you why she invited Miss Pennicott?' Lady Ridgeworth demanded.

Bea shook her head. 'It would have been very rude of me to ask, but I assume it was to make the acquaintance of the young lady I will be chaperoning this season.'

The old woman pursed her lips and her eyes raked them like claws. 'There is something havey-cavey going on. If Mary Leith only found out you were in Bath yesterday, how did she know about you chaperoning Miss Pennicott? And if she knew that, why did she not invite Iris, too?'

'I cannot know the workings of Lady Leith's mind. She is your neighbour. Perhaps you could make a call and ask her yourself.'

Lady Ridgeworth thumped the arms of her chair in disapproval. 'Don't get pert with me!' She muttered something under her breath just as John and Iris joined them. Joanna shivered as she watched a malicious smile grow on her hostess's lips. It reminded her of a spider waiting to pounce on its unsuspecting prey. 'Now,' she turned to Bea, 'why did you not mention that Mr Maxwell was also present?'

Iris gave a sob and turned her face into John's sleeve. Clearly she had given the game away and been unable to face Joanna.

'What was he doing there?' Lady Ridgeworth demanded. 'Did you arrange this clandestine meeting thinking I would not find out?'

'It was hardly clandestine, Mother-in-law. Lady Leith—'

'Be quiet! If this an example of how you act as chaperone, I forbid Iris to go to London with you. I will not have my grand—'

This time it was Bea who cut in. 'You cannot forbid her. Iris is in my charge with the permission of her father and my husband.'

'And her brother,' John added.

'Fools! All the men in my family are fools!' Lady Ridgeworth looked fit to burst with rage. 'Each and every one of them seduced by trade instead of upholding the honour of our name!' She almost spat out the words. 'I have warned Iris how it will be. She—' a bony finger pointed at Joanna '—has been using my family's connections for her own benefit for years. Being seen constantly in her company will lower Iris's standing. I won't have it!'

Now Iris was actually crying and Joanna felt a wave of protectiveness for her friend. Joanna had a fine temper that went with her red hair but she seldom felt the need to let it loose. She usually let irritations slide past but she hated bullying. She stared at Lady Ridgeworth and said proudly, 'I am not ashamed of my background. It has already been pointed out to me that my expectations far outweigh my birth. I will not lack for introductions.'

'Then I wash my hands of you. Get out of my house! Go with that jumped-up shopkeeper, but you will not take my granddaughter with you!'

As one, Bea and Joanna turned towards the door. Iris stood with bent head, reluctant to leave the shelter of her brother's arm, and moved with him as he turned to follow the others, ignoring his grandmother's command for Iris to stay.

Out in the hall, Bea touched Joanna's hand. 'I am sorry.'

Joanna smiled. 'You do not need to apologise for someone else's rudeness. It is wrong of me to criticise my hostess, but I am really glad she will not be going to London with us.'

'I am so sorry, Joanna,' Iris whispered. 'I did not mean to tell her. I was speaking to John and Grandmother overheard.'

Joanna hugged her. 'I know that. But what do we do now?'

John took command. 'Get your coats. Bea will take you to Lady Leith while I make arrangements for us to leave.'

If Lady Leith was surprised to see them so early and in a slightly dishevelled state, she hid it well. 'How lovely to see you. Angus has gone for a ride as we expected to call on you later in the day.' She saw them comfortably seated and raised an enquiring eyebrow. 'Now, what can I do for you?'

'John is arranging for us to return to London today. I just beg shelter for an hour or two,' Bea replied.

'You are welcome here at any time, my dear. I will ring for refreshments and you shall tell me what has changed your plans.'

Lady Leith listened to Bea's potted version of the recent quarrel. She did not voice an opinion but her understanding nods spoke volumes. 'I would ask you to stay here, but Bath is a small town and it would give rise to gossip. And gossip is the last thing you want to take to London with you.'

94

Joanna shifted position on the sofa she was sharing with Iris and a strange crunching sound came from the region of her pocket. She suddenly remembered the slice of toast and started to laugh, drawing the attention of the two older ladies.

'I am glad you can find some humour in the situation,' Bea said in some surprise. 'You were grossly insulted.'

Joanna withdrew a handful of crumbs from her pocket. 'It was my breakfast toast.'

'Dry toast!' Lady Leith said, scandalised. 'Lady Ridgeworth is not known for her generosity, but that is worse than I ever expected of her.'

Joanna was still laughing. 'We did not have time to finish breakfast so I stole a slice to eat later. It would have made much more mess if I had stayed to spread it with butter and jam!'

In the lightened atmosphere, Bea said, 'Frugal breakfasts were why we were out so early yesterday. It was lucky for us, otherwise we would not have known Mr Maxwell was in Bath.'

Joanna wished he were here now; if he was gone from the house for much longer, he would miss them.

They drank tea and ate the sandwiches Lady Leith had ordered, making casual conversation as though this were an ordinary visit. Joanna had to admire the older ladies' poise and the way they ignored the recent unpleasantness as though it had not happened. She was still seething inwardly, not just on her own account but for the way it had upset Iris. Lady Bea had received her own share of insults with quiet dignity. Joanna wondered about the 'jumped-up shopkeeper' gibe. In her opinion, Lady Bea had better manners than the dowager.

Lady Leith's butler entered the room and bowed to his mistress. 'My lady, Lady Ridgeworth's maid has arrived with a footman and…'

'No!' Iris's wail cut him off as she rushed across the room and threw herself down in front of Lady Bea, pleading, 'Please don't let them take me back!'

The butler smiled and softened his rigid posture. 'It is Lady Beatrice's maid,' he said reassuringly. 'With a large valise.'

Bea disentangled Iris's hands from the material of her skirt and went out into the hall. 'Vera! What would I do without you?'

Vera Cotton had again proved her worth. When ordered to pack, she had separated suitable travelling clothes for Bea and the girls and ordered a footman to carry the valise along the street to Lady Leith's house.

Bea relayed the information to Lady Leith, who told her butler to get a maid to show her guests up to a bedroom so they might change. They were, in fact, shown two bedrooms: one for Lady Bea and one for the girls. Vera unpacked the clothes they had worn on their journey to Bath and left to help Lady Bea dress.

Joanna was worried about Iris. Even with the assurance that she would not be returned to her grandmother, her friend had still not regained her sparkle. As Iris finished pinning up Joanna's hair, Joanna watched her in the mirror. It was not just due to the earlier unpleasantness; her unhappiness stemmed from whatever had happen last evening. She risked a question. 'Why won't you talk to me?'

Iris's startled eyes skittered to Joanna's reflection and away again. 'It is all my fault. If I had not spoken to John about Max, Grandmother...' Iris broke off mid-sentence and chewed at her lower lip.

Joanna turned around on the stool and took hold of Iris's hands. 'It was not your fault. And even if Lady Ridgeworth overheard, there was no need for her to be so nasty this morning.' She released one of Iris's hands to lift her chin. Eye to eye, she said, 'I know it is rude of me to comment but I have never met anyone as rude as your grandmother!'

Iris managed a small smile. 'Be as rude as you wish. Grandmother has always been difficult to please but I was never frightened of her before.'

'Frightened?' Joanna's mind was racing. 'This is not about this morning, is it? Something happened while Bea and I were out last evening.'

Iris nodded. 'Grandmother does not like Bea. She was planning to write to Papa to say she had taken over my care.' She gulped down a bitter laugh. 'Care! All Grandmother cares about is how things look in society. I would not have been allowed to even meet you.'

Joanna grinned. 'Well, I think it is all for the best. Now Lady Ridgeworth will not be in London to interfere with our fun! Buck up. Bring back the Fairy sunshine.'

Iris threw her arms around Joanna's neck. 'Thank you. I can always rely on you to see the best of a situation.'

Joanna thought it was all down to practice; looking for a positive aspect in any situation had sustained her in the early years at the school. She had enjoyed school life, had an easy relationship with the other pupils and the approval of the teachers. Being invited to visit Iris's family was a high note, but there had been many occasions when mention of a family event had made her feel very lonely indeed. She had made a practice of concentrating on the positives, like the extra treats Miss Waring provided for the girls who did not have accessible families. The 'stayers', as they were called, were taken on visits to the playhouse in Gloucester, on day trips to the Forest of Dean and other places. And always Joanna could look forward to Max's letters.

Oh, she hoped he would return before they had to leave. There was bound to be at least one London train in the next hour or two.

Vera entered the room to say that Lady Bea had gone downstairs. 'I'll finish packing your things. It is a pity Miss Iris's new travelling dress is not finished, but you look very smart, Miss Pennicott.'

'Oh,' Joanna said, worriedly, 'I must ask Lady Bea to arrange for Mrs Down to be paid, even though we do not have all the dresses. Papa was very strict about not owing money.' She laughed. 'Being a tradesman himself, he abhorred unpaid bills!'

John and Max arrived while the girls were still upstairs; they had met in the street and John had quickly reported their change of plans. He repeated the information to the two ladies adding, 'There is a train at a quarter past twelve and I have booked us seats. I have also sent a telegram to Uncle Simon giving the time of our arrival.'

'Well done, John,' Lady Bea applauded. 'I shall be glad to get home.' She looked at Lady Leith and smiled. 'Not that I am eager to leave your company.'

'I quite understand. I think that I may come to Town in a week or so to see how you are all getting along. I have not had so much excitement for years!'

She looked towards the clock on the mantlepiece. 'Iris and Joanna will need to hurry if you are to catch that train. We were very glad Miss Cotton had the foresight to bring them suitable clothing.' She looked John up and down. 'You will have to go as you are. When you get to London, I advise you to hire a valet.'

Although he accompanied them to the station, Joanna had no chance of a private conversation with Max. She listened as he spoke to Lady Bea, asking for her address and thanking her for taking care of Joanna. 'I will let you know in good time about the launch,' he said.

The porter was moving towards them, urging passengers to take their seats. 'When will I see you again?' Joanna asked as Max helped her to board.

He shook his head. 'I don't know, but I will write,' he promised. He reluctantly let go of her hand and stepped back as the porter came between them to slam the carriage door. Joanna's seat was on the other side of the carriage so she could not even wave goodbye as the train pulled away on the next step of her adventure.

Chapter 16

Iris's spirits started to improve as soon as the train left the station whereas Joanna's dipped in the opposite direction. She was so disappointed not to have spent more time with Max. He had been a friend, a constant presence in her mind for years, but nebulous and unformed as a man. Now, having met him, the shadow had taken flesh. Being close to him engendered feelings she had never experienced before, but just when she wanted to explore those feelings they had had to part for an unspecified time. Would it be weeks, months? No, surely not that long until the new ship was ready to be launched.

Iris squeezed her hand and distracted her thoughts. 'I can't wait to get to London and start replenishing my wardrobe,' she enthused, with a grimace at the school cloak and bonnet she was wearing. 'Papa would call it vanity, but I look more like a maid than Mrs Cotton.'

'You look like a young lady fresh out of the schoolroom, Miss Iris,' Vera replied. 'Nothing wrong with that. My lady will soon have you looking like a young lady ready to enchant London.'

'Oh, I don't want to do that!' Iris protested. 'It will just be nice to wear pretty clothes.'

Joanna smiled. Even dressed as she was, Iris had drawn admiring looks from the other passengers. New clothes would only enhance her angelic looks and sweet expression. Sitting beside her, Joanna felt over-large and ungainly. Lady Ridgeworth's assessment had been blunt but very near the truth; ladies were expected to be dainty and helpless because it was a sign of good breeding. New clothes would not achieve that.

Mention of clothes reminded Joanna of the dressmaker's unpaid bill and she asked Lady Bea about it. 'I have already made arrangements with Lady Leith,' Bea replied. 'The bill will be sent to me. Mrs Down must not be the loser because our arrangements have changed.' She laughed quietly and smiled at Joanna. 'My father owned a bookshop and suffered greatly if people did not pay their bills.'

Joanna nodded understandingly. It was another reason for Lady Ridgeworth to despise her daughter-in-law, and it also helped to explain the Armitage family's unusually egalitarian attitude. She had put the reverend's acceptance down to his Christian beliefs but hearing that a viscount could marry a shopkeeper's daughter encouraged her to think that her own commercial connections would not be an insurmountable problem. Not that she was looking for a husband any time soon. Unless it was Max.

Joanna's thoughts juddered to a halt. Given her newly awakened feelings for Max, the thought of marriage to any other man filled her with revulsion. Thank goodness no one had the power to make that decision for her.

Deep in her own thoughts, Joanna lost track of the conversation around her. A direct question from Lady Bea made her apologise and request it be repeated.

'I asked if you would like to make contact with your family. I know there has been an estrangement, but you are bound to meet them at some point. It would be better if the first meeting was in private.'

Joanna smiled suddenly, an imp of mischief riding her shoulder. How it would annoy Aunt Louisa to see her dressed in the height of fashion and sponsored by a viscountess! The meeting would probably be unpleasant but, having survived old Lady Ridgeworth, Joanna knew her aunt's taunts would lack the power to hurt her. She was no longer a frightened child. Miss Waring had taught her to value her own worth.

'I think you are right, Lady Bea. I will leave it to your judgement as to when and where we meet.' She wrinkled her nose in distaste. 'I doubt my aunt will be pleased to see me, but I would like to see Uncle Herbert again. He was the only family member to keep in touch.'

'Joanna, Lady Fulton is a widow.'

Joanna's mind blanked for a moment. 'Uncle Herbert is dead?'

Lady Bea nodded sadly. 'Were you not informed?'

'Who would tell me?' Joanna asked bitterly. 'Certainly not my aunt. I did wonder why Uncle Herbert stopped sending me birthday and Christmas gifts. I thought Aunt Louisa had stopped him.' At Lady Bea's incredulous look, she added, 'Papa said he was under her thumb.'

Iris squeezed Joanna's hand. 'I am sorry. You said he was a kind man.'

'He was. He once braved Aunt Louisa's displeasure for my sake, but I am sure he paid for it later.' Joanna felt a pang of regret though it was hard to find any real grief. Their meeting had been so long ago and quite brief, and she had not really known him. By the time his letters stopped arriving, she was more focussed on hearing from Max.

Lady Bea turned the conversation into brighter channels and said how eager she was to see her young son again. 'And Cynthia, of course,' she added with a slight frown.

Joanna wondered about the frown. She knew Cynthia was Lady Bea's step-daughter, but even on short acquaintance Bea did not give the impression of being a wicked stepmother. Oh well, she would find out for herself soon enough.

Alighting from the train at Paddington Station, Joanna was assailed by memories of arriving here with her father. It had been rather frightening trying to keep up with his long strides across the crowded concourse. He did not like her to hold his hand and she had been jostled to one side and lost sight of him. When she caught up with him again, he did not seem to have noticed their separation; his mind was already focused on hailing a cab to take them to a business meeting.

Now she was being shepherded through the crowd as though she were a person of importance. Fellow travellers moved aside as John led the way, Iris and Bea each holding one of his arms. Vera Cotton took hold of Joanna's arm and followed close behind, daring anyone to step into her path.

As soon as they cleared the barrier, Bea dropped John's arm and rushed into the embrace of her husband. Joanna only had a few moments to see how closely the viscount resembled his brother and nephew before she was being introduced and welcomed.

'The carriage is waiting,' Lord Ridgeworth said, leading the way with his wife who was hanging onto his arm, talking non-stop and making him smile.

In the shuffle, Joanna had somehow changed places with Iris. Supported by John's arm, she relished the admiring glances cast her way. She was not fooled into thinking she was the focus and basked in the glory of being escorted by such a handsome man.

In fact two carriages, both with crests on their doors, were waiting outside the station. John urged his uncle to take the ladies while he and Miss Cotton saw to the luggage. It was only then that Joanna noticed a porter with a laden trolley standing respectfully behind them.

Ridgeworth House in London was huge, and Joanna's eyes nearly popped out of her head when the carriage stopped in front of a gleaming white mansion. Steps led up to an open door flanked by columns and clipped bay trees in red pots. The butler bowed in welcome and two footmen hurried down to the second carriage. Everywhere Joanna looked spoke of money and good taste, from the gleaming wooden floor to the flower arrangements on console tables set under gilt-framed mirrors.

After he had greeted his employers, the butler spoke to Iris. 'Welcome back to London, Miss Armitage.'

'Thank you, Bassett. This is my friend, Miss Pennicott.'

Joanna received a bow and a murmured 'Miss Pennicott', before his place was taken by the housekeeper, Mrs Walker. The greetings and introductions were repeated, giving Joanna little chance to look around.

A maid took the girls up to their rooms. 'This is your room, Miss Armitage. Miss Pennicott is next door.'

'Oh,' Iris said, 'I thought we would still be sharing.' She looked rather lost in the middle of her large room. It was decorated in shades of rose and cream and had a huge bed. 'It would be more fun if you were here with me, Joanna.'

Joanna did not feel confident enough to question the arrangements and had not even seen the room allocated to her, but the two girls had shared a bedroom for more than eight years both at the school and on her visits to the vicarage. They even slept in the same bed. The only time Joanna had slept alone, discounting the two other girls who shared the room, was during the short periods when Iris was away on family visits. It suddenly occurred to her that her friend was equally out of her depth in these surroundings.

The maid who had been their guide said, 'Shall I ask for your things to be brought in here?' As their possessions had been packed together, it would make changing rooms easier so Joanna said, 'Yes, please. Is this the room you had when you visited before?' Joanna asked Iris after the maid had left.

'No, I always slept up on the nursery floor with Ralph and Peter. Goodness knows what my brothers would have got up to if I had not been there to keep an eye on them.'

'You are a young lady now, and fit to be with the adults,' Joanna laughed.

Iris sat down on the edge of the bed and motioned for Joanna to join her. She clasped her hand and confided, 'I'm not sure I am ready to be a young lady. It seemed fun when we spoke of it before, but we will have to go into other houses like this and meet lots of strangers. I don't think I could have borne it without you.'

Joanna gathered her into a hug. 'Goose! What help do you think I will be? Your grandmother was right, I don't belong in your kind of society.'

'I don't either,' Iris wailed. 'Even at the station people were looking at us. It will be worse when we are dressed up and going to balls. I wish I were back at school.'

Lady Bea arrived in time to hear Iris's last statement. 'What is this?' She sat on the other side of Iris and took her hand. 'What has upset you, love? It cannot be anything dreadful.'

Iris tried to explain and Bea laughed. 'Stage fright! I felt exactly the same when I was thrown head first in society. And remember, I was even less well-prepared than you. You will get over it. Just hold your head high and people will value you as you value yourself. Now, we are informal for dinner so one of your day dresses will do. And Cynthia will be coming down to join us. I popped in to tell her after I had seen Nicholas. She became so excited that Miss Payne threatened to withhold her permission.'

Bea's genial face took on a frown. 'It is high time Miss Payne was replaced. I shall mention school to Simon as soon as possible.' She headed for the door, only to turn back and ask, 'Do you want a maid sent up?'

Joanna said they were used to helping each other and mentioned Iris's request that they share a room. 'Of course, if that is what you want. The storage will be a bit of a squeeze once you have new clothes, but you can use the next room as well.'

'Who is Miss Payne?' Joanna asked as soon as the door closed.

'Cynthia's governess. Payne by name and pain by nature. I do believe she thinks a smile is a deadly sin.'

Joanna and Iris were dressed and debating whether to go down when there was a gentle knock on the door. Joanna went to open it and a thin, dark-haired girl rushed past her to hug Iris, babbling an incoherent welcome. A short, plump, middle-aged woman stepped in after her and said severely, 'Miss Cynthia! Your manners, if you please.'

Standing half-hidden by the door, Joanna watched the young girl stiffen, step back and curtsey. 'Welcome to London, Cousin Iris,' she said in a voice devoid of emotion as though all the joy had been sucked out of the reunion. The transformation was heart breaking.

Joanna moved from her position and faced the governess. Using every inch of her height, she looked down at the stern-faced woman who reminded her forcibly of Aunt Louisa. 'Thank you, Miss Payne. We will take Cynthia down to dinner.'

Miss Payne looked up in surprise but recovered quickly. 'After that display, Miss Cynthia does not deserve to eat with adults.'

Joanna's action had given Iris time to rally her protective instincts. She placed an arm around Cynthia's waist; what she lacked in size she made up for in breeding. 'Cynthia will come with us,' she said, echoing Joanna's words. She nodded to Joanna who started to close the door, forcing the governess to back out of the room.

Joanna turned back to the cousins who were again in each other's arms. They did not look much alike. Although not yet twelve years old, Cynthia was already a head taller than Iris. Her dark-brown hair was combed so tightly back into a braid that Joanna could imagine the arranging must have been painful. *Payne by name and pain in execution*, Joanna thought.

Cynthia also lacked Iris's sunny smile; even with the governess dismissed there was a slightly worried expression on her face. 'Miss Payne will be very cross. She says I am too young to eat in the dining room.'

Iris and Joanna exchanged a frowning glance over the child's head. Something was very wrong here. Iris pulled her cousin to sit on the edge of the bed. Keeping a comforting grasp on her hand, she asked, 'Is Miss Payne often cross?'

Cynthia nodded. 'I keep getting things wrong. I have to go without puddings or supper if I am sent to bed early.'

Joanna came to sit on Cynthia's other side. 'Does she smack you or say nasty things?'

'Just nasty things,' the child whispered in the direction of her lap.

The worst form of punishment, Joanna thought. Words left no visible marks but they sank claws deep into one's sense of self. She knew exactly how that felt. 'Have you told your parents?'

'No!' Cynthia cried in alarm. 'She would tell them even worse things about me. They will really hate me.'

'I don't believe you are so very naughty that Uncle Simon and Aunt Bea could ever do that,' Iris protested. 'And I am quite sure they do not want you to be unhappy.' She looked at Joanna and read equal concern on her friend's face.

Joanna mouthed the word 'Later' and spoke in a rallying tone to Cynthia. 'Will you take us downstairs now, please? I, for one, am very ready for my dinner.'

They met Lord Ridgeworth and Bea as they emerged from their bedroom. Cynthia kept her eyes down and dipped a wobbly curtsey. Lord Ridgeworth frowned in disappointment and withdrew the hand he had extended. Cynthia moved closer to Iris, who caught her uncle's eye and shook her head.

Lord Ridgeworth frowned again, but Bea took his arm and led the way down the stairs to where John was waiting in the hall.

The dining table was long enough to seat thirty, but six places had been laid at one end. Cynthia clung to Iris's hand and slid into the seat between her cousin and stepmother. John pulled out a chair for Joanna so she was seated between him and Lord Ridgeworth.

Despite the grand surrounding, it was a very relaxed meal. Iris and Bea looked after Cynthia, helping her to the dishes offered by a footman. From her side of the table, Joanna watched the girl enjoying her food. She ate quickly but not untidily and cleared each plate. She was unnaturally thin and Joanna wondered if she missed more than the occasional pudding.

After a few queries as to her comfort, Lord Ridgeworth begged Joanna's pardon and spoke across her to John. 'I have arranged for you to go to Ridgeworth tomorrow. My steward will show you the books and general routine. A week or so should be adequate, then you will come back to London to be introduced into the political side of being a lord.'

Joanna found their discussion fascinating and dared to ask, 'Are all lords involved in politics?'

Lord Ridgeworth shook his head. 'Not as many as ought to be, I am afraid. There are those who prefer enjoying themselves instead of using their influence for the betterment of the nation.' He smiled. 'But we must not bore you. Tell me, what are you most wanting to see in London?'

Joanna had not been at all bored but she accepted the change of topic. 'Lady Bea says we will have to wait for our new clothes before we can go out and about.' She chuckled. 'Lady Ridgeworth was most adamant on that point.' Then she blushed. Would Lord Ridgeworth be annoyed at the implied criticism of his mother?

He exchanged a quick, twinkling glance with his wife before replying, 'I hear she does not approve of pink blouses.' Joanna and Iris laughed and Cynthia had to be let in to the story of Bea's school adventure.

Servants came between them to collect the used dishes and conversation stopped until the desserts were placed on the table. In the lull, Bea said to Cynthia, 'I have been talking to Papa about sending you to Iris's school. I had…'

Cynthia leapt out of her chair and threw herself onto her knees at her father's side. 'Please don't send me away. I promise I will be good.'

Lord Ridgeworth pushed back his chair and gathered his weeping daughter onto his lap. He looked helplessly at Bea, who left her seat to join in the family embrace. 'You don't have to go,' she said quietly. 'We just thought you would like to be with other girls. I had such a lovely day at Miss Waring's school.'

'We loved it there, Cynthia,' Iris added. Joanna backed her up by saying she would have been content to stay there until she was an old lady.

Bea dismissed the servants and drew a chair close to her husband so she could hold Cynthia's hand. 'Cynthia, my dear, please don't be upset. You need a new governess anyway and I thought...'

Cynthia lifted her face from where it had been buried in her father's cravat and asked shakily, 'Miss Payne will leave?' The ringing hope in her voice told the adults all they needed to know.

'And about time too!' Joanna blurted out and then apologised for interfering in a family matter.

'Joanna is right,' Iris insisted. 'Cynthia is afraid of Miss Payne. I did not like her when I stayed here before and I thought her too strict. But she always had an excuse.'

'She does insist that Cynthia is easily over-excited,' Bea said thoughtfully. She smiled at her stepdaughter. 'You do seem to always have a bad night after I have taken you out for a treat.'

Lord Ridgeworth kissed the top of his daughter's head and transferred her into Bea's arms. 'Take her to the drawing room. I am going to speak to Miss Payne.' He strode from the room like a general going into battle. Joanna would have given half her fortune to be a witness to the coming interview.

John hovered uncertainly as the women shepherded Cynthia from the room. He had no idea whether his presence in the drawing room would help or aggravate his cousin's distress. The only gently bred young girl he had ever known was Iris, and he could not remember her ever being upset. Until today. Her distress this morning had left him at a loss as how to comfort her. On the whole, he thought he would be better out of the present situation.

He caught Joanna's sleeve and said, 'I won't join you. Better not,' and made for the safety of his room.

In the drawing room, Bea settled on a sofa with Cynthia tucked closely into her side. Iris and Joanna sat opposite and, with gentle questions, gradually coaxed Cynthia into telling Bea how Miss Payne had been undermining her confidence with criticism and withholding her food. Worst of all, the governess had shut her in a cupboard and sometimes forgotten to let her out.

'Everything will be alright now,' Bea promised. 'I doubt you will ever have to see Mis Payne again. And you will not go to school.'

'Oh, that would be a shame,' Iris told her cousin. 'I enjoyed it so much that I am going back for a while to learn to be a teacher.'

'That is news to me,' Bea remarked wryly, making Iris blush.

'Well, I haven't convinced Mama yet. She thinks I will turn into a lady!'

Joanna smiled. She was the only person besides Miss Waring who knew of Iris's ambition. Mrs Armitage was so concerned that her mill-owner background would hamper her children that she insisted they take every opportunity to associate with their titled relatives.

They talked more about Miss Waring, the school regime, the buildings, gardens and happy experiences until Cynthia started asking eager questions. It was a joy to see the child gradually gaining confidence. Finally she asked shyly, 'Could I go just to see how I like it?'

Bea hugged her and agreed. 'Papa and I will come with you and make sure everything is to your liking.'

Cynthia sighed in contentment and nestled closer to Bea. 'I knew you loved me, even though Miss Payne said I was a thorn in your side.'

'We will forget Miss Payne ever existed', Bea said firmly. 'Now, is there anything else we can do to make you happy?'

Cynthia thought for a moment. 'I missed pudding again.' The other three laughed and Bea told Iris to ring the bell and order a portion of pudding sent up straight away.

Cynthia was happily scraping the last of the cream and pastry from her dish when Lord Ridgeworth returned. He still looked very stern, but Joanna began to suspect his austere manner hid a heart as open and generous as his brother, Reverend Armitage.

'All clear, little one,' he told Cynthia with a smile. 'Whether you decide to go to school or not, Miss Payne will be out of this house at daybreak.'

Cynthia's face fell. 'Not until the morning?'

Iris remembered that Miss Payne's bedroom was next to the nursery. She looked at Bea for permission and suggested,

'Perhaps I could sleep upstairs with you?' Bea nodded and Iris added, 'If Joanna does not mind?'

'Is there another bed? I would like to join you, if I may.'

Bea laughed and wondered aloud if they intended to try out every room in the house.

Chapter 17

Joanna's first week in London was a whirl of dress fittings and shopping. When they were not engaged in preparing for their coming out, Joanna and Iris spent most of their time in the nursery. They were not overly surprised to find that Cynthia spent little time with her young half-brother. Admittedly he was only four years old but he already had the looks and charisma of his male relative.

'Miss Payne's influence again,' Joanna whispered to Iris as Cynthia sat on the floor happily piling bricks for her brother.

They were more appalled by Cynthia's lack of education, which had nothing to do with the girl's intelligence. The educational materials were more suited to an eight year old than a girl approaching puberty. New books were added to their shopping lists and they played at schools, often joined by Bea, to show Cynthia that learning could be fun.

Fun had been in short supply in Cynthia's life. Miss Payne had always contrived to be present when Bea visited the schoolroom, curbing the child's natural impulse to respond to her stepmother's loving overtures. When Bea had insisted on taking Cynthia out the governess had reported that the excitement had made her ill, but it was not excitement just the after-effects of a punishment.

Joanna had found a bottle of emetic in the governess's room and Polly, the nursery maid, had told her Cynthia was always given a dose after an outing with Lady Bea. 'Miss is often sick or wets herself if she is upset, but it doesn't seem to do much good,' the maid confided. The girl clearly did not know the vomiting was the result of the emetic. Joanna was horrified and shared the information with Bea at the first opportunity.

Other bits of information emerged slowly as Cynthia gained confidence. Miss Payne was a sadistic bully and, if Joanna had had her way, would have been brought to justice for ill-treatment.

'Best just to let it go now,' Bea advised. 'The less said about that woman, the better.'

Removed from the governess's tyranny, Cynthia began to show her true nature. She acted much younger than her age as a result of neglect, but she was intelligent and eager for new experiences. She worshipped Iris and always wanted assurances that Iris would return whenever they went out without her.

Away from Cynthia, Iris cried. 'How could anyone treat a child so?' she sobbed to Joanna when told of the emetic. 'I am determined to go with her if Uncle Simon agrees to her attending Miss Waring's school.'

Where Iris was overly gentle and coaxing, Joanna challenged Cynthia to sing louder, run faster and to aim a ball at more and more distant targets, then she heaped praise on her achievements.

The biggest breakthrough came through music. There was an upright piano in the schoolroom that Cynthia regarded as a monster. 'That is my worst thing,' she confided. 'I do practise but I can never get it right.' It was not surprising: the instrument was so badly out of tune that even Iris could not coax a true melody out of it. A piano tuner was called in and music sheets were added to their shopping lists.

As Joanna loved to sing, the nursery often echoed with lively songs. Singing had always been her way of giving vent to her emotions. It had started when she was a child, when she would sing to her mother who never had the energy for more active pursuits. Later, at school, songs had been a way to express the feelings she did not share even with Iris.

Everyone had praised her, which was a novel experience. Right from the start, the other girls had found Joanna rather strange because her early life had been so different to theirs. She had never learned to play; the artefacts her father brought home were not toys and he had taught her to handle them with care. There were no story books, only business papers.

By the time she was eight years old, Joanna was taking notes at her father's dictation, unaware that this was his way of concealing his illiteracy. This all added up to make her an ideal student but not overly friendly, which was why she understood Cynthia so well. They had both been lonely.

Lord Ridgeworth was also a regular visitor to the nursery and lost all his stiffness as he romped with his son. Sometimes, while

Iris was engaged in giving Cynthia a lesson, he spoke to Joanna about her own ambitions.

'I did not really have any,' Joanna admitted. 'I just took each day at a time.' She smiled ruefully. 'I suppose I was just waiting. I came to accept that Papa would never return so I supposed I would stay with Miss Waring until I was old enough to live independently. I am not even sure what I meant by that.'

Joanna liked Lord Simon, as he asked to be called. He was considerably older than his wife and always looked very stern, standing with his hands behind his back and taking note of everything and everyone. But when he smiled, the years fell away and revealed how devastatingly handsome he must have been in his youth. He also had a quick sense of humour and abundant love for his wife, son and daughter.

He had been told about the impending ship launch and said he would be happy to escort them. That led to him revealing some of his Parliamentary work to improve the living and working conditions of the poorer classes. 'Shipyards will be a new experience for me, too.'

Joanna was beginning to wonder if the launch would ever take place. There had been no word from Max although she had written several, as yet, unposted pages to him. She did not know where to send them; she did not know if he was still in England or on the Continent. At least he would not be on his way back to India for another eight years. It was very frustrating, but surely it could not be much longer. He had been quite insistent that he had things to tell her.

Joanna had heard from Mr Ebstone. Two days after her arrival, a special courier had delivered some of her mother's jewellery. Mr Ebstone's covering letter explained that the most expensive pieces were still lodged in a Bristol bank. He had added: *Even I know diamonds are not considered suitable for young girls.*

Bea considered most of the pieces were also too sophisticated for a young girl. She selected a few modest necklaces and bracelets for immediate use and placed the rest in Lord Ridgeworth's safe. Joanna was to have an opportunity to wear her finery the next day.

Lady Bea has arranged for the girls' first official appearance to be at the theatre. It would give them an overview of polite society without having to engage too closely with multiple strangers. Keeping to a light atmosphere, she had chosen a musical comedy staged at the Gaiety Theatre. They were to be escorted by Lord Ridgeworth, John Armitage and a young male acquaintance to make up the numbers.

Cynthia perched on the bed, watching as Vera supervised the dressing of Joanna and Iris. They had been given a maid of their own and, although she was very young and inexperienced, she was a natural hairdresser. Joanna's thick tresses had been looped over her ears and swept up into a complicated knot at the back. She thought it looked very well.

The two maids lifted her dress over her head, being careful not to disarrange her hair. It was of heavy silk in her favourite shade of moss green, severely cut and with minimal frills. It had been made by Lucy Moscomb, an old friend of Lady Beatrice. She was much sought after and only accepted clients she felt would do justice to her designs. She did not usually dress debutantes but had agreed to see Joanna as a favour to Lady Bea.

She was unlike anything Joanna had expected of a fashionable modiste. Middle-aged and on the plump side, the clothes she was wearing did not pose much of an advertisement; in fact, she was untidy from her greying hair down to her scuffed slippers. She spoke with a sing-song East Anglian accent and did not mince her words.

'Not in the usual style,' Lucy remarked, walking around Joanna to view her from all angles. She smiled to soften the apparent criticism. 'You will never be conventionally beautiful but I can make you stand out.'

'I am not sure I want that,' Joanna replied. She waved a hand down her front and pulled a wry face. 'I do that too much already.'

Lady Bea and the dressmaker had laughed and, ignoring Joanna's protests, set about planning her wardrobe.

This dress exposed more of Joanna's shoulders and chest than she was really comfortable with, although the dressmaker had assured her the neckline was quite modest. The corset foundation emphasised her natural curves and the smooth line of the skirt front drew attention to her height. The back was drawn into a series of folds over a hip-pad. With the addition of long gloves and a gold locket, Joanna was pronounced, 'Very fine indeed.'

She looked at herself in the long mirror and had a sudden wish that Max could see her now. Fine clothes did seem to make fine ladies, but she was still too tall, too curvy and had too many freckles. Her eyes swivelled to Iris, who looked even more beautiful than usual in a white dress sprinkled with silver embroidery and accepted that no-one was going to notice her when her friend was near. It had always been so and, in the absence of Max, it still did not matter.

The ladies travelled to the theatre with Lord Ridgeworth. He paid gallant compliments to all three, saying he was reluctant to share them. That eased some of Joanna's apprehension and she was able to enter the theatre foyer with confidence.

John and Mr Whiley, the young man with whom he had struck up a friendship, were waiting for them and made the introductions. Mr Whiley was a good head shorter than Joanna, and quickly looked away from her to gaze adoringly at Iris as he offered her his arm and they followed the Ridgeworths deeper into the building.

That left Joanna beside John. It was the first time he had seen her since their arrival in London and he was taken aback by her transformation. He hid his surprise with a smile as he tilted his head closer and whispered, 'Lady Bea is going to have her hands full with the pair of you looking so lovely.'

Joanna accepted the implied compliment gratefully. Being considered favourably in the same breath as Iris was a novel experience. 'You look very fine yourself,' she replied.

Several other women in the vicinity appeared to agree as they cast their eyes over John. The severity of his evening clothes accentuated his blond hair and tall, athletic build; Joanna could not have asked for a more handsome escort. She ignored a tiny voice in her head that whispered 'Max' and placed her hand on John's sleeve with a smile.

They were led to a box close to the stage from which Joanna could look around at the gilded décor and finely dressed audience. High above, huge chandeliers cast their light over the packed floor of the theatre and, more dimly, the rows of lesser seats that she had heard referred to as 'the gods'. Everyone seemed to be in party mood as they nodded or waved to acquaintances until the babble of voices was drowned out by the orchestra striking up a rousing overture. The lights dimmed and the performance began.

Joanna had never seen anything like it. From the moment the curtains opened, she was enthralled by the music, the costumes and the sheer exuberance of the opera. Thankfully it was in English with enough spoken words between the songs to explain the plot. She loved every minute.

During the interval, servants brought them refreshments and several people came to be introduced, but Joanna only paid polite attention. That was hardly noticed because everyone was more interested in Iris and John. In fact, Joanna resented their intrusion when she was eager to get back to the rest of the performance.

'That was wonderful!' she exclaimed when the applause died down after the final curtain call. People were moving towards the exits but she wanted it to start all over again.

Lord Ridgeworth smiled at her enthusiasm. 'I am not a great lover of opera, but I have to admit that was most entertaining.'

'I thought it would be in a foreign language. I would have enjoyed it anyway,' she added hastily, 'but it helps to know what they are singing about.'

The evening was not over; they adjourned to the Savoy Hotel for a late supper. The ladies went straight to the retiring room, where Bea introduced them to several other ladies. Joanna could not help overhearing them praising Iris's looks and saying she would be the rage of the season. Enquiries about Joanna were whispered, but not beyond her hearing.

'A friend of Iris's whom I have agreed to sponsor,' Bea replied briefly before being asked about John.

Iris rolled her eyes and whispered, 'I knew how it would be. I am sure a girl in the opposite box spent more time looking at John than she did at the stage.'

Joanna laughed. 'Why were *you* looking around instead of looking at the stage? Didn't you enjoy it?'

Iris gave the closest she could achieve to a frown. 'The next time I come to the theatre, I am going to sit up in the gods instead of being put on display.' Then her smile reappeared and she nudged Joanna playfully. 'And I was also looking at you. I thought you were going to jump out of the box and join the players.'

That was just as Joanna had felt. She loved music. Listening was good but actually singing was better. Some of the songs were still echoing in her head.

Bea asked if they were ready and led them down to the restaurant. Lord Ridgeworth had ordered champagne and Bea allowed the girls one glass each. Joanna would not have wanted any more because she did not really enjoy it; she did not need any more bubbles inside her or she would surely have floated up to the ceiling.

She did not want the evening to end. Excitement had added a glow to her usually pale skin and she was unaware of how lovely she looked. She attributed the admiring glances cast towards their table to Iris and John.

'Well, I am glad that is over,' Iris declared when they eventually reached home and their bedroom. She pulled the combs from her hair and wriggled out of her dress as soon as the maid unfastened it.

Joanna, still floating on a cloud, stared at her in confusion. 'Didn't you enjoy the opera? I thought it was wonderful.'

'Oh, the opera was good but I wish we had come straight home.' Iris sounded unnaturally cross and went behind the screen while the maid assisted Joanna. Free of her dress, Joanna dismissed her, saying they could manage alone now. 'Iris?' she called. 'Are you finished?'

Iris emerged in her nightgown and Joanna stepped towards the screened toilet facilities, but Iris caught her hand as she passed. 'I am sorry to dampen your mood,' she said quietly.

'What is wrong?' Joanna asked, taking in Iris's woebegone expression.

'I hate being stared at. Mr Wiley made me feel most uncomfortable. And he has threatened to call tomorrow. Well, I suppose it is today now, which makes it much more imminent.'

'He was rather taken with you,' Joanna replied. 'Your first beau.'

'I don't want a beau!' Iris said emphatically. 'I don't want to be showered with compliments – especially by someone who looks like a wet spaniel.'

Joanna laughed. 'He didn't look very wet to me.'

'It was the spaniel part I meant,' Iris moaned. 'Those brown, pleading eyes never seemed to look anywhere else.'

Joanna pulled Iris to sit beside her on the bed. 'Iris, I think you are going to have to get used to it. You always look lovely but tonight even more so. I felt like a big lump beside you.'

'John did not seem to think so. He was watching you almost as closely as Mr Wiley was staring at me.'

'John!' Joanna spluttered. 'Don't be silly. He is the big brother I never had. Come to bed. I think you are just over-tired.'

She attended to her own toilet and joined Iris under the covers before dousing the lamp. She could feel Iris lying stiff as a board and in no way composed for sleep. She reached for Iris's arm and slid her fingers down to her friend's tightly curled fist. Gently she prised her fingers apart and linked them with her own. 'Iris? I don't understand why you are so upset. Everyone who knows you says how beautiful you are.'

Iris jerked her hand free and sat up. 'That is just it! He does not know me. None of the people staring at me tonight know me. I felt…' She could not find words to describe the feeling of being a prized object in a shop window. 'Oh…' she wailed and slid back under the covers until only a froth of blonde curls were visible in the muted light.

Joanna gathered her weeping friend into her arms and crooned soft sounds of comfort. It was so unlike Iris to display any emotion other than a sunny joie de vivre.

'I want to go home,' Iris whispered on a hiccup.

Joanna lay quietly and considered Iris's complaint. The two compliments she had received had come from Lord Simon and John, both of whom could almost be regarded as relatives. Strangers had only given her a cursory glance, very few of which were approving. In that she was wrong, but she was too inexperienced to recognise the difference between disapproval and speculation. On the other hand, everyone had smiled at Iris just as they had done during the whole of Joanna's acquaintance with her.

She eased her arm out from beneath the now-sleeping Iris and stared up at the ceiling, trying to grasp the difference between the smiles of friends and strangers. Looking at Iris made her feel happy and it seemed to have the same effect on everyone, which should be a good thing. Iris was performing a public service by bringing beauty into other people's lives.

Joanna yawned, too tired to puzzle over Iris's problem any longer. Nothing would change: Iris would remain beautiful and people would want to look at her. All Joanna could hope for was that Iris would become accustomed to the attention.

***

Over the following days, Iris collected a court of unwanted admirers. She was always polite and, on the surface, her usual happy self. Only Joanna recognised her growing tension before any public appearance. Whenever she could Iris sat with the wallflowers; her admirers followed and Iris skilfully palmed them off to the less popular girls. It did not always work, however, and she was forced to dance with men who, unwittingly, made her uncomfortable.

As usual when she had something on her mind, Joanna wrote to Max. She still did not know where to send the letters but the very act of putting her thoughts on paper helped to clarify them. She came to the conclusion that friends saw more than Iris's face; they saw her kindness and willingness to help others and that, despite her open friendliness, she was basically very shy.

Joanna received her own share of attention. When it became generally known that she was the sole heiress to the Pennicott Shipping Company, she was besieged by impoverished gentleman and mamas with marriageable sons. Bea had her hands full vetting the invitations that came through the post and the direct requests made at the social events they attended. Overall, Joanna found it highly amusing.

She had no illusions as to the source of their interest. She had been a plain child and an awkward adolescent, a fact of life that she accepted. Maturity and fashionable clothes had improved matters, but she was well aware she did not fit the ideal of blonde daintiness society demanded. That being so, she accepted the attention with a healthy dose of scepticism. She treated the young men, mostly second or third sons with no expectations, much as she treated Iris's younger brothers.

Joanna's down-to-earth attitude found favour with the arbiters of fashionable behaviour. Men in search of a wife considered her fortune; titled men in search of a more basic relationship saw her lush curves and counted her background as an asset, supposing she would be open to offers other than marriage. Joanna accepted the compliments demurely and did not believe a word of them. She simply enjoyed being asked to dance, to take carriage rides and to be included in other outings.

Joanna had even enjoyed meeting her Aunt Louisa. Bea had taken her to call on Lady Fulton as soon as she had acquired a suitable walking dress, saying that unpleasant tasks were best dealt with promptly. Joanna had taken a mischievous delight in her aunt's shocked expression when she literally had to look up at her despised niece.

Lady Bea had covered the moment of awkwardness with social chit-chat and the brief visit passed without any direct conversation between aunt and niece. Subsequent meetings had been cool but polite, and Joanna rarely gave her relative another thought.

Only her continued worry about Iris prevented her enjoyment of the season from being complete.

One morning at breakfast Lady Bea gave a small sound of dismay as she went through the post. 'Oh, dear.' She looked at Joanna sorrowfully. 'Joanna, Iris has been invited to a presentation. I did try to get you included but…' Her voice trailed off.

'I won't go without her,' Iris declared.

'Nonsense,' Joanna replied. 'You have a right to be presented formally. No, don't argue. It will please your mama – and I never expected it anyway.'

Lord Simon commended her for her generous attitude. 'It is not generous, just realistic,' Joanna said with a shrug. 'I have overheard comments that I am only accepted because Lady Bea is sponsoring me.'

Her breakfast companions tried to reassure her but Joanna did not really care one way or the other. 'I am enjoying being in town, but I would not like to live like this all the time.'

When asked what she wanted to do, Joanna could not put it into words. It would be insulting to tell her hosts that she found most of her new acquaintances shallow, with little purpose to their lives beyond a continual round of entertainment. She much preferred the company of Lord Simon's friends, who were generally older businessmen or politicians. They did not try to flatter her and were easily diverted into talking about their own activities in the wider world. Some were startled by her knowledge and interest in current affairs, but most were happy just to air their opinions.

'I miss being busy,' Joanna said eventually. When the others laughed, she added, 'I don't mean rushing around shopping or going to parties, I mean busy with my mind. Teaching Cynthia has made me think about asking Miss Waring if I may go back and help at the school.'

That was only part of the idea that had been forming. Her father was quite obviously not going to come home, and a single lady had very limited scope when it came to employment. With the future in mind, Joanna had been toying with the idea of opening a school of her own when she was older. She had the house in Bristol, which was well-situated and large enough to start a small establishment. She did not even need her father to finance it; her investments were doing nicely and, given a few more years, would make her independent.

'But you have no reason to work,' Lord Simon insisted. 'You will marry and have a home to run. That should keep you busy.'

Joanna astonished her hosts by saying she had never given serious thought to marriage and none of the gentlemen she had met recently had made her change her mind. *Except Max,* she thought privately. Meeting him had given rise to thoughts of intimacy that she wanted to share with him, but which were totally abhorrent in connection with any other man.

Max had given no indication that he felt the same way. Their one evening together had been wonderful but far too short. She did wonder from time to time about what he had hinted they needed to talk about, but it could not have been very urgent.

'I sympathise with Joanna,' Bea said. 'Very few men are like you, my dear, and they would not tolerate a wife who wanted to use her intelligence. Add the fact that married women are now entitled to keep any money they earn,' she laughed ruefully, 'well, that is a very sore point with some men.'

Iris had been quiet during this discussion. She waited until they were alone before giving Joanna a hug. 'Will you really come back to school?' she asked eagerly. 'Everything would go back to the way it was. It is like a dream come true.'

Joanna was glad to see Iris happy again but she no longer wanted everything to be the way it was. That phase of her life was over; even if she did go back as a teacher, things would never be the same again.

Chapter 18

Two days later, the ladies returned from ordering Iris's presentation gown to be greeted by the very worried butler. 'My lady, this telegram arrived. I sent a message to the dressmaker but you had already left.'

Bea took the envelope and murmured vaguely, 'We made some calls.' She opened the envelope and gasped. The message from Reverend Armitage was brief and threw the whole party into panic: Mrs Armitage had suffered a heart attack and Iris was to return home immediately.

Iris burst into tears. 'It's all my fault. I never meant...'

Joanna pulled her friend into her arms saying, 'Hush. It is no such thing. Come upstairs and I will help you to pack.'

Lady Bea did not understand why Iris should think it was her fault, but a shake of Joanna's head advised her not to ask. Before she could decide what to do next, the front door opened to admit Lord Simon and John. 'Oh, thank goodness you are here!' she cried, rushing forward.

Lord Simon saw the telegram in his wife's hand and took charge. 'I received the same news. Fortunately John was with me so we came straight here.'

In the privacy of their bedroom, Iris wept on Joanna's shoulder. 'This is my fault. I prayed to go home, but not like this.'

Joanna gave her a little shake. 'Iris, this is *not* your fault. Your papa would say you are presumptuous to think the Almighty would punish your mama for your discontent.'

'I did not mean to be ungrateful,' Iris sobbed.

'Now don't talk nonsense. You *are* grateful to Lady Bea. You just dislike a lot of attention.'

Joanna fetched a cold, wet cloth and was holding it to Iris's eyes when Vera Cotton arrived to supervise the packing. As Iris tried to pull herself together, Vera was as bracing as Joanna. 'You'll not need to take much. I dare say your mama will be as right as rain in a few days. You'll be back before we have time to miss you.'

'I won't be...'

Joanna quickly forestalled the protest she could see on Iris's lips. No-one needed to know Iris would be glad to stay at home; time enough to sort that out when they knew how things stood with Mrs Armitage. 'This coat will be more comfortable for travelling,' she said, holding it ready. 'Your uncle will have the carriage at the door before we have you ready.'

In a very short space of time, Bea and Joanna were on the front steps waving goodbye to Iris, John and Lord Simon on their way to the station.

Bea heaved a sigh. 'I need tea.'

'And we will need to tell Cynthia. It would not do for her to learn of Iris leaving from the servants.'

'Tea first. And you can tell me why Iris reacted that way.'

The delay gave Joanna time to concoct a plausible story. She could not betray Iris's confidences with the truth. Over the teacups, she told Bea that Iris felt guilty for enjoying a London season instead of going home to help her mama with her parish duties.

'It is nonsense, of course. Mrs Armitage has everything well in hand and still finds time to oversee the factory. But if I know Iris, she will insist on staying home and cosseting her mother to death. Oh!' Joanna clapped her hands over her mouth. 'That was an unfortunate turn of phrase.'

Bea managed a smile. 'Best not to repeat that in Cynthia's hearing.'

Cynthia reacted exactly as expected to the news of Iris's departure. She had developed what the schoolgirls called a *crush* on her cousin, and only saw the situation from her own perspective. She showed scant concern for the aunt she had never met. 'Iris will be coming back, won't see?'

Bea wiped her stepdaughter's eyes and said quietly, 'I cannot say for sure, Cynthia, but it seems unlikely.'

'What about her presentation?' The girl was becoming hysterical and slapped away Bea's comforting hands. 'I want Iris. She did not even say goodbye to me.'

Joanna whispered, 'Leave her to me,' and Bea gratefully slipped out of the room.

Joanna allowed Cynthia another minute of self-pity before saying coldly, 'You are being very selfish. Iris had no thought but to get to her sick mother. What she will do in the future depends on the situation she finds at home.'

The shock of being taken to task dried Cynthia's tears, though she stared resentfully at Joanna. 'Iris is supposed to be your friend but you don't look very upset.'

'I have learned to control by feelings. I will miss Iris more than you will ever know. She was my first friend at a time when I felt all alone in the world. You are not alone, and you are quite old enough to think of others besides yourself.'

Cynthia glared and pouted, but when Joanna simply stared back she was the first to lower her eyes. 'I hope Iris's mama gets better in time for her to go to school with me,' she said in a flat voice.

Joanna sighed. From being repressed, Cynthia had gone to the other extreme and always wanted her own way. The sooner she went to school and mixed with other girls, the better it would be for all concerned. It was time for another piece of advice.

'If Iris does return to the school while you are there, things will be very different,' she warned. That caught Cynthia's attention and Joanna continued. 'You will be just one of her pupils. There will be no special treatment because you are cousins. If she singled you out, you would be called a teacher's pet and shunned by the other girls. It won't mean that Iris loves you less, just that it would undermine her position. You would not want that, would you?'

'Then I won't go. I want Iris!' Cynthia flounced away to look out of the window and only turned around when Joanna said calmly, 'I was taught that "I want" shows a serious lack of manners. Now stop behaving like a baby and draw a get-well picture for your aunt. Make Iris proud of you,' she added as a clincher.

Joanna left to mull over what she had said to Cynthia. Perhaps she had spoken out of turn; she was not a relative and it really was none of her business how Cynthia behaved. But she had never shied from facing the truth and, in the long run, it would be better for Cynthia to do the same.

She went to reassure Bea that the storm had passed. 'I don't know how you do it,' Bea said gratefully. 'I suppose it is because you seem much older than your years and she respects you.'

Joanna was not sure about the respect – Cynthia was more likely to resent her straight talking – but Bea was still pondering her relationship with her stepdaughter. 'I have never been able to get close to Cynthia. Before I married Simon, she lived with her maternal grandmother. After our marriage, Mrs Prentiss begged for Cynthia to stay in her charge.' Bea gave a grimace. 'I am afraid she was of much the same opinion of me as Lady Ridgeworth, and only grudgingly allowed Cynthia to visit. She only came to live with us permanently a few months ago.'

It explained a great deal, but Joanna decided it was time to change the subject and asked what they were to do for the rest of the day.

'We are invited to tea with Lady Brockley,' Bea replied, 'but I will send a note if you do not wish to go.'

One of the last things Iris had said to Joanna was an order that she should enjoy the rest of the season and write her a full account. 'I shall enjoy it much more at second hand,' Iris had whispered as they clung together in a parting hug. 'And you write such good letters.'

Joanna smiled at her hostess, said there was little point in their sitting around moping and went to change her gown.

The rest of the day was spent in a determined effort to hide their concern. Iris's absence had to be explained many times and the well-wishers only added to Joanna's hidden depression. She was very fond of Mrs Armitage, who had treated her like another daughter. The little lady ruled her family with a firm hand, lots of love and a large dose of common sense. It was worrying to imagine her life in danger. If prayers really helped, Joanna pestered God with every second thought and hoped for the best.

There were one or two queries as to what would happen to Joanna now, but Bea squashed the speculation by declaring that her sponsorship of Joanna was not dependent upon Iris's presence. But it still worried Joanna; she could not expect to stay with Bea forever. That left returning to the school as her only viable option, and now that it seemed a distinct possibility the idea was not so alluring. Oh, well, there was no point in fretting about it just yet.

She spent a restless night alternately praying for Mrs Armitage and conjuring images of Max inviting her to go back to India. She had little faith in either.

When she went down for breakfast next morning, Bea told her she had received a telegram from Simon to say all was well and he would be returning to town. 'We cannot expect him until after luncheon, so I will go and cancel Iris's presentation gown.' She looked up as though expecting some comment and, when none was forthcoming, remarked, 'I see you agree with me. Iris will not be returning to us.'

Joanna started to say, 'I don't think she will leave her mother,' then decided on honesty. 'Iris was not comfortable with all the attention. She is so kind hearted that no-one realises how shy she is.'

'I was beginning to think the same.' Bea made a wry face. 'May I prevail upon you to break the news to Cynthia?'

Joanna went up to the nursery floor as soon as she had finished breakfast. Cynthia stood up as she entered the school room but did not immediately return her greeting. She looked very tense and Joanna steeled herself for another scene, then Cynthia startled her by rushing forward and throwing herself to her knees. 'I am very sorry,' she gasped.

Joanna had to stifle a laugh. She pulled Cynthia to her feet and led her to the table. When they were both seated, she said, 'That was very dramatic but I don't know why you are apologising to me.'

'I thought about what you said. I don't want to be selfish or make trouble for Iris.'

Joanna reached out and took hold of the child's hand. 'You have been too much alone. First that horrid woman treated you like a prisoner, then Iris and your mama,' Joanna held up a finger to forestall Cynthia's protest, 'Iris and your mama let you do whatever you liked. They did it because they love you, but you are old enough to be responsible. When you live with other girls you will learn to see their needs and consider their feelings.'

She gave Cynthia's hand a squeeze. 'You have already made a start and Iris will be proud of you.' Joanna looked the girl in the eye. 'I am proud of you, which is a much greater achievement.' She was rewarded with a rather wan smile and briskly suggested they go to walk in the park.

Lord Simon returned home in the late afternoon. The ladies were in the drawing room and Joanna asked if Cynthia could join them. 'It will save you having to repeat everything,' she said with a smile. While they waited for her to come down, Joanna quickly outlined their daughter's resolve to behave in a more grown-up way. 'She really needs some friends.'

Cynthia joined them. As they sat drinking tea, Lord Simon said he had seen his sister-in-law sitting up in bed and issuing instructions. 'The doctor is hopeful it was just a passing spasm but has ordered her to rest more. Iris is staying to make sure she obeys.'

Iris had also sent a letter to Joanna. This, more than anything, convinced them that Mary Armitage was in no danger. Joanna scanned the letter and shared most of its contents with the others, though some parts were for her eyes only. 'And to end, she sends her love and urges Cynthia to keep up with her lessons.'

Joanna missed Iris and spent more time with Cynthia. There was no miraculous change in the girl's demeanour, but she was trying. Unfortunately, she transferred her idolatry of Iris to Joanna, which made Joanna uncomfortable.

She was not used to admiration. She had got on well with all but one or two of her school companions, but she had had few close friends. Most of the girls at school had seen her down-to-earth attitude as unsympathetic. She was not uncaring, just unable to enter into the extreme highs and lows of teenage emotions. She gave practical help, such as checking their written work before it was handed in or explaining lesson points. That may not have encouraged true friendship, but her brisk attitude was certainly helping Cynthia.

A letter arrived from Max addressed to Lord Ridgeworth giving details of the launch date and the assurance that accommodation had been booked for the party at the Grand Hotel in Glasgow. All expenses would be covered by Pennicotts. *I am grateful to you and Lady Ridgeworth for taking care of Joanna and look forward to making your acquaintance.*

Lord Simon said he would rearrange his schedule to allow time for them to do some sightseeing and Bea suggested that Cynthia should go with them.

Joanna was at first peeved that Max had not written to her but a little reflection made her realise he had acted correctly; it would not have done for Joanna to relay the information to her titled hosts. A later post brought a personal letter that lifted her spirits. He hoped she was enjoying her time in London. The rest of the letter was filled with details of his activities and ended with: *So looking forward to seeing you again.* Did that mean he had missed her?

She posed this question in her next letter to Iris and was heartened by her reply. Iris was a romantic and pointed out how promptly Max had always replied to Joanna's letters, his interest in her activities and, most of all, how concerned he had been about her when he had first visited the school. *I believe he was falling in love with you even before you met,* she wrote. *He was very upset when we had to leave Bath so suddenly.*

She ended with the comment: *And, he respects your intelligence and has even taken your advice. That has to be significant.*

Joanna stifled a wish that he also admired her person but that was a bit too much to ask.

She had expected less attention at social events without Iris to act as a magnet but it was not so. Initially Iris's admirers approached her for news of her friend, but gradually her elderly escorts were replaced by a younger, livelier group who sought her out because they enjoyed her company. All in all, she was having a wonderful time, boosted by the knowledge that she would soon be seeing Max.

Chapter 19

Bea was alone going over the household accounts when the butler brought in a visitor's card on a tray. She picked it up and frowned for a moment before she remembered that Earl Stanley was Joanna's grandfather. 'Please tell Lord Stanley I will be with him directly.'

Bassett gave a nod and added, 'I have taken the liberty of showing him into the small drawing room, my lady, as the gentleman has trouble walking.'

Bea thanked him and followed him from the room, though not to the downstairs drawing room. Instead she nipped up the back stairs to where Joanna was giving Cynthia a lesson in the schoolroom. 'Joanna, please come downstairs with me. Your grandfather has called.'

'I did not know you had a grandfather,' Cynthia remarked.

'I had forgotten about him,' Joanna replied. Before Cynthia could follow up on this intriguing comment, she whisked out of the room. 'What does he want?' she asked Bea as soon as they were alone.

'I assume he has come to renew your acquaintance.'

Joanna snorted. 'That will be a first!'

Lord Stanley rose carefully to his feet when the ladies entered the small drawing room. He was painfully thin and leaned heavily on an ebony cane. His face was lined, with deep grooves beside his unsmiling mouth.

Bea rushed forward. 'My lord, please resume your seat.' She waited until he had done so before urging Joanna forward. 'I expect Joanna is much changed since you saw her last,' she said brightly.

The old man took his time examining Joanna from head to foot with pale but very sharp eyes. Joanna bore the scrutiny with an equally assessing gaze. She recognised him, but he seemed a poor shadow of the man she remembered. A nudge from Bea reminded her to curtsey and say, 'Good morning, my lord.'

'When did you get back from India?' he asked sharply.

'I have never been to India.'

129

As briefly as possible, and interspersed by questions, Joanna outlined her history. She said her father had never returned to England. Stanley's face gave away nothing of his thoughts but his fingers beat an angry tattoo on the side of his cane. He turned to Bea. 'How is it that you are harbouring my granddaughter when she has family and a parcel of aunts to sponsor her?'

Joanna spoke first. 'My father parted from you on bad terms, my lord. He appointed his lawyer, Mr Ebstone, to be my guardian and it was he who arranged for me to come to Lady Ridgeworth. Your family has never shown any interest in my welfare and I do not understand why you are here now.' It was verging on rudeness, but Joanna did not like his attitude.

Lord Stanley ignored the question and said crossly, 'It will not do. I am your next of kin, not some provincial lawyer!'

Bea intervened. 'My lord, with all due respect, even in his absence Mr Pennicott is still Joanna's father. His wishes are paramount. If you are so concerned with appearances, perhaps you will tell us why you have delayed so long in making an approach. Joanna has been out in society for several weeks.'

'I have been incapacitated. I only heard she was here in a letter I received this morning.'

'Aunt Louisa knew I was here. We called upon her almost as soon as I arrived in town,' Joanna said indignantly.

Lord Stanley's lips tightened in annoyance and his cane thumped on the floor. 'That will need to be explained,' he said ominously, and Joanna felt a reluctant sympathy for her aunt. 'In the meantime I will arrange for Joanna to live with one of her other aunts.' He paused when Bea sat forward as though to speak and held up a hand. 'I thank you for your services, but they were never necessary. This matter has been bungled from start to finish.'

'But it is not finished,' Joanna insisted. 'I wish to stay with Lady Ridgeworth.'

'It is quite legal, my lord,' Bea assured him. 'I have a contract signed by Joanna's appointed guardian. In any case, we will be travelling to Scotland in a few days' time.' To soften the blow she suggested, 'Perhaps, when we return, Joanna can make the acquaintance of her other relatives.' She smiled at Joanna. 'It will be nice to meet your cousins.'

Joanna noticed there was no mention of aunts. In fact, she had completely forgotten her mother had had other sisters, presumably now married and with families of their own. There had also been a brother. It felt strange and rather sad to think she had family she had never met.

Lord Stanley was not happy with the state of affairs and said he would speak to Lord Ridgeworth. He got to his feet and swayed slightly. Joanna rushed forward to steady him and was batted away. 'I am not helpless yet,' he growled.

'But you are clearly unwell, sir. If it please you, I will visit as soon as we return from Scotland.' The offer seemed to mollify him a little, and he departed on better terms than either Bea or Joanna had hoped for.

True to his word, Lord Stanley summoned Lord Ridgeworth to call upon him. They learned of Lord Simon's response later that afternoon. 'Apparently your aunt gave him the impression you had sailed to India with your father. It was very much a case of out of sight, out of mind. Now you are, as he put it, adrift in society, it does not suit his consequence for people to know he has been spurned – not that he put *that* into words!'

The outcome of the meeting was unclear. Lord Stanley was still not happy, but Simon had pointed out that there would be a lot of gossip if he tried to wrest control from Joanna's appointed guardian.

'So that is that, then?' Joanna asked hopefully.

'Not quite. He still wishes to speak to you.' Lord Ridgeworth grinned. 'I think that means getting to know you, but it will be more in the form of an interrogation.' He shook his head at Joanna's grimace. 'It is reasonable request. He is very involved in the lives of all his children and grandchildren.'

'Interfering,' Bea muttered.

'Yes. It must be very galling for him to excluded from arranging Joanna's future. His health is causing the family concern, but he still keeps a tight rein on their affairs. I have assured him that Joanna will visit when we return from Scotland.'

Joanna breathed a sigh of relief and put family out of her mind to concentrate on preparations for their trip.

Chapter 20

Joanna and the Ridgeworths set off for Scotland five days before the launch. It was almost a cavalcade, with the Ridgeworths and Joanna in the lead coach, Simon's valet, Vera Cotton and Joanna's maid, Sally, following in a the second, and a footman riding guard on the luggage wagon that brought up the rear.

Cynthia had been allowed to accompany them, much to the annoyance of four-year-old Nickolas. 'Boats are for men, not girls,' he had declared, disregarding the fact that Joanna was to launch the ship. He was only slightly mollified by his father's promise of a 'men only' treat when they returned.

Cynthia had been inclined to crow until Lord Simon pointed out that she could also be excluded from the trip if she continued to act so childishly. The rebuke worked, but Cynthia was beside herself with excitement by the time they were ready to leave.

Whether it was that or the motion of the train, Cynthia was sick before they had gone twenty miles. Lord Simon quit their private compartment at the first opportunity and sent Vera Cotton to deal with the mess and dose Cynthia with one of her famous remedies. Whatever it contained, Cynthia slept for the rest of the journey. Joanna thought of asking if she might have a dose of the mixture as the residual smell was making her feel queasy. Lady Bea sprinkled perfume on her wrists, handkerchief and on her companions, but it only seemed to make matters worse.

Joanna was very glad that Lord Simon had decided to spread their journey over two days. He was a busy man and was taking this opportunity to combine business with pleasure. They were to break their journey in Manchester so he could consult a parliamentary colleague on the question of the upcoming private voting system.

Cynthia recovered as soon as they left the train. Lord Simon saw them installed in an hotel before going about his business, telling them he would not be back until late evening. After a change of clothes and a light meal, Cynthia was full of energy again so the ladies went exploring accompanied by the footman. They saw some fine buildings, shops and many statues, but the general opinion was that it did not compare with London. They dined in their private suite and were all three in bed before Lord Simon returned.

The next morning Vera only allowed Cynthia toast and jam, no butter, for breakfast, washed down with camomile tea. 'Just to settle your stomach,' Vera said when Cynthia turned up her nose. Vera was to travel with the ladies again and declared that Cynthia must travel facing forward. 'You will not be sick now.' It sounded like an order, but Lord Simon was not taking any chances and travelled second class with his valet.

The second stage of their journey was shorter and without any unpleasant events. They reached Glasgow mid-afternoon. There was rain in the wind that hit Joanna as she made to exit the train. Head down, she accepted the outstretched hand for balance and was about to murmur thank you when a voice said, 'Joanna.'

Joanna looked up to see Max standing in front of her. For a moment she could only stare; she had not expected him to actually meet the train. He offered his arm and hurried her out to a waiting carriage.

Max helped her into the carriage and took the seat beside her. Lord and Lady Ridgeworth sat opposite with Cynthia squeezed between them. Everyone except Joanna had something to say about the weather, the journey, why Iris was not with them and where they were going, but Joanna just sat and revelled in the feel of Max's leg and shoulder touching her as the carriage rounded corners and bumped over cobblestones. She dared not look at his face and she did not want him to look at hers because she was sure she was blushing. Combined with her freckles, that would not be a pretty sight.

There was no time for conversation in the flurry of booking into the hotel and being shown to their rooms. Before her door closed, Joanna heard Max tell Lord Simon that he was staying in the same hotel and would join them for dinner.

Luncheon was served in the Ridgeworths' suite but, to Joanna's disappointment Max did not join them. Lord Simon left them soon afterwards and Bea went to lie down, which left Joanna to amuse Cynthia. It was not an easy task as it was too wet to go out and none of the activities Joanna suggested held the child's attention for long. Things improved when they were served tea with a selection of delicious sandwiches and cakes, but it was a tedious afternoon and Joanna was relieved when it was time for her to dress for dinner.

In something of a daze, she submitted to Sally's ministrations. Her heart was going nineteen to the dozen at the thought of seeing Max again, and her mind whirling at an even faster pace. Had Max really looked pleased to see her? Had the touch of his arm in the carriage only been due to the motion? His hand had rested in the small of her back more than was strictly necessary when he had helped her to alight at the hotel and had stayed there until they were inside the foyer.

'There you go, miss.' Sally stood back to admire Joanna, who was dressed in a dinner gown of amber silk. She gave her a sly look. 'Your young man will be bowled over.'

My young man, Joanna thought. If only he were. She had longed to see Max again and had become a mindless idiot in his presence. None of the men she had met in London had made her pulse race and none of their compliments had made her blush, but one look at Max and she had been flooded with impossible dreams. How was she to face him at dinner with any semblance of normality?

***

On the floor above, Max was trying to escape from his Indian servant, Abdul. The little man was as pernickety as the most starched valet in the Ton. 'That will do,' Max grumbled as Abdul tried to adjust the set of his jacket. 'I am going to dinner with friends, not meeting the Queen.'

Abdul looked offended. It was unusual for Mr Maxwell to be so abrupt, though he had not been himself for several weeks now, not since their visit to Bath. But his mood had been of a brooding nature, not impatience.

Max was impatient to be out of the room and downstairs to take Joanna in to dinner. He had done a lot of thinking in the last few weeks and reached a decision. He had come to England to see if he could marry her.

The thought had not occurred to him until George Pennicott had suggested it. After his initial surprise, he had realised that he was not averse to the idea. He had corresponded with Joanna for years and felt he knew her sufficiently to make an offer.

Conversely, she ought to know him well enough to accept. He was not foolish enough to think they were in love, but it would be a very practical arrangement. He had just needed to meet her in person and to make sure she was equally happy with the arrangement.

Max had not been best pleased when George had written a new will making him his heir. George has sprung it on him at the last moment when they were actually on the ship that would carry Max to England. Max told George that it was unfair to Joanna, and the ensuing row had threatened to sever their relationship. He still thrummed with annoyance as he recalled the event. 'It smacks of bribery,' he had protested.

'I don't know what the fuss is about,' George had replied gruffly. 'It will all be yours anyway when you marry the girl.'

Max held on to his temper and pointed out that married women were now allowed to keep control of their earnings and inherited monies.

'All the more reason for you to own it,' George insisted. 'Heaven only knows what a woman would do with my hard-earned business.'

That was too much for Max. 'Joanna is an astute investor and has managed her own portfolio for several years. We have even acted on some of her suggestions – very profitably, I might add. If you took any interest in your daughter, you would be proud of her achievements.' George listened, open-mouthed as Max waved the will under his nose and continued, 'You can't just give away her inheritance.'

'I'll do what I like with my own money!'

'Well, I won't accept it.'

George laughed derisively. 'No-one refuses a fortune!'

Max ripped the document in half. 'I just have. If I am to marry Joanna, it will be on fair terms.'

A cry rang through the ship, 'All ashore as going ashore!'

Max had shoved the older man in the direction of the gangway. His parting words were, 'Change that will.' He turned away and ignored George's shout that he had something else for Max to take with him.

The memory still left a bad taste in Max's mouth, even more so now that he had genuine feelings for Joanna. He was not sure

135

when their paper friendship had changed to something more personal; perhaps it had been his protective instinct when he saw Joanna looking so ill and misused at the school. He had wanted to whisk her away and take care of her.

Seeing her again in Bath had confirmed everything he thought he knew about her. She had grown into a very desirable woman, although she seemed totally unaware of her appeal. He had felt really jealous of her relationship with John Armitage.

But Joanna's enthusiasm for a spell in London had made him look at the situation from her point of view. She had been incarcerated in a girls' school for the past eight years. Was it fair to ask her to make a commitment before she had chance to see what the rest of the world had to offer?

It was a risk that had kept him on tenterhooks for weeks. Suppose she met someone else? The men in London would not be blind either to her looks or fortune, nor could he reasonably expect them not to make a move on both. Had they? And how had Joanna reacted to their overtures? The dilemma kept him awake at night.

It seemed he had cause to be worried. Far from falling on his neck like a long-lost lover, Joanna had treated him coolly, barely glancing at him before she hurried away to her room. Dinner together might turn into a nightmare.

Max was waiting in the foyer when Joanna descended the stairs behind Lord and Lady Ridgeworth. At first, he could only see her head with her glorious hair swept up into a mass of intertwined braids and secured with amber combs. Then her shoulders and upper-breast came into view, and he had to consciously restrain his jaw from dropping onto his chest.

The Ridgeworths stepped to one side after the last step and Max saw Joanna full length. The smooth lines of her dress accentuated her height, bosom and waist and the bunched material at the back hinted at generous hips. He could hardly breathe. She was magnificent, like a gilded Amazon goddess.

Then she smiled and he stepped forward to take her hand. 'Words fail me,' he said. 'I am honoured to be your escort.'

Joanna could not find any words to reply. Lady Bea had taught her it was considered gauche to compliment a man on his appearance, which was more the pity because formal evening wear set off Max's physique and dark hair to perfection.

She smiled again as he placed her hand on his arm and covered it with his free hand. Both were warm and solid, and he was tall enough to make her feel not exactly dainty but small enough to be cherished.

They followed Lord and Lady Ridgeworth into the dining room. It was large, with widely spaced tables through which they passed drawing admiring looks from the other diners. Their table was at the far end; a column on the left and a huge flower arrangement on a plinth on the right gave the illusion of privacy, but they – and half the room – were reflected in a large wall mirror.

Joanna forgot her nervousness as she was seated sideways on to Max and Lord Simon with Lady Bea directly opposite. A waiter offered her a menu while Max and Lord Simon discussed wines with the sommelier.

'This is rather grand,' Lady Bea said looking around. 'I had not expected such opulence in Glasgow.'

Max laughed. 'Scotland is not the back of beyond! We have a long history and culture and some of the finest universities in the world,' he added with pride.

'And a renowned ship-building industry,' Lord Simon said. This led to a discussion of the launch and other items on the itinerary.

'Will we be allowed to sail on the new ship?' Lady Bea asked, causing her companions to almost choke with mirth.

'It will not be ready to sail!' Joanna told her.

Bea looked confused. 'But I thought you would hit it with a bottle and send it sliding into the water?'

Joanna laughed ruefully. 'Even I could not push a fifteen-hundred-ton ship down the slipway.'

The men listened indulgently and with growing admiration as Joanna explained. 'Workmen will knock out the supports and sheer weight of the ship will start it moving controlled by heavy chains, but it will have to be moved to another berth to test the engines. Then there will be all the interior fittings and furniture to install.' Joanna turned to Max. 'Has the interior been decided?

Mama was allowed to choose some of the furnishings when she launched the *Veronica*.'

'I am sure you will be allowed a say. In fact, I shall insist upon it.' Max had seen all the specifications, right down to the choice of linen and china, but if it would please Joanna he would make sure she was consulted.

Max had listened to her speaking confidently with pride . He knew that many men would be daunted by her intelligence and disapproving of her having aired her knowledge. Not that she had done so boastfully, but she was confident in all practical matters. It was only on a physical level that she displayed insecurity, something that was totally unjustified in his opinion. Animation lent her a glow that was utterly captivating. He could hardly wait to speak to her about the future.

They had finished their meal and were preparing to leave when Max happened to glance at the mirror and froze. Seated at a table half way down the room was his father. Although Max had not seen him for over a decade, he knew he was not mistaken: the Earl of Strathcairn had aged, but not sufficiently to disguise his arrogant features or forceful attitude. He was speaking earnestly to a younger man who did not looked pleased at what he was hearing.

Max's attention was recalled by Lord Simon suggesting they take coffee in the lounge. As he stood and pulled out Joanna's chair, Max looked back at the mirror and tried to gauge his father's sight line. It looked possible to leave the room without being recognised, as long as his father did not turn his head. The last thing Max wanted was a confrontation in the middle of the dining room.

Max angled his body towards Joanna as they walked towards the door. No-one hailed him and he breathed a sigh of relief when they gained the foyer. Joanna looked up at him with a worried frown. 'Is something wrong?'

'No,' he assured her. 'Will you excuse me for a moment? I need to check at the desk as I am expecting a message.' He left Lord Simon to escort the ladies into the lounge and hurried away. The receptionist was willing allowed him to view the visitors' book and, much to his relief, his father was not a resident. But he could come into the lounge, a place just as public as the dining room.

Max went back to his companions with a concocted excuse for not joining them for coffee. 'I need to go out, but will see you at breakfast then take you on a tour of the city.' Only Joanna noticed that he headed for the stairs, not the exit.

Max held his breath until he was safely past the entrance to the dining room. The first flight of stairs seemed endless and at every step he expected to hear his name called. Reaching the landing, he risked a glance over his shoulder just in time to see his father step out of the dining room. Max took the second flight two treads at a time and almost wrenched his bedroom door from its hinges in his haste to get inside.

Abdul shot up from the floor where he had been sitting cross-legged, meditating. 'Sir?' He was too sensible to ask if something was wrong; that was obvious. Never in his four years of service had he seen Mr Maxwell so discomposed.

Max closed the door and leant back against it. 'Sorry to have startled you.' He took in his valet's loose-fitting clothes and apologised again. 'I have broken your meditation.'

'Perhaps sir should join me?' The implication was clear and Max laughed.

'It will take more than a few "oms" to calm the fright I have just suffered.' But it was not such a bad idea. They did yoga practice together every morning. It had started soon after Abdul had joined him and he had wondered at the Indian's agility. The deep breathing and disciplined movements also helped to clear the mind.

Max stripped down to his underwear and joined Abdul on the carpet.

***

Joanna made a rather more sedate progress to her room a little later. Her mind was not at all calm. During the drinking of coffee and polite 'good nights', she had been wracking her brains about the cause of Max's sudden change of mood. He had been an attentive companion, listening to her comments with nods of approval and smiles that did strange things to her insides. One moment, he had been quite relaxed and the next he was as jerky as a puppet on a string. She had watched him approach the

139

reception desk and seen the visitors' book handed to him rather than a note, then he had gone upstairs and not come down again, which he surely would have done if he had an urgent errand.

It was very strange and probably none of her business but Joanna could never resist a puzzle.

Chapter 21

Max seemed quite back to normal when he joined them for breakfast. Joanna was itching to ask questions, but Cynthia was with them and had questions of her own. She wanted to know if Max had ridden an elephant, shot a tiger or been seasick. He answered yes, no and never. Bea commented that they had a fine day for their tour of the city and Lord Simon drew Max's attention to a headline in the newspaper.

He responded cheerfully, all the while wondering how he was to get Joanna alone to alert her to possible disaster. He wanted her to be in full possession of the facts before she met his father.

Joanna ate her breakfast and wondered if she would ever be allowed a private moment with Max, but it was very much a communal event with everyone having something to say about the day ahead.

Max had hired an open carriage and a reliable guide for the tour. Although he had been born and spent his childhood in Scotland, he had rarely visited Glasgow and was almost as ignorant of the city's amenities as his guests. The guide was knowledgeable and proud of his city, but in moments of enthusiasm his accent became so thick that Max had to interpret. That caused much good-natured laughter and left them with a list of places to return to for closer inspection. Lady Bea and Cynthia wanted to visit the shops and Joanna expressed a ghoulish interest in the ornate monuments in the Necropolis. They were unanimous about seeing the cathedral and the Hunterian Museum – but that was all for another day.

The carriage took them back to the hotel. Much to Joanna's disappointment, Max was unable to join them for lunch. 'I will be back in time to accompany you to the shipyard,' he said. 'The carriage will return at two o'clock.'

Lord Simon was going to the shipyard with Max and Joanna because he was keen to observe the working conditions and assess the demeanour of the labourers. For the sake of propriety, Vera Cotton would go with them as chaperone.

Joanna could hardly contain her excitement as the carriage left the grand buildings behind. She could smell the river and glimpse it occasionally as they passed between huge warehouses and untidy open spaces, and she heard the noise of the shipyard long before they reached it. A gatekeeper came out of his lodge to enquire as to their business and, at a word from Max, sent a boy running with a message before directing them to the main office building.

By the time they arrived, Mr Cameron, the company chairman, was on the steps to greet them. He was a large, prosperous looking man with a bald head and round belly. Behind him was ranged a small army of minions who all bowed humbly and tried not to stare at Joanna. Max made the introductions.

'Lord Ridgeworth, it is an honour to meet you,' Mr Cameron said and shook Lord Simon's hand. He turned to Joanna and smiled in an avuncular fashion. 'Miss Pennicott, I was not expecting you today. My wife will be here tomorrow to look after you, but you will be quite alright in my office with your maid.' He waved a vague hand towards the interior of the building.

'Later, perhaps,' Joanna replied. 'May we see the ship first?'

Mr Cameron looked flustered and sought support from her male escorts. 'It is not really the…'

'Miss Pennicott is here to represent her father,' Max said quickly. 'Please show her all that you would show the man who commissioned the ship.'

Mr Cameron sighed and offered Joanna his arm. Lord Simon and Max fell in behind, with the minions bringing up the rear.

Joanna's first sight of the ship was of two black-painted funnels towering above low buildings. As the party emerged into an open area, the superstructure came into view. The rest of the vessel was in a deep trench. She dropped Mr Cameron's arm and stepped closer to the edge. Max was beside her in an instant, but she was too engrossed to notice; her eyes were riveted on the ship.

Her mind knew that it was three hundred feet long but she was not prepared for its height. The hull seemed to balance on its keel, held upright partly by scaffolding and partly by thick poles. It towered above her so that she had to crane her neck far back to see the company logo of a red P in a white square painted on one of the funnels. All she could say was, 'Oh!'

Mr Cameron, standing a little further away from the edge, preened. 'I am quite proud of this beauty,' he said, as though he had built it himself. Then he seemed to become aware of the sudden silence and glared at the men who had stopped work to stare.

'There still seems to be a lot of work going on,' Joanna remarked. 'May we go aboard now?'

Mr Cameron looked alarmed. 'On board?' he croaked. 'My dear young lady, it is not that easy.' He pointed to a narrow walkway spanning the chasm between dock and ship. 'That is the only way across.'

'Very well,' Joanna replied. 'Will you lead the way?'

Mr Cameron blanched and actually took a step back. He beckoned to one of his followers, a lean, middle-aged man in a suit that had seen better days. Not quite introducing him, Cameron said, 'McTavish will show you around.'

Vera gave a squeak of alarm as Joanna made to follow McTavish, but Max placed a hand on her shoulder and said, 'I will see she comes to no harm.'

McTavish offered Joanna his hand but she stepped confidently onto the walkway. Halfway across, she paused to look down. She had seen many ships before but never out of the water. Seen in its entirety, it looked top-heavy. A novice might have wondered why it did not tip over but Joanna understood that most of the weight was below the water line.

She moved on and accepted Mr McTavish's hand to step down onto the deck. Max was a step behind and smiled at her obvious delight. She stared up at the two funnels. 'It seems funny not to have any sails,' she commented.

'Not needed,' McTavish replied. 'She will be under power the whole time.' Joanna had plenty of questions and McTavish answered her plainly, not trying to dumb down the information because she was a woman. Together they peered into the cavernous holds, at present half-filled with ballast. A steep staircase led down to the silent engine room where the gleaming rods and dials promised power when needed. McTavish advised against visiting the boilers as she would get coal-dust on her clothes and there was not much to see anyway.

They had a quick look at the crew accommodation and galley before going up to the passenger area. The ship was built for cargo and only had six passenger cabins, each panelled in light wood but otherwise unfurnished. A large lounge with windows level with the deck was positioned below the bridge.

The view from the bridge took Joanna's breath away. She placed her hands on the wheel and thought how wonderful it would be to have control of the vessel, to decide where it should go and to feel the power of the engines as they cut through the waves.

She was not aware she had spoken the thoughts aloud until Max chuckled. He gave her a mock salute and said, 'Captain Pennicott. How do you like your new command?'

'The new master was here yesterday,' McTavish remarked. ''Giving her a look over and proud as a peacock.'

'The captain was here?' Max asked.

'Aye. Captain Urquhart, a Navy man with long experience. She will be safe in his hands.'

Joanna did not understand Max's sudden frown and asked, 'Is he not allowed to come before the launch?'

Max seemed to be struggling to find words, then he smiled. 'Well, technically the ship still belongs to Cameron. I was just surprised. I knew no more than that Captain Fogarty had found his replacement.' He turned to McTavish. 'You approve of him?'

'Very business-like. Knew what he was talking about.' McTavish chuckled. 'Don't think he has dealt with merchantmen before. He will run things according to Navy rules.'

Having seen all that was accessible, the party returned to the dock where a workman told them Mr Cameron had taken the other visitors back to his office. After being thanked for his time, McTavish left them with a clerk who took them to the office.

Mr Cameron rose from behind his desk and came forward beaming. 'Did you see all you wanted? I admit my heart was in my mouth when you stepped onto that gangplank. Did you not feel dizzy looking over the edge?'

Joanna laughed. 'Not at all. I felt far dizzier looking up at the funnels.' She went to sit beside Vera who was nursing a cup of tea. 'Oh, miss,' Vera sighed. 'Fancy you going off with those two men. Whatever will Lady Beatrice say?'

'Lady Bea will not mind a bit.' Joanna pulled a face. 'Though her mother-in-law would be appalled if she knew.'

She was served refreshments and listened to Max questioning Mr Cameron about the captain. 'He came with an authority from Captain Fogarty. I would not have accepted it if you had not already told me about it,' Cameron told Max. 'He arrived barely a half-hour after you left.'

'I have never met him. May I see Captain Fogarty's letter?'

Cameron shook his head. 'He took it away with him. But we did talk.' He continued with the information that Captain Robertson Urquhart had been in the Royal Navy, man and boy, for more than twenty years. He had experience both under sail and, latterly, steam. 'He said he left the Navy because he was too far down the lists to get a command in peacetime. It appears he does not really need to go to sea again as he is heir to an earldom. You may be looking for another captain before too long.' Max muttered some under his breath and changed the subject.

They left soon afterwards. In the carriage, Lord Simon said he had spent a profitable hour talking about trade unions and the general satisfaction of the workforce. 'Cameron has plenty of orders on his books and most of his men are glad to have steady employment.' He laughed. 'He quivered like a jelly when I mentioned the unions, but they have not been unreasonable in their demands.'

He turned to Joanna. 'Cameron also gave me a detailed rundown on tomorrow's launch ceremony. You will be the guest of honour at the evening banquet.' He smiled at her. 'Be prepared to stand and shake hands with people you will likely never see again, from the mayor down to I don't know who. It is surprising how many people manage to get invitations to these events.'

'A launching is a big event for any company,' Max remarked. 'Cameron's is quite small compared to some of the other shipyards so it will do him no harm to trumpet his success.' It was the first time he had spoken since they left Mr Cameron's office. Joanna had watched him covertly and noted a faraway look in his eyes. Something was on his mind, and she wondered

145

if it had anything to do with his strange behaviour after dinner yesterday.

Max certainly did have something on his mind. It had been a shock to hear the name and aspirations of the newly appointed captain. Max did not know Robertson Urquhart personally but had worked out who he was.

Max's father, the Earl of Strathcairn, was not a likeable man. He was arrogant and short tempered; over the years he had alienated most of his relatives and there was little interaction between the branches of the family. If Max remembered rightly, Robertson was the son of his father's great-cousin, far enough removed from the succession never to have been directly referred to. Max only knew of him through his grandmother, Lady Leith, who had an encyclopaedic memory for family trees.

Max also had a firm suspicion that Robertson had been dining with Lord Strathcairn last night. Was there a chance they would be at the hotel again this evening? Max did not think he would be lucky enough to escape his father's notice twice.

He had no further time to ponder the question because they had arrived back at the hotel. When Cynthia came running to meet them full of questions. Max saw a solution to his dilemma and suggested they dine privately in his suite so that the child could join them.

She grabbed his hand, jumping up and down with excitement. 'Thank you, thank you! Joanna has been having all the fun. We went to the shops, but Mama just wanted to try on hats!'

Lady Bea told her to calm down and behave like a lady if she wished to dine with the adults. It was close enough to Miss Payne's threats to subdue Cynthis instantly. She smiled at Max and thanked him demurely for the invitation before climbing the stairs with her parents and Joanna. Max watched them out of sight before going to the reception desk to order dinner served in his suite.

When he entered his room, Max went straight to the tray of previously untouched decanters. He poured himself a large measure of whisky and drank half of it down in one gulp. Abdul poked his head out of the dressing room door, took stock of the situation and retreated.

The spirit burned its way down Max's throat but did little to settle the knot in his stomach. He loosened his collar and slumped into an armchair. He was ashamed to notice that his hand was shaking, causing the whisky to swirl around in imitation of his swirling thoughts.

It had been like a blow to his gut to hear that Robertson Urquhart was flaunting himself as heir to an earldom. It had to be Strathcairn – there were not that many earldoms available. Max ground his teeth. Strathcairn was his, his birthright! For years he had pushed it to the back of his mind, but he had always known that he would go back one day. Had he left it too late? Had his father declared him dead? The thought was too awful to contemplate. Max put back his head and felt like howling.

There was a knock at the door; when told to enter, a waiter presented him with a menu and waited while Max chose the meal. He also ordered wine, and lemonade for Cynthia. The waiter bowed and said a servant would come and lay the table.

The interruption was just what Max needed to pull him out of his black mood. He had guests arriving soon and he would have to appear a genial host. He looked at the whisky but decided the solution to his problems was not going to be found in a glass, nor was it to be found that night or tomorrow. He owed it to Joanna to support her through the coming ceremonies.

He would try to find out if his father was still in Glasgow. A meeting was long overdue. He set his glass down on a side table and went through to change for the evening.

Abdul was aware that Max had a problem; he was more friend than servant, but wise enough not to ask questions. He went about his duties, trimming Max's beard and laying out his evening clothes. His consideration did not go unnoticed and Max managed a rueful smile and a thank you before he returned to the sitting room to await his guests.

***

Joanna's maid was not so reticent. Sally was disgruntled at not being allowed to accompany her mistress to the shipyard. She had already heard of events from Vera and said, 'I would not have been scared to cross that gangplank and leave you alone with two men.'

Joanna laughed. 'It was not a clandestine meeting! Mr McTavish was old enough to be my father, and Max – well, Max would not do anything he ought not.' *Unfortunately,* she added silently. 'Anyway, you would have been bored. Now, may we just get on?'

Sally huffed a bit but soon returned to her usual sunny demeanour and took pride in turning out Joanna to the best of her ability. As a result, Joanna arrived in Max's suite looking every inch a fine lady. Her hair was styled in a smooth chignon low on her neck, and her amber silk dress showed off her fine figure. It was the same one she had worn the night before because she only had one other evening gown with her and that was reserved for tomorrow's banquet. Joanna looked in the long mirror, wishing she were small and dainty; perhaps then Max would look at her with more interest.

***

Max was certainly interested. Every time he saw Joanna he wanted to sweep her into his arms, but first they needed to talk. He crushed the thought; there was another conversation looming but he could not allow himself to think about it just now. Instead he took pleasure in watching Joanna's lively participation in the conversations that took place around the table.

Dinner was a pleasant interval, made even livelier by Cynthia's enjoyment of being treated like a grown-up. Max welcomed her naïve comments on the dishes; she was not used to seeing such an array of different foods and said she had nothing like it at home. 'Is this how grown-ups dine every day?' she asked.

Lord Simon chuckled. 'Unfortunately not. I shall do full justice to all these tempting dishes.' That led to a good-natured squabble with his wife, who pretended to be offended at the slur on her housekeeping. Joanna broke them up by reminding them of the lunch Lady Bea had been served at Miss Waring's school. Everyone laughed when they were told that Bea had even offered to help with the washing up.

The party broke up as soon as the meal was over, when Lady Bea insisted it was past Cynthia's bedtime. Max invited her to return after seeing Cynthia to her room but Bea declined politely. Joanna was disappointed by the knowledge that she could not be left with the men; it was a silly convention but not worth challenging, so she thanked Max for the meal and reluctantly followed Bea.

Lord Simon stayed to share a glass of port and they settled into comfortable chairs to enjoy manly, after-dinner conversation. Max liked the viscount but wished him anywhere but there. The strain of quelling his thoughts was giving him a headache.

Chapter 22

The day of the launch began with an overcast sky and a drizzle of rain. Joanna was worried that it would ruin the ceremony and kept going to the window of the Ridgeworths' sitting room to check for any sign of blue sky.

'Joanna, you will not change the weather by wishing,' Bea said sympathetically. She had become very fond of Joanna and treated her more as a friend; she had even told her to drop the 'Lady' when they were alone. 'Sit down and find something to do,' she advised. 'It will make the time pass faster.'

Cynthia was also in a grumpy mood because she wanted to visit the Hunterian Museum. 'Why can't we go out? It is only a little rain,' she complained. 'Papa went out.'

'Papa had an appointment,' Lady Bea said reasonably.

'And Mr Maxwell,' Cynthia added with a pout. From being scared to open her mouth, the child had become very demanding. Bea thought the sooner she went to school the better.

'How many times must I tell you that there is not enough time? We need to be at the shipyard by two o'clock.' Lady Bea was losing patience and looked at Joanna helplessly.

They still had two hours to fill before an early lunch and dressing so Joanna gave a resigned sigh and challenged Cynthia to a game of draughts. Perhaps allowing her to win would save Vera and Sally from a wearying afternoon.

Bea smiled her thanks and settled down with her book. Joanna set up the board and, to make it more interesting, suggested forfeits for the loser. 'And a prize for the winner,' Cynthia insisted. 'If I win, I want…'

Joanna gave the girl a direct look and murmured, 'Remember what I told you about "I want".'

Cynthia whispered, 'Sorry,' and added magnanimously, 'You can go first.'

Seated with her back to the window, Joanna did not notice the improvement in the weather until a shaft of sunlight fell across the draughts board. She jumped up and ran to look outside. 'The clouds have gone!' she exclaimed. 'It is going to be a fine day after all.'

Bea and Cynthia joined her, Bea with relief and Cynthia with renewed demands to be allowed to go out. 'Mrs Cotton and Sally may take you to the museum this afternoon,' Bea reassured her. Vera would not be too pleased, but Cynthia and Joanna's young maid could not be allowed loose in a strange city without a sensible older person.

Lord Simon returned in time to join the ladies for luncheon, but there was no sign of Max until they descended the stairs to meet the carriage. He was waiting for them in the foyer and apologised for not sending a message, though he gave no indication of what he had been doing. He joined in the general conversation on the way to the shipyard but Joanna was sure he had something on his mind.

They were taken straight to Mr Cameron's office and introduced to the other board members and their wives, one of whom presented Joanna with a small bouquet. Mr Cameron repeated the instructions he had given Joanna the day before then offered his arm to lead the small procession out to the dock.

The area had been decorated with flags, and a flower-bedecked platform had been built close to the prow of the ship. Shipyard workers lined the dock and several more were in the depths ready to knock out the restraining blocks. Joanna noticed that most of the scaffolding had been removed and the huge gates at the end of the dock opened, giving a view of the river.

The launch had been timed to coincide with the high tide and water was already creeping halfway along the length of the ship. Mr McTavish stood below the platform, his worried glance passing between the rising water and the gathered dignitaries. 'The time, Mr Cameron. We need to move things on.'

'Yes, yes,' Cameron replied and urged Joanna to climb the steps to the platform. He and his two co-directors followed, together with Max. The rest of the party was swiftly ushered to a row of benches and chairs that was placed to give a good view of the proceedings.

When he reached the platform, Max noticed a photographer angling his camera and turned slightly so his face would not be visible. He suspected the picture would be front cover in the local paper next day and the Scottish nationals the day after. He really did not want his father to see it before Max had seen him.

Positioned as he was, he was free to look at Joanna. Dressed in her favourite moss green, with a perky little hat of the same colour set far back on her glorious hair, she looked poised and not at all nervous. As she leaned forward to look down, Max thought she would have been an ideal model for a figurehead on an old-fashioned sailing ship.

Mr Cameron stepped to the front of the platform and started to make a speech. Below him Mr McTavish was making frantic signals to the men in the bottom of the dock. The two furthest back swung their sledgehammers to release the blocks and retreated. Mr Cameron, at last realising the urgency of the situation, handed Joanna the bottle of champagne.

She did not waste any time. In a strong, clear voice she said, 'I name this ship *Joanna*. May God bless her and all who sail in her.'

She flung the bottle forward and it smashed on the prow, sending shards of glass and a spray of wine into the air. Everyone cheered as the final blocks were knocked away. For a moment the ship seemed to wobble, and Joanna grasped the rail in front of her and held her breath. She had enough knowledge to know that the water flowing into the dock was not deep enough to support the ship's weight and she feared it would to tip over. Then, with a rattle of the restraining chains, it began to slide backwards into the water.

Everyone cheered again as the *Joanna* sent up a huge wave and settled on an even keel. Tug boats chugged forward to nudge the ship into a position parallel to the dock and the men on board released the drag chains. The steamship *Joanna* was launched!

Joanna turned to Max with stars in her eyes, and he had to restrain the impulse to sweep her into his arms and kiss her smiling lips, 'Well done,' was all he managed to say before Mr Cameron shepherded the party from the platform.

There followed a champagne reception where Max and Joanna were presented to civic dignitaries, including the mayor. Mr McTavish was formally presented as the chief engineer, and Joanna thanked him again for his informative tour the day before.

After that she lost count of the people who thought they had a right to recognition.

One man caught her attention; he was dressed in a smart frock coat and wearing a top hat and was making his way straight towards them. He removed his hat and bowed to Lady Bea. 'Lady Ridgeworth, forgive me for introducing myself. I am Robertson Urquhart, newly appointed as master of the *Joanna*.'

He certainly did not lack confidence, Joanna thought, taking a moment to sum him up. He was a slim, sandy-haired man who appeared taller at a distance than he did close up – she had barely to raise her eyes to look at his face. His features were regular and tanned by exposure to the elements, and a neatly trimmed beard added a touch of gravity. He had a nicely shaped mouth and his smile reached his silvery-grey eyes so that the skin crinkled at their corners. It was difficult to assess his age but, given his years of experience, he had to be at least forty. He moved like a man accustomed to command.

Lady Bea acknowledged him with a nod and introduced Joanna, who shook his proffered hand and said, 'I am pleased to meet you, captain.'

'Miss Pennicott, it is a pleasure to meet you too. I was not expecting such a fine young lady.' His voice was cultured and the tone warm with approval.

Joanna tilted her head in enquiry.

'Captain Fogarty described you as a child.'

Joanna laughed. 'So I was the only time I met him, but that was eight years ago. I know nothing of you beyond your name. I hope we will be able to spend longer together at the banquet this evening. I would like to learn more about your naval experience.'

Urquhart looked a little surprised. It sounded as though she intended to interview him! The absurdity made him smile again. Before he could reply, Joanna felt Max at her side forcing the captain to take a step back.

Joanna introduced the men, adding that Max was her father's partner. They shook hands but she was aware of a strange undercurrent. They were both polite but she detected a coldness, almost a challenge, in the glances they exchanged.

'I was not aware Mr Pennicott had a partner,' the captain said suspiciously.

153

'How would you be?' Max replied coolly. 'Your appointment is recent and not expected to be operative for some weeks.'

Captain Urquhart drew himself up to his full height, which was still several inches less than Max though he still contrived to look down his nose. He opened his mouth but thought better of what he had been about to say.

Before Urquhart could think of a more suitable comment, Max came back with another remark. He looked the captain up and down and said, 'I believe I noticed you in the Grand Hotel dining room the evening before last? With an older gentleman?'

'My uncle, the Earl of Strathcairn,' the captain replied proudly. 'I cannot say I noticed you.'

Max merely laughed at the snub and scanned the gathering. He turned back and asked casually, 'Your uncle is not here?'

Captain Urquhart gave a grunt of annoyance. 'Mr Cameron said all the invitations had been sent out,' he said coldly. 'My uncle was most put out and has returned to his estate.'

Max reached for Joanna's hand, looped it in his bent arm and told her they ought to circulate. With a curt nod he drew her away, leaving the captain to stare after them with a thoughtful frown.

'I like him,' Joanna said, looking back over her shoulder to where the captain was still watching them. 'I am glad he is going to be captain of my ship.'

Max smiled at her use of the possessive and patted the hand resting on his sleeve. 'You can be quite confident in Captain Fogarty's assessment of his seamanship. It is a little early to be forming an assessment of his character.' It was quietly said, but Joanna had a feeling Max did not share her opinion.

Max had taken an instant dislike to his distant cousin and, having caught him in a downright lie, knew he needed to contact his father without delay. But delay there must be, for at that moment they were approached by the mayor and his wife who wanted to know if Joanna expected to sail on the ship's maiden voyage.

**

Captain Urquhart asked Joanna the same question when he managed to corner her as the guests assembled before the banquet. 'I would be happy to surrender my cabin,' he said with a smile.

'I had not given it any thought.' She gave a small laugh. 'But it sounds appealing now you mention it. Have you been to India before?'

Captain Urquhart indulged her with a resumé of his career. He had joined the Navy as a boy and progressed through the ranks by his own efforts. 'One may not purchase a commission in the Navy as they do in the Army,' he said scornfully. He had commanded a ship in the Caribbean for three years after the captain had been struck down by yellow fever. On returning to England, the Admiralty had neither confirmed his rank nor offered him another command. Joanna heard a note wounded pride when he added, 'There seemed no future there so I searched for a suitable merchant vessel.'

'So you found Fogarty rather than the other way around?' Max asked. Joanna had not seen him approach and disliked his apparent accusation. What was wrong with him? The captain was showing laudable ambition; when one path had closed, he had sought another.

At Max's sudden appearance, the captain half-turned ready to complain at the interruption but one look at Max's scowling face made him think better of it. Instead he bent his head towards Joanna and said quietly, 'I hope to see you again soon so we may continue our conversation.' To Max he said, 'I was about to offer Miss Pennicott my escort in to dinner.'

'Thank you, but that will not be necessary. I shall take Joanna in as we are both seated at the top table. I suggest you go through and find your own place.' It was a superb snub, delivered with insincere politeness. The captain had no option than to retreat with as much dignity as he could manage.

'You were very rude,' Joanna declared as soon as they were out of earshot. 'He has been telling me about his career.'

'And about his expectation of a title?'

'It was not mentioned. Why? Are you jealous?'

Max yanked her aside so abruptly that she landed flat against his chest. She looked up into his stormy eyes and wondered what on earth had come over him. 'Max?' She could feel his heart pounding through the layers of clothing between them and would have stayed there forever if Max had not suddenly drawn back. Without another word he led her into the dining room and to her place between Mr Cameron and Lord Ridgeworth.

Max was seated far to her left between Lady Bea and the mayor's wife. Joanna thought it just as well as they had been on the verge of a quarrel – or something even more indiscreet. She was grateful for the undemanding conversation of her dinner partners and tried to forget his odd behaviour.

Between courses she looked around and saw Captain Urquhart at one of the side tables. Each time she caught his eye, he smiled and nodded. She could find nothing untoward in his manner and racked her brains for the cause of Max's antipathy.

Lord Simon leant towards her and asked if she were feeling unwell. Joanna jerked her attention back to the present and replied with a smile, 'I was just admiring the décor.' He followed her lead and surveyed the high, painted ceiling, carved fireplace and pedimented door frames. He knew Joanna well enough to be aware that she was not really enjoying herself and kept the conversation on trivial topics until Mr Cameron rose to make a speech.

Max replied on behalf of Pennicott Shipping, saying all the right things but with less verbosity than the ship builder. Joanna heaved a sigh of relief when everyone rose to toast the Queen, bringing the banquet to an end.

People milled about in the entrance hall, commenting on the excellence of the meal and saying their goodbyes while they waited for their carriages. Joanna noticed that Captain Urquhart had stationed himself to the side of the main door. They would have to pass close by and she hoped Max would not snub him again. But Max had already seen him and moved from Joanna's left side to her right, in effect giving the captain his shoulder.

Their carriage was announced. Joanna allowed Max to help her up the step but refused to look at him when he took the seat opposite. Lord Simon must have said something to his wife because Bea touched Joanna's arm and said, 'You are looking tired. It has been a very exciting day. Tomorrow will seem like an anti-climax.' She smiled across at Max. 'Do you have anything special planned for tomorrow?'

'I am afraid I will have to be away very early. I have a meeting on the east coast that cannot be delayed.'

Joanna looked up in surprise. Max smiled at her apologetically. 'If all goes well, I will see you in London in a few days.'

She longed to ask questions. Max had been so adamant that he could not be seen in London, so what had changed? He had been behaving very out of character since dinner on their first evening in Glasgow. She wondered how she recognised that; after all, they barely knew each other apart from through their letters.

The hour was quite late when they arrived back at the hotel. Lady Bea wanted to go straight upstairs but Max asked for a private word with Joanna. Lady Bea noted his grave expression and moved out of earshot with her husband.

Max took hold of Joanna's hands and looked down at her seriously. 'Joanna, there is so much I want to say to you. I have left it too long.' He lifted her hands and placed a kiss on each knuckle, all the time looking deeply into her eyes. It felt like an unspoken promise. 'I am sorry I did not tell you sooner,' he added.

He swallowed hard and squeezed her fingers. 'I will see you in London, as soon as I can get there.' He turned her gently towards Lady Bea and beckoned to Lord Simon.

Joanna was confused. Max had seemed both happy and worried at the same time. Surely he could not have bad news when he had kissed her hands so tenderly? She looked back over her shoulder as she climbed the stairs. Max and Lord Simon were watching and Max lifted his hand, but it was not really a wave. Joanna had the whimsical thought that it looked like a blessing! Oh, well, there was no point in worrying about it. All would become clear when he saw her in London.

The men stood at the foot of the stairs until the ladies were out of sight before ordering brandy and taking seats in the lounge.

'I am going to see my father,' Max said when their drinks arrived. 'We have been estranged for many years. I need to set my affairs in order before I speak to Joanna.'

157

Lord Simon understood what had been left out and nodded. 'Don't worry. We will look after her.' He raised his glass in a toast. 'Good luck.'

Chapter 23

Joanna and the Ridgeworths stayed in Glasgow for a further two days. They visited places of interest on the first day and on the second took a boat ride down the river.

A cab took them to the Broomielaw pier where they joined a small crowd waiting to board the steam ferry. The man in the ticket office told Lord Simon they would have plenty of room; the crowds did not usually come until later in the year. They chose seats at the front of the deck where they had a good view of both sides of the river. Cynthia squealed when the huge paddle wheels started to turn and the vessel vibrated with a regular thumping sound.

Joanna searched the bankside docks for a sight of her ship but could not pick it out from the many crafts under construction. Her spirits rose when they cleared the industrial area, the river widened and she had a glimpse of distant, wooded hills. They looked both tempting and mysterious; now she understood Max's occasional references to his homeland. He had willingly left it for years but it was still dear to his heart. She wondered if proximity to the place of his birth was causing him to re-evaluate his life.

As the river widened, they felt a difference in the movement. The tide was coming in and a stiff breeze whipped the water into waves. Joanna found the movement exhilarating. The wind had teased strands of her hair loose and she wondered what it would feel like to be out on the ocean in a gale. She suddenly threw her head back and started to laugh. 'I have never been to sea before. My father owns a shipping company and I have never been on the water!'

'I don't like it,' Cynthia cried, working herself up into a tantrum. 'I want to get off.'

'I did not know you could swim,' Joanna said with mock surprise. 'I think you might find the water is very cold.'

The diversion worked and Cynthia looked scornful. 'I did not mean here! You do say the silliest things sometimes, Joanna.'

'And thank God for it,' Simon whispered to his wife. Aloud he remarked, 'We will be getting off soon.' He drew his daughter into the shelter of his arm and pointed to Rothesay harbour, backed by thickly wooded hills. 'I am told there are some lovely walks along the shore and a ruined castle.'

The town of Rothesay was larger than it appeared from the water. There were some fine buildings and rows of smaller houses, all built of grey stone, but everything seemed fresh and clean. They decided to have lunch before visiting the castle, where they spent a happy hour exploring the ruins.

The time passed swiftly, so they went back into the shopping area and allowed Cynthia to browse in the small shops and buy souvenirs. Then it was time for tea before re-joining the ferry for the return trip.

Their fellow passengers were in a merry mood. 'Bottle merry,' Lord Simon remarked dryly when they began singing. They could not fully understand the broad accents but the chorus, 'Doon the watter to Rothesay', was repeated frequently enough for Joanna and Cynthia to join in quietly. When their participation was noticed, two young girls approached and invited them into the increasingly raucous group. Bea declined politely and softened her refusal by offering the girls some of the sweetmeats they had purchased. Cynthia was inclined to argue until Joanna whispered, 'I want,' and encouraged the girl to show the other things she had bought.

Bea leaned closer to Joanna and thanked her. 'You have a talent for managing Cynthia. I am afraid she tries my patience. I would turn into a storybook wicked stepmother if I had sole charge of her.'

Joanna brushed the thanks aside. 'I am used to young girls. And it is little enough thanks for all you have done for me.'

Bea settled down to discuss the events they would attend on their return to London. 'Your admirers will be pleased to see you back.'

Joanna smiled, her eyes sparkling with anticipation. 'Max says he will come to London when his business is complete.' She refused to consider his caveat: *if all goes well.* It had to.

Bea kept her answering smile hidden. She had not been blind to the growing awareness between the young couple and decided to help matters along. Making a grab for her hat that was in danger of being blown away, she said, 'Captain Urquhart is rather taken with you. He has promised to call.'

From below her upraised arm Bea had the satisfaction of seeing Joanna's interest. The captain was a well set-up man, perhaps not so young – but there was nothing like a little competition. She could well remember Max's reaction to John Armitage. She just hoped the captain called at the same time as Max. That young man needed a little nudge to make him realise what a prize he had in Joanna. Bea suspected Joanna was already in love with him.

'I shall look forward to seeing Captain Urquhart again,' Joanna replied. 'We had little time to talk the other day and I am interested in finding out more about his career and experience. He seems very ambitious.'

'Oh, career!' Bea scoffed. 'I am talking about the man. He is not wildly handsome but there is a comforting air of reliability about him. And he has expectations of a title,' she added. 'You could do a lot worse.'

'Are you match-making?' Joanna laughed.

'The connection could be to your advantage. You are heiress to a shipping line and he has experience of ships.'

'So do many other captains. But what does he know about trade?' Joanna asked scornfully. 'And anyway, even if I *were* looking for a husband, he is too old.'

Lord Simon had been listening with half an ear. 'Too old?' he said in an offended tone. 'Then I must be in dotage.'

'Not you,' Joanna replied, laughing. 'And anyway, you are already married.'

'I think you should marry Mr Maxwell,' Cynthia piped up. 'He likes you and you like him.'

Joanna could not have agreed more but Lord Simon told Cynthia, with a straight look at his wife, that people must be allowed to decide such things for themselves.

***

Robertson Urquhart was a worried man. He had called twice at the hotel during the day in the hope of seeing Miss Pennicott, and this time was determined to wait until she returned. Perhaps she could give him a clue to Mr Maxwell's unwarranted antipathy.

Samuel Fogarty had spoken of Maxwell, saying he had begun as Mr Pennicott's apprentice and proved to be an asset, but he had not mentioned a partnership. That gave Maxwell the authority to influence appointments, and his comment that the captaincy had not yet been activated had sounded rather like a threat.

Urquhart was not wealthy and a laid-off lieutenant's half-pay barely covered his commitments. Cautiously, he had not resigned from the Navy until he was offered the captaincy of a new ship. If this appointment fell through, his boats were well and truly burnt and he would be forced to take whatever post came up, however lowly. It would be too humiliating.

Another thought occupied his mind. Miss Pennicott was a young lady of marriageable age and an heiress. It was reasonable to expect whomever she married would have control of her fortune. Was Mr Maxwell a candidate? He had twice been quick to remove Miss Pennicott from his – Robertson's – company. *Was he jealous of my interest?* It was a novel thought, although not an unpleasant one. Joanna Pennicott was an attractive woman whom any man would be proud to call his wife. He would use the coming meeting to arrange to see her in London.

Voices from the foyer announcing the return of the Ridgeworth party. Urquhart stepped forward, all smiles. 'My Lord, Lady Ridgeworth, Miss Pennicott, good evening.' Cynthia took a step forward and he added, 'And this young lady must be your daughter.'

Lord Ridgeworth replied, 'My daughter, Cynthia.' He applied light pressure to Cynthia's shoulder and she bobbed a curtsey.

Urquhart gave her a kind smile before turning his attention back to Joanna. 'I am hoping you will all agree to dine with me this evening.'

'That would have been delightful, Captain Urquhart,' Bea replied. 'But as you can see, we are sadly dishevelled. We have had a busy day.'

'We have been "Doon the watter to Rothesay",' Cynthia sang making the captain laugh. 'We did not understand all the other words,' she added regretfully.

'Just as well,' Lord Simon said in an aside to the captain. 'Those I caught were not the kind to be repeated by young girls.'

Bea smiled sweetly and took regretful leave of the captain. 'We have had a long day and need to prepare for our journey home tomorrow. Perhaps you will renew your invitation if you should find yourself in London.' She shook his hand before heading to the stairs and taking Joanna and Cynthia with her.

Lord Ridgeworth lingered, watching the expression on Captain Urquhart's face. Bearing in mind Mr Maxell's implied intentions, he wanted to know how serious the captain was in his pursuit of Joanna. 'Perhaps you would care to join me for a drink? Drown your disappointment, what?'

Encouraged by Lord Ridgeworth's affable tone Urquhart accepted. Once they had been served, he said how proud he was to be given command of such a fine ship. The viscount asked gently leading questions, and the captain was more than willing to talk about his naval experience, his reasons for leaving the service and his hopes for the future.

With becoming modesty, he also mentioned his surprise at finding himself heir to an earldom. 'Lord Strathcairn's only son disappeared many years ago and is presumed dead.' Bolstered by Lord Ridgeworth's interest, he brought the conversation round to Joanna. 'I was surprised to find Miss Pennicott such a fine young lady. I was under the impression she was just a child. I was hoping for the opportunity to get to know her better. Captain Fogarty is not a gossip and only mentioned Joanna briefly when he explained the company's background.'

Lord Ridgeworth smiled. 'It has been a pleasure to house Joanna while my wife organises her entrance into society. She has made many friends.' His half-smile and the lift of his eyebrow conveyed the information that Joanna had a male following. 'Including Mr Maxwell.' He was gratified to note the slight tightening of the captain's lips. 'Lady Beatrice has hopes of an advantageous marriage.'

Captain Urquhart's smile was strained. 'Her inheritance would make her an attractive prospect for a man with a humble background.'

Ridgeworth did not respond to the implied question. 'Oh, I believe Joanna would be attractive if she were penniless.'

'Yes, quite so. A lovely young lady.'

Ridgeworth finished his drink, stood up and held out his hand. 'Perhaps we will meet again. You know our direction in London?'

Urquhart said yes. At the present time he had no idea where the Ridgeworths lived but it would be quite easy to find out.

'Captain Urquhart has ambitions,' Lord Simon remarked to his wife later that evening as they were preparing for bed. 'I heard you extolling his virtues to Joanna.'

Bea laughed. 'You must know she has her heart set on Mr Maxwell. He would be much the better option. As Joanna remarked, the captain is a bit too old for her.'

'So why are you encouraging him?'

Bea continued to brush her hair. 'Mr Maxwell needs a little competition. He relies too much on their long acquaintance. He has no background to speak of, so a titled rival should prod him to make a move.'

'Maxwell has already indicated his interest to me.' Simon drew his wife into his arms. 'Don't meddle, Bea. Let them sort themselves out. We did,' he said before he kissed her.

Chapter 24

Max hired a carriage that he could drive himself for the last stage of his journey to Strathcairn. The familiar landscape caused a tightening in his chest. These were the hills he had roamed as a boy; there was the stream where he had swum and fished. He took the inland road – the coast would conjure the memory of pulling his mother's body from the sea, a memory that did not need to be refreshed before he faced his father.

His first view of the grey stone house made his hands shake and the horse took it to be a signal to break into a canter. Max hauled back on the reins. He had envisaged the coming meeting in many ways but cantering up to the door had not been one of them. He did not want to appear too eager; his main fear was that he would be turned away. The horse shook its head and stamped a hoof, bringing Max back to the task in hand. He relaxed his grip on the reins and rode the rest of the way at a walking pace. The nearer he drew to the house, the more nervous he became.

He was reassured that the place looked the same, the same as it had looked for three centuries. It was a fortified manor with a massive front door eight feet above the ground for security. The horseshoe steps had been added later when the threat of marauders had passed. Later still, some ancestor had planted gardens to soften the aspect but it still looked forbidding. Over the years this was what he had remembered whenever his father crept into his mind: the grey stone and a man's craggy features merging into one.

But it had not always been that way. His first memories were of a happy home when the thick walls had contained warmth, music, laughter, even love, before his mother had become bored. With maturity, he could understand her wish for company. Edinburgh and all its entertainments sat tantalisingly across the Firth. She had been made for laughter and gaiety and he could remember her excitement before a trip to London or the arrival of guests.

She had come to regard Strathcairn as a prison and her husband as her goaler. There had been loud arguments, broken ornaments and storms of tears whenever she could not get her own way. She had never been an outdoor person and was blind to the natural beauty of the area. He could not remember her ever walking beyond the gardens until that fateful day when she ran down to the shore – and her death.

The horse had walked into the shadow of the house and Max tried to believe his sudden chill was from the loss of the sunshine. What was he going to say? How would his father react? He raised his eyes to the window of the room that had been his. Was it the same, or had his father burned all the childhood mementoes? He hoped…

No, that was asking for disappointment. How things played out depended upon his father. This was a duty Max had to perform before he could embark on the next phase of his life.

A man Max had not previously noticed among the flower beds threw down his hoe and hurried forward. 'Master Angus? Is that really you?'

Max reined in the horse and sighed with relief. Someone was glad to see him! Jonas Todd had taught him to ride his first pony and tanned his bottom for stealing apples from the loft! 'Jonas!' he cried. 'You still here?'

'And where else would I be?' the old man replied, coming to place a hand on the edge of the carriage. 'Does His Lordship know you were coming?'

Max shook his head and Jonas tutted. 'Well, get you to the house. I'll take care of this.' He took hold of the horse's bridle while Max climbed down.

'Good luck, lad,' Jonas said softly as Max approached the steps. He waited to see the door open and Max step inside before leading the horse away.

A stranger opened the door in response to Max's knock. 'Whom shall I say is calling?' he asked in reply to Max's request to see Lord Strathcairn. Max could not bring himself to baldly say, 'I am his son.' Instead he handed the servant a card. It bore the name Angus Maxwell but his father would recognise it. There was no knowing if he would receive him; it would be less humiliating to be turned away as plain Mr Maxwell than Lord Robert Urquhart.

Max was shown into a small, sparsely furnished room, the one used for dubious visitors rather than the main salon. He smiled wryly. What else had he expected? The servant did not know him and, unless he had changed dramatically over the years, his father could be testy about receiving strangers.

He did not have long to wait. The servant returned, said, 'Lord Strathcairn will see you,' and led the way up to his father's study.

'There is no need to announce me,' Max said firmly when they reached the door. He backed up his words with a stare until the servant moved away. He was sorry to discomfort someone who was only doing his job, but this was his home. He would not creep in under a false name.

Lord Strathcairn was seated behind his desk. He was thinner and more lined than Max remembered but the stern expression was the same. It was an echo of so many other occasions when Max – no, Angus – had been summoned for a lecture or worse. 'You took your time,' his father said by way of greeting.

'Good day, Father. I hope I find you well.'

Strathcairn gave a snort. 'For God's sake, sit down!' He frowned and waited for Max to pull forward a straight chair. 'Explain yourself.'

Max was no longer intimidated by that glare. He was now considerably larger than his parent and there would be no bending over the desk for a whipping. On the other hand, if his father wanted strict formality he could have it. 'I heard you have a new heir. I am planning to marry and it would be helpful to know the date of my assumed demise.'

Max had the pleasure of seeing his father taken aback. 'Demise? You are not dead!'

'Obviously not. But Robertson Urquhart is announcing himself as your heir.'

'I allowed him to assume you were dead. He was as eager as a puppy to trumpet his expectations abroad.' Distaste twisted Strathcairn's lips but his eyes gleamed with triumph. 'It was my way of getting you back where you belong. The news would reach your grandmother and sister, both of whom knew you were alive and took great delight in hiding your whereabouts.'

'Acquit Megan. She did not know.'

'So where have you been?'

'India.'

With many interruptions, questions and explosions of parental wrath, Max gave a broad outline of the last decade. His father knew of the two years before his son had joined George Pennicott because Max had kept his promise to his grandmother on that score. He was surprised to learn that his father had been well aware of his activities during that period but dismissed it with a shrug.

'I gave you time to work off your ire. I did not expect you to disappear completely,' Lord Strathcairn complained.

Max refused to apologise and kept to a strict account of his years with George Pennicott. He ended his story with the news that he was now a partner in the prosperous shipping line, wealthy in his own right and about the marry the owner's daughter.

'You have done well,' Lord Strathcairn said with warm approval. The trade connection did not worry him. Money was money, and the more of it the better. He flicked the small white card on his desk and giving a soft chuckle. 'When that was brought in, I thought the son had returned – *prodigal!*'

Max suppressed a shudder at the thought of his reception had he come home with his tail between his legs. His success gave him the upper hand and he could afford to meet his father half way. 'Your fatted calf is quite safe, Father, but I would not say no to a meal.'

Things had gone better than he had expected, but the following days were not entirely free of strife. Max fretted to be away, back to London and Joanna, but his father wanted him to stay and take his rightful place in the house, the community and eventually in Parliament. They reached a compromise: for the time being, Max would travel between Scotland and India. Lord Strathcairn was still in vigorous health and not ready to hand over the reins just yet but insisted that his son needed to know what was expected of him.

Max had no intention of giving up his interest in the shipping company but it mollified his father to think *he* was laying down the terms. Time enough for confrontation when it could no longer be avoided.

He wrote to Joanna explaining he had been delayed but would be with her as soon as possible.

***

On the day Max confronted his father, the Ridgeworth party were up and about early to catch the nine o'clock train to London. The station platform was crowded with people waiting to board but Lord Simon had reserved a private compartment. He led the way, advising Joanna to keep up and not let go of Cynthia's hand.

'Oh, there is the captain!' Bea exclaimed. She waved her hand and Captain Urquhart touched his hat in response.

As they drew level with him, Joanna paused. 'I did not know you were travelling to London,' she said.

He bowed. 'If I don't make a push to get a seat, I shall be standing all the way,' he smiled and made to move away.

'No, wait!' Bea called. She turned to her husband with a beguiling smile. 'May we offer the captain a place in our carriage? He fears he will not get a seat.' Simon hid his annoyance and pretended not to see Bea's smirk, but what could he do but agree?

Before they had gone far, Lord Simon was glad he had given in to his wife's request. He had been dreading a recurrence of Cynthia's travel sickness, even though she had been given another dose of Vera's magic mixture and been told very firmly that she would *NOT* be sick! The captain paid for his comfortable seat by entertaining them with stories of his travels. At one point, Joanna expressed concern that he had never been in the Indian Ocean and warned him of typhoons. 'My dear Miss Pennicott, I brought my ship safely through West Indian cyclones. I feel confident I can weather a typhoon.'

'I didn't like being on a boat,' Cynthia said. 'It went up and down and made me feel ill. So does this train.'

'That is nothing to be ashamed of,' Urquhart told her. 'Even Lord Nelson suffered from seasickness. The trick is to find something to take your mind off it.' He opened his valise, took out a length of cord and amused Cynthia by teaching her to tie complicated knots.

'You are very patient,' Lord Simon remarked when the captain tried to untangle the cord after one of Cynthia's less successful attempts.

'I had a little sister.' Urquhart tweaked the child's braid. 'I taught her to plait her hair and tie her ribbons.'

'Do you have any children?' Cynthia asked innocently.

Urquhart glossed over her father's reprimand with a shake of his head and answered simply, 'I am not married. It seemed very unfair to marry a lady and then leave her for months, even years at a time.'

Joanna grinned at him. 'Our captains are allowed to take their wives with them.'

'I was told so, but I am surprised *you* know about that.'

'There is very little I do not know about the company. Max keeps me informed.'

Cynthia flourished the re-tied knot under Urquhart's nose and said with pride, 'This is a good one. May I keep it to show Mr Maxwell?'

'No!' Urquhart said in alarm then floundered for an explanation.

Cynthia's mouth fell open at the abrupt denial, but Joanna had remembered Max's antagonism and rushed to the rescue. 'We do not know when we will be seeing Mr Maxwell again.' She smiled sideways at the captain. 'And I am sure Captain Urquhart know lots of other knots.'

Urquhart waited until Cynthia was concentrating on unpicking the cord before whispering, 'Thank you.'

Joanna was intrigued. The captain was obviously aware of Max's dislike and did not want to antagonise him further. Whatever could he have done that was so bad Max did not want her to talk to him? She rather liked the captain; he was intelligent, well-mannered and patient, which all seemed desirable attributes.

For one joyful moment she wondered if Max was jealous that she enjoyed Captain Urquhart's company. How wonderful that would be. The next second she had to dismiss the thought. Max had not been pleased to learn the name of the Joanna's future captain. But why? Captain Fogarty was satisfied with his seamanship and suitability, so it could not be that. And they could not have met; Max had been in India for eight years and Urquhart had never been that far east. It was a puzzle and Joanna determined to ask Max about it the next time she saw him.

The rest of the journey passed without incident. Captain Urquhart progressed from knots to teaching them some of the less risqué sea shanties. People passing along the corridor looked in at the merry party and smiled.

By the time they reached London, Lord Simon was so in charity with his fellow traveller that he offered to convey him to wherever he was staying. The captain declined politely. 'I am visiting my mother south of the river. It would be too far out of your way.' He shook hands all round and asked Bea's permission to call on Miss Pennicott in a few days' time.

'That would be very pleasant,' Bea replied, ignoring her husband's frown. 'We shall look forward to it.'

On their arrival at Ridgeworth House, Bassett greeted them with the hope that they had enjoyed a pleasant visit to Scotland. 'Your post is on your desk, my lord. My lady, I have placed yours in the small drawing room.'

Lord Simon disappeared into his study and Bea sent Cynthia up to the nursery with Vera and Sally. The butler handed Joanna a letter that had arrived for her in the afternoon post. At a quick glance Joanna recognised Max's writing and skipped up the stairs to read it in the privacy of her room.

It was short and rather disjointed, almost like the letters Max had written in the early days of their correspondence. He apologised for the delay but he was waiting on a confirmation telegram from her father. He would explain when he saw her. To save time, he had sent word to Mr Ebstone to forward the package left with him for safekeeping into the care of Lord Ridgeworth. He hoped Joanna would be pleased, and he would try to get to London in two or three days.

Joanna frowned and read the letter through again. If she had not known better, she would have thought Max was nervous.

A maid came to ask her to join Lord Ridgeworth in his study. Joanna put Max's letter in her writing box with all his other missives and went downstairs, curious but in no way alarmed.

Bea was with her husband when Joanna went in and she could see that Bea, at least, was bursting with news. Lord Simon looked stern, but Joanna had come to accept that as his usual expression and not an indication of his thoughts.

'Joanna,' Bea began, 'Simon has heard from Mr Ebstone.'

Lord Simon smiled indulgently at his wife but spoke to Joanna. 'Indeed. Despite his incapacity, Lord Stanley visited Mr Ebstone in Bristol.' He waved the letter in his hand. 'Mr Ebstone writes to inform me that Lord Stanley tried to get him to revoke the arrangement with Bea and place you in his charge.'

Joanna gasped but Lord Simon went on. 'He did not succeed. I quote, from Mr Ebstone's letter: *"That would be against the express wishes of Mr Pennicott. I suggested such an arrangement before Mr Pennicott left the country but he was most adamant that he did not want Lord Stanley to have anything to do with Joanna."'*

'But Lord Stanley has not given up,' Bea interrupted. 'Simon has—'

'Bea! Please allow me to finish,' her husband said. Bea held her tongue with difficulty while he continued. 'I have also received a note from Lord Stanley asking me to call at the earliest possible moment. I shall go tomorrow, but you have no need to worry. You will stay with us at least until the end of the season.'

'That is a relief.' Joanna sighed. 'I have received a letter from Max. He hopes to be with us in a few days. If anyone knows if my father has changed his mind, it will be him.' She frowned. 'But I do not think that is likely. My father parted from Lord Stanley on very bad terms and he was barely civil to Aunt Louisa.' They had to leave the matter there. As she left the room she added, 'Max said he is sending you a package for safe keeping until he can get here. I hope it is soon.'

Next day, after his visit to Lord Stanley, Lord Simon was able to fill in a few more details. Lord Stanley had started off reasonably, pointing out the impropriety of Joanna being in the care of anyone other than her family. He did not mention having already been denied, or his trip to Bristol. 'When I told him of Mr Ebstone's letter, he raged about Pennicott's ingratitude saying your father owed his success to him.' Lord Simon looked up at Joanna and asked, 'Have you any idea what he meant by that?'

Joanna nodded. 'When my parents married, Lord Stanley introduced Papa to other wealthy collectors. In return, Papa made him regular, expensive gifts. Not money, of course –Lord Stanley would not want anyone to think he was dabbling in trade,' she said cynically.

'How do you know this? Surely you were only a child at the time.' Bea was wide-eyed with amazement.

Joanna shrugged. 'Papa told me. He said it was a bad bargain but one should never renege on an agreement.'

'How odd,' Lord Simon murmured almost to himself. 'I would not dream of mentioning such things to Cynthia.'

'Of course not!' Joanna laughed. 'She would not understand.' It was said in a matter-of-fact way, as though that would be the only reason not to discuss serious matters with her.

Bea collapsed in giggles. 'Joanna even owns shares in the Suez Canal Company.'

Her husband shook his head in amazement. 'Joanna, you are a wonder! What else do you know?'

'About the business? Just about everything. Max sends regular reports and Mr Ebstone answers any questions that need a more immediate response.' Joanna paused to think, her brow creased in concentration. 'What I cannot understand is why... Oh, never mind.' She looked up and smiled. 'When would be the best time for me to call on Lord Stanley?'

'Call on him?' Bea echoed. 'Have you changed your mind?'

'Oh, not about leaving you,' Joanna reassured her. 'But I did promise to see him when we got back from Glasgow.' Her smile widened and she said gleefully, 'I have family, Bea! Aunts and cousins I have never met. They cannot *all* be as awful as Aunt Louisa. Do you understand what that means? I am not alone any more. If being polite to my grandfather is the price for meeting them, I will do it.'

'Well said, Joanna,' Lord Simon applauded. 'I – we – are both, proud of you.'

Joanna glowed with happiness. It only needed Max to feel the same and her joy would be complete.

Lord Simon suggested that Lord Stanley be invited to visit Joanna. 'If you go there, Bea will have to go with you. If he comes here we can arrange for you to have a private talk. I think it will be less embarrassing for all concerned.'

It was agreed, and Lord Stanley came to dinner the following evening. Joanna saw his carriage arrive from the drawing-room window. Now the moment had come, she felt nervous; not afraid, just apprehensive. How would Lord Stanley behave? Would he continue to insist on her leaving Bea's care? She knew that would not happen but she hated confrontation. Her real fear was that he would prevent her from meeting the rest of the family.

In deference to Lord Stanley's incapacity, they were using the small downstairs drawing room. When Lord Simon went out into the hall to greet his guest, Bea gave Joanna a reassuring smile. 'Relax. We will greet him with courtesy and, as a guest, he will follow our lead.'

Joanna surely hoped so. Lord Stanley did not seem the kind of man to follow anyone's lead. She moved away from the window and sat beside Bea on a sofa, but they both rose as Lord Simon ushered her grandfather into the room.

Bea stepped forward. 'Welcome, my lord.' They were the same words she had used on his last visit. This time, he bowed over her hand and thanked her for the invitation. Then he turned to Joanna.

She dipped into a curtsey. As she rose, she looked up into his face. Lord Stanley appeared to be ill; deep grooves bracketed his mouth and they deepened as he moved. *He is in pain,* Joanna thought and felt a sudden sympathy. This matter of her place of residence was important enough to him to brave a long journey to the opposite side of the country. It made her voice gentle as she urged him to sit down.

Lord Simon offered his guest a drink, which was accepted, and the group arranged themselves in a rather stiff circle. Lord Stanley sipped his whisky and regarded Joanna over the rim of the glass. She found it difficult to meet his eyes and took a too-hasty sip of her sherry. Bea covered her cough with a light comment about dinner soon being announced. 'I hope you will not mind, but we usually allow Ridgeworth's daughter, Cynthia, to join us for dessert.'

Lord Stanley followed her lead and asked about Cynthia, a conversation that lasted just long enough for Bassett to arrive and announce dinner. Joanna watched as the old man hauled himself upright. She could see it cost him an effort, but the way he squared his shoulders spoke of pride that would be offended if anyone offered him help. He led the way with Bea on his arm.

Lord Simon smiled at Joanna and whispered, 'Don't look so worried. All will be well.' There was no time to tell him that her frown was one of concern for Lord Stanley.

With the servants coming and going, conversation at the table was kept to impersonal topics. Joanna was conscious of being watched and it quite ruined her appetite. It was a relief when Cynthia joined them. 'Good evening, Lord Stanley,' the girl said politely when she was introduced. 'I did not know Joanna had a grandfather. I wish I had one.'

Lord Stanley smiled at her, and Joanna was surprised at his gentle tone when he replied. 'Perhaps Joanna will be willing to share me.'

'Oh, that would be lovely. Will you, Joanna? Please?'

Joanna avoided looking at Lord Stanley and smiled at Cynthia. 'I am not sure how we are to do that. What do you suggest?'

Having neatly passed the conversation back to Cynthia, Joanna listened as the girl outlined possible meetings and activities. 'We could go for ices. I love desserts.' Cynthia demonstrated by taking a spoonful of the fruit cream in her dish and closing her eyes in an expression of ecstasy. After she had swallowed, she told the old man about the wicked governess who had confiscated the desserts and eaten them herself. Everyone laughed, and soon after Cynthia was sent up to bed.

The adults went back to the drawing room. When she had seen Lord Stanley comfortably seated, Bea said, 'Thank you for being so kind to Cynthia.'

'I am very fond of young children,' Lord Stanley replied. 'That was why I wanted Joanna to live with me when her father went away.'

Lord Simon touched his wife's arm before she could speak. 'My dear, I believe this is out cue to leave Joanna to talk to her grandfather.'

When they were alone, Joanna asked, 'Please, my lord, what did you mean?'

She did not need to define the question. Lord Stanley looked at her sadly. 'That was why your father and I quarrelled. I did not want you to be exposed to the Indian climate.' He shook his head. 'I worded it too strongly and accused him of ruining your mother's health. I won't bother you with the rest of our angry words. Suffice to say I was told it was none of my business. But I did not give up and I wrote a last appeal and sent it with Louisa.'

'I did not know.'

'No, and I did not know you had been sent to that school.' Lord Stanley looked suddenly fierce. 'I assure you I have shown Louisa my displeasure.'

Joanna tried to be glad that Louisa had been punished, but overall was the regret that she had been deprived the comfort of family for so long. 'Please will you tell me about the rest of my family, my lord?'

Lord Stanley smiled. 'Family comes with a grandfather. Do you think you could stop calling me "my lord"?'

Joanna moved to the chair next to him and took the old man's hand. It felt frail in her strong clasp and she sensed his weakness was due to more than normal ageing. 'Grandfather,' she whispered, 'for years I have taken my cue from Papa and thought badly of you. That was wrong. I wish we had not lost so much time.'

By the time Lord Stanley left, arrangements had been made for Joanna to meet her other relatives. There were two other aunts besides Louisa, both married and with children of their own; there should have been three aunts, but one of his daughters had died in childbirth. Joanna also had an uncle and seven cousins ranging in age from twenty-two years down to four years.

She went to bed that night in a glow of happiness. She had been so lonely that even the kindness of Iris and her family had never really filled the void but now she was no longer alone. She felt tears running down her cheeks, but tears of happiness were mingled with sadness for the lost years. She brushed them away, telling herself not to be silly. She was happier than she could ever remember, and she could hardly wait to share the news with Max. He should arrive soon; he had said two or three days and it was already past that.

Joana got out of bed and retrieved Max's last letter from her writing box to see when it had been posted. The date stamp was blurred and she could not read it, so too was the name of the postal office. Max had mentioned travelling to the east coast and she wondered if he was still there or if the letter had been sent from somewhere else. Whatever he had been doing was taking longer than he had expected. Oh, well, he would surely explain when he arrived.

Joanna went back to bed with the letter under her pillow and prayed Max would come soon.

Chapter 25

For the next two days, Joanna's life was a whirlwind of calls and visits. Her first caller was her Aunt Claudia, Lady Bassett, one of her mother's younger sisters. She was warm and welcoming, the antithesis of Aunt Louisa, and Joanna liked her on sight. Claudia was Mama's youngest sister, in her late twenties and the mother of two little girls still in the nursery.

She swept Joanna off to meet another aunt, Lady Sylvia Westwood, a slightly older lady. Her boys were aged twelve and fourteen and away at school. Claudia mentioned Louisa's daughter, Pamela, but said Louisa was in disgrace and had been banished to the country.

'Hard luck on Pamela,' Claudia said with feeling. 'The poor girl will have to bear the brunt of Louisa's ill-temper.'

Claudia and Sylvia enjoyed a few minutes tearing their eldest sister to ribbons but even at their harshest, Joanna could not detect real venom. Their conversation was so different to Louisa's sugar-coated gibes. Apparently, Louisa had always been selfish and discontented, and Joanna took comfort from the fact that she had not been singled out for her aunt's spite.

Both aunts assured her that had they known Joanna was still in the country they would have taken an interest in her as soon as they were old enough. Another sister, Julia, the closest in age to Veronica, would certainly have done so, but she had died in childbirth at the age of twenty-two.

Joanna thought of the lost years but was given no time to brood because her aunts had planned a full programme of visits and introductions.

Much as she enjoyed meeting her family, Joanna was becoming anxious about Max's non-arrival. It was now over a week since she had received his letter. Whatever could be keeping him so long? She could not even write to ask him about the delay because she did not know where he was.

Instead she poured all her news into a long letter to Iris. *I still miss you,* she wrote. That was true, but she was finding more pleasure in the social events without having to worry about how her friend was coping with all the attention. It made her feel rather disloyal since Iris had always been there for her during her darkest times. Now Iris needed support, Joanna was gadding about, meeting family, dancing and laughing with a bevy of suitors, none of whom made her pulse race as did the mere thought of Max.

When Joanna mentioned this to Bea, her mentor replied, 'Iris is doing what she likes best. I know how hard she tried to look as though she was enjoying the season, but we both know the attention made her uncomfortable.'

'I never realised before that Iris is actually very shy. She likes people and tries to be helpful, but I think that is just her way of distracting them from her looks.'

Bea nodded agreement. 'Most girls do all they can to attract attention and envy. They do not see that extreme beauty can be a burden – and Iris is a beauty.'

Joanna laughed. 'I would not mind a little more burden!'

'You do yourself an injustice. Your face might not be conventionally beautiful but you have beautiful hair, a magnificent figure and an honesty that is lacking in so many debutantes. Believe me, it is not just your fortune that brings you admirers.'

'I don't want admirers.'

'You want Mr Maxwell.' Bea laughed when Joanna blushed. 'I think he wants you, too. Be patient. I am sure all will work out for the best.'

That evening, before she got into bed Joanna stood in front of her mirror and tried to see herself as others did. She had never considered red hair, a bosom and a straightforward manner to be assets; to her mind they equated with garish, lumpy and too frank for most people's comfort. The girls at school had considered her rather odd. She had never tried to change her appearance and she did not weave impossible dreams of the future, she just made the best of each day. If she did not wish for more, she could not be rejected and disappointed.

The only person to whom she had ever really poured out her heart was Max and that had been easy because distance formed a kind of shield. He knew her more intimately than anyone else on earth. But was that enough?

Joanna sighed and turned away from her reflection.

***

The next day Joanna joined a party of young friends on an excursion to Richmond. She arrived back cold, tired and hungry but brightened when the butler greeted her with the news that a letter had arrived for her in the afternoon post. He had sent it up to her room. She forgot her fatigue and skipped up the stairs, hoping it was from Max.

She was disappointed. The letter had come from India via Mr Ebstone, with a copy of its covering note.

Mr Lloyd apologised for the delay in sending the enclosed; it had been found caught in the clip holding invoices that Mr Pennicott had collected from the warehouse on the day that Mr Maxwell left. He asked for it to be forwarded to Miss Pennicott as soon as possible and hoped the contents were not urgent.

The enclosed envelope carried her father's scrawled words: *Joanna were she is.* If it were not so sad, Joanna would have laughed. Her father did not write to her often, but she was too tired, cold and hungry to decipher the letter at that moment and put it aside to read later.

A bath and a hot cup of tea restored her sufficiently to join Bea for dinner but the disappointment that her letter had not been from Max still left her depressed. The ladies dined alone as Lord Simon had another commitment.

'Did you enjoy your day?' Bea asked, and then listened sympathetically to Joanna's tale of woe. The weather had been awful and prevented them from exploring the park; arrangements for luncheon had not been confirmed and the party had trailed from inn to inn trying to find an establishment that could cater for a party of twelve. And she was weary from the incessant bickering of the brother and sister who had been the day's hosts.

'It was just my luck to be in the carriage with them,' she groaned. 'I wanted to knock their silly heads together.'

Bea commiserated. 'Things will look better in the morning. Mr Maxwell should be here soon and you have Captain Urquhart's visit to look forward to.'

'You sound just like Iris,' Joanna laughed. 'But I think I will go up and try to decipher that letter from my father.'

She waited until she was in bed before taking out her father's letter. It took several readings to unjumble the higgledy-piggledy letters, bad spelling and multiple crossings out and at first Joanna could not believe what she was reading. There must be some mistake.

The letter said,

Dear Jo. Lady Robert Urquart if maried. Soon a Cowntess. No need for delay now he has seen you.

I have been a bad father but this is for the best.

Max will do the arrangements. I have made him my heir. The son I never had. Company in good hands.

Confusion gave way to anger and unbelievable pain. She knew her father had always wanted a son, but to see it written down made her feel worthless. That was how he saw her – how else could he hand her over to a stranger like an unwanted parcel?

And Max: she had thought him her friend and latterly something more. Was this the news he had been reluctant to share with her? Were his smiles false? They had to be. He had wormed his way into her father's affection and stolen her inheritance.

The rat! The snake! If he were here now, she would rip out his heart! Claw the false smile from his face! She would…

Joanna turned her face into the pillow and gave way to tears of betrayal. She had never felt so alone, abandoned. This was worse than being left behind when Papa went to India, worse than Aunt Louisa's contempt. At school she had found friendship and learned self-esteem, and there had been Iris and letters from Max.

Max. A fresh wave of sobs added physical pain to the ache in her chest.

She did not hear the knock on her door and only knew Bea was there when she felt herself being turned over and a soft hand pushing her wet and tumbled hair out of her eyes.

'Whatever is wrong?' Bea asked, kneeling on the floor, her face inches from Joanna's. 'I heard you crying. Can you tell me?'

'Max,' Joanna croaked. 'My father. Oh, I wish I were dead.' She wrenched free of Bea's hand and burrowed into the damp pillow again.

Bea did not know what to do. Hoping for inspiration, she looked around the room and her eyes lit on the crumpled letter. It went against her instincts to read private correspondence but this was an emergency.

At first, she just looked at it with an unbelieving frown. Could this really be from Joanna's father? It took a great effort to decipher George Pennicott's rambling thoughts and even more tangled words, but she gleaned enough to understand Joanna's distress. Men! Selfish, arrogant, heartless men! 'Joanna,' she said firmly. 'Come out of there. We can sort this out.'

'How?' Joanna moaned. She rolled over and looked at Bea. 'How? I am worthless. Papa could not wait to get away from me – and now this. Did he ever love me at all? He has given everything to Max!'

Bea hitched herself up onto the bed and took Joanna into her arms. 'I think it is Max you are crying for,' she said gently. 'I must say I am surprised. I do not know him well but he does not seem the kind of man …' She could not put the betrayal into words, but on one point she could be reassuring. 'You do not have to marry Captain Urquhart. There are laws. You cannot be married without your consent. This is not the Dark Ages.'

Bea hoped she was right. Simon would know. But for the moment it was enough to comfort Joanna. The girl gave a shuddering sigh and attempted to mop her tears with the sheet. She was not alone and that thought gave her courage and, gradually, a return of her natural resilience. She managed a tremulous smile and thanked Bea. 'I am alright now,' she said untruthfully. She would never be alright again, but the words formed themselves.

'Of course you are,' Bea lied in return. 'Now, I am going to send Vera in with something to help you sleep and we will sort this out in the morning.'

Vera Cotton's remedy was a cup of warm milk with a splash of brandy – well, nearly half and half with a dollop of cream to soften the burn. While Joanna sipped the brew, Vera straightened the bed and turned the pillows. She asked no questions and tucked Joanna up with a kiss on her cheek and a whispered, 'Sleep well.'

Vera's potion ensured that Joanna slept, but in the early hours she dreamed she was being attacked by an unknown man. She cried out to Max to help her but he turned away. Frantically she fought the hands that were tearing at her clothes until she awoke with tears streaming down her face to the realisation that the hands were her own.

She sat up, clammy with sweat and trembling. She wanted to get up, to wash away the dream, but exhaustion reclaimed her.

She woke again later unrefreshed. The details of the dream had faded but she was left with an impression of disappointment and betrayal. She had a slight headache and a mottled complexion that made her shudder at her reflection in the mirror. What a mess! She could not remember the last time she had cried and if this was the result, she had best not do it again! Instinctively she thought that it was a good thing Max could not see her now.

That brought everything back and almost started the tears again. *Oh, Max, why…?*

Vera bustled into the room saying that Sally was with Miss Cynthia. She did not add that she had sent the maid upstairs. Keeping up a stream of bracing comments, Vera helped Joanna to dress and applied a cucumber cream and a dusting of powder to her face to repair some of the ravages. Unfortunately, she did not possess a remedy for a broken heart.

In a midnight conference, Bea had given her husband an outline of the situation. When Joanna joined them for breakfast, Lord Simon gave her a reassuring smile. The main topic of interest was not mentioned in front of the servants, and Joanna managed to eat a meagre breakfast. After the meal, they retired to Lord Simon's study. 'Now, let us see what we can do to help you,' he said.

Joanna laid out the crumpled letter and apologised. 'Papa has difficulty writing,' she explained. 'He is very clever in other ways, it is just words on paper that he finds difficult.' She went through each sentence, which Lord Simon re-wrote on a separate sheet.

'Do you know when your father met the captain?' he asked.

Joanna shook her head. 'I don't see how he could have done. The captain told us he had never been to India, and to the best of my knowledge Papa has never left there. I only know that Captain Fogarty, our senior captain, was given permission to appoint his successor.'

'Very well. Let us take this point by point. Firstly, if you marry,' he raised a finger to forestall Joanna's protest, 'I say *if* you marry the captain, you will not automatically become Lady Urquhart. I am quite sure the courtesy title of Lord would not pass to a mere nephew. Whether he eventually succeeds to the title is in the lap of the gods.'

'I hope he drowns first,' Joanna declared. Then added, 'But I hope he does not take my ship down with him.' As her words sunk in, she bit her lips. 'Sorry. I don't mean that. I would not wish death on anyone. And it isn't my ship – Papa has given everything to Max.'

'An heir is not a possessor, Joanna,' Bea pointed out. 'Perhaps you can persuade your father to change his will again.'

'Fat chance,' Joanna snorted, then apologised again. The older couple laughed.

'Seriously,' Lord Simon continued, 'we cannot know why Mr Maxwell was made the heir.'

'He is the son my father never had,' Joanna said bitterly. 'He says so in the letter. I am just a girl! Not fit to accompany him to India, never receiving a visit and only scant messages added to Max's letters.'

Bea covered Joanna's clenched fist with her hand. 'I still cannot believe Mr Maxwell has been so devious.'

'Nor I,' Lord Simon added. 'Inheritance apart, he gave me the distinct impression that he wished to marry you himself.'

'He did?' Joanna whispered. 'Then why…?'

Lord Simon stood up and patted Joanna's shoulder. 'That we cannot know until he gets here.' He waited until Joanna looked up at him before adding, 'You do not dislike Captain Urquhart?'

'No,' Joanna replied quickly. 'But I don't want to marry him.'

There was no point in further discussion and Lord Simon left them to go about his business. Joanna went up to supervise Cynthia's lessons, which took her mind off the problem for a few hours.

She and Bea were drinking coffee in the drawing room when two cabs drew up outside the house. From the window Joanna looked down on Max and Captain Urquhart talking on the pavement.

Chapter 26

Max found the journey to London frustrating. The train seemed to stop at every station and the changing company in his carriage meant a repetition of inane comments about the weather and their various reasons for the journey. He was impatient to reach Joanna and tell her all about his background and his hopes for the future.

George had sent word that he had reconsidered his will and sent a revised version directly to Mr Ebstone. That had made Max suspicious; George could be very stubborn on occasion and was not above using diversionary tactics to get his own way. Max had felt compelled to go to Bristol to check on his partner's plans before travelling to London. He wanted everything fair and above board when he proposed to Joanna.

Captain Urquhart was paying off his driver when Max's cab drew up behind him. Max jumped down and tossed some money to his cabbie before striding forward. 'What are you doing here?' he demanded.

'I have permission to call on Miss Pennicott,' Urquhart replied haughtily and made to approach the steps.

Max scowled at the bouquet Urquhart was carrying and stepped in front of the captain to reach the door first and bang the knocker. The butler opened the door but blocked the entrance. 'The ladies are not receiving,' he told them solemnly. A shriek from the upper floor made him turn and Max took advantage of his distraction to enter the hall.

Joanna came flying down the stairs and Max instinctively held out his hands in greeting. She batted them away and punched him hard in the chest for good measure. 'You traitor!' she screamed. 'I thought you were my friend!'

Max was stunned and confused, even as his body reacted to her magnificence. She was fury personified, a Valkyrie ready to reap vengeance!

Before he could gather his wits, Joanna whirled around to the man standing just behind him. 'And as for you,' she took a swipe at the bouquet, sending a shower of petals to the floor, 'you can take those where they will be appreciated! I will not marry you.'

'I haven't asked you,' Urquhart stammered in surprise.

Max grabbed Joanna's arm. 'You're upset. What is the matter?'

'Upset?' Joanna yelled before he had finished speaking. She gave a harsh laugh. 'Upset because you have seduced my father into making you his heir? Upset because my absentee father has already arranged for me to marry him?' A glare and a pointed finger made the captain take a step back. 'If Father wants to give me away like an unwanted parcel, he can damn well come home and do it himself!'

A tide of pain added to her rage and she tried to free her arm, which Max still held in a firm grip. 'Let me go,' she hissed. He was not hurting her, but she could not bear him to touch her.

Her words gave Max a clue as to the reason for her outrage: somehow she had found out about George's scheme but got the details wrong.

Bea came down to the hall and gently disengaged Max's hand from Joanna's arm. 'I suggest we all go into Simon's office and sort this out.'

'I do not know what is going on,' Captain Urquhart protested. 'I think I should leave.'

'Oh no, you don't,' Max growled. 'You will stay and explain what you have been up to.'

Bea ushered them into the study and closed the door. She guided Joanna to a chair and stood by her side with a comforting hand on her shoulder. Her calming presence diluted some of Joanna's emotions and she whispered, 'I think I swore.'

'You did,' Bea replied smoothly, trying not to laugh.

'Joanna,' Max began gently, only to have Joanna turn her head away.

'I don't want to talk to you,' she muttered

'I think there has been some mistake,' Captain Urquhart suggested from his position near the door. 'I ought to leave,' he repeated, his face red with embarrassment.

Max ignored him and looked appealingly at Bea, who reached out and picked up the crumped letter from the desk. It was not really her place to do so but she handed it to Max. He read it through and started to laugh while the others stared at him in varying degrees of amazement.

Max hunkered down in front of Joanna and waved the paper under her nose. 'This doesn't refer to Urquhart. Well, it *does* – but not the one you think. It's me. My name is Robert Angus Maxwell Urquhart. My father is the Ear of Strathcairn.' He smiled as though offering her a prize.

Joanna gave him a hard shove so that he toppled over. 'And that makes it alright, does it?'

Max heaved himself to his feet. 'I meant to tell you, but there was never an opportunity.'

'You had *eight years*!' Joanna screeched.

'I could not put it in a letter and wait months for your response. I went to see my father to find out why *he*,' he gave a curt nod towards the captain, 'was posing as Strathcairn's heir.'

'It was not my doing,' Urquhart made haste to assure him. 'I received a lawyer's letter and…'

'I know about that,' Max said impatiently. He looked at Lady Bea and smiled. 'My lady, will you allow me a little time alone with Joanna?' His gaze switched to Urquhart and he added, 'Don't go far. I will talk to you later.'

Bea took the captain away and closed the door.

It took time to unravel the mystery. Joanna listened, at first stony faced but gradually thawing. 'And what about the will? Am I to be left a pauper?'

Max reminded her of the papers he had asked Mr Ebstone to send. 'I did not register your father's will – I tore it up in front of him. I told him it was unfair and that there was a chance you would not want to marry me. I could not accept what was rightfully yours.'

The sincerity in his voice leached some of Joanna anger – but not all. 'But you agreed to his suggestion,' she accused.

Max took advantage of the fact that Joanna was willing to talk to him and knelt in front of her again. He took hold of her tightly clenched fists. 'Joanna, George did not need to bribe or persuade me. I *want* to marry you.'

'Really?' Joanna rage was replaced by wonder. *Max wanted to marry her!*

Max smiled tenderly and Joanna smiled shyly in return. 'Miss Pennicott, will you do me the honour of becoming my wife?'

Joanna gave a whoop and threw her arms around his neck, unbalancing him so that they both ended up on the carpet. Max rolled her beneath him and kissed her until she melted into a puddle of sensations. Exuberance gave way to an aching tenderness and everything else ceased to exist.

Max eventually eased back and rested his weight on one elbow. Joanna took a deep breath and her magnificent bosom strained against the neckline of her dress. Max growled and buried his face in the enticing valley. When he lifted his head, his face wore an expression usually reserved for cream-covered chocolate cake. He even licked his lips.

For the first time in her life, Joanna felt beautiful. When his large hand cradled her breast, he groaned and she gave thanks for its abundance. The feeling was beyond anything she could have imagined; her hot little dreams were reduced to the status a child's picture book.

He kissed her again and they were still in a blissful tangle when Bea came back into the room. Joanna gazed up at her friend with a beaming smile. 'We are going to be married.'

'I am glad to hear it,' Bea told them. 'But until then, I have to insist that you behave with more decorum.' Her accompanying smile robbed her words of any censure.

Max helped Joanna to her feet and into a chair then drew another one close so he could still hold her hand. Bea sat close by and listened to a potted version of events before Max remembered the captain. 'What have you done with Urquhart?' he asked. 'I still want to know how he managed to get the captaincy.'

Bea laughed. 'I let the poor man go because he was so embarrassed, but I have asked him to join us for dinner. He will give you the details himself – but your Captain Fogarty is his godfather.'

Before dinner that evening, Captain Urquhart joined Joanna, Max and the Ridgeworths for a celebratory drink in the drawing room. He gave his reasons for thinking himself Lord Strathcairn's heir and Max explained how it had come about.

'My devious father thought it would bring me home, that the rumour of a new heir would get back to my grandmother, Lady Leith. He knew she had been in constant touch with me all the time I was away and would pass on the news.' He held out a hand to his distant cousin. 'I am sorry for your disappointment.'

'Not at all,' Urquhart replied, giving Max's hand a hearty shake. 'The sea is my life, and if I still have the captaincy...' He let the question hang.

Max put him out of his misery. 'If Fogarty vouches for you, that is good enough.' He crossed to Joanna and placed an arm around her waist. 'How would you like to sail to India on the *Joanna*'s maiden voyage?'

'Oh, Joanna can't stand the heat,' Bea said, torn between the idea of a romantic voyage and fear of disappointment.

Joanna laughed. 'That was a fiction I created to stop people feeling sorry for me.' She turned to Max with stars in her eyes. 'It could be our honeymoon.'

Chapter 27

Joanna had never known a month to pass so quickly or so slowly. Individual days were too short to accomplish all the shopping, dress fittings and discussions Bea and Joanna's aunts considered vital to prepare for her wedding. Conversely, those same hours seemed to drag until she could see Max again – and then they were seldom alone since Bea had turned into the strictest of chaperones.

When Joanna complained, Bea said it was very easy to get carried away with disastrous results if something happened to prevent their marriage. Her words were delivered with such tenderness that Joanna wondered if Bea was speaking from experience.

The times they were allowed to be alone were precious jewels that Joanna hugged to herself in Max's absence. He seemed to enjoy kissing her, but she had no romantic illusions; she had been in society long enough to realise that her ample figure kindled interest in men who did not know her or want a serious relationship. She clung to the knowledge that Max was her friend and he knew and liked her, although he had never mentioned love.

Neither had he made any further mention of his position as her father's heir. Yes, he said he had torn up the will but another could easily be written. Was he expecting to manage anything that her father left to her? Joanna decided it did not matter; being married to Max was beyond anything she had ever expected. It would have to be enough.

Max had also come in for his share of pre-wedding negotiations. Lord Stanley had tried to find out about any settlements and dowry and been very annoyed when Max told him it was all arranged. Then there were constant letters from Max's father asking about the same things. Max laughingly suggested to Joanna that they run away from all the fuss and the idea appealed, but Joanna had learned patience. Over the years she had taught herself to live very much in the present, not hankering for the past or dreaming of a halcyon future. What would be would be – but she still wished the future would hurry up and arrive.

Her activities were not exclusively about the wedding. She was also enjoying getting to know her aunts, whose love was gradually filling the void she had never acknowledged. They both wanted to tell her stories about her mother's youth, which had not been as bleak as Joanna had imagined. Lord Stanley had emerged as a strict but loving parent..

Her grandfather was a sick man but still a force to be reckoned with. He did not take kindly to being denied a hand in arranging Joanna's financial future, or her insistence on staying with Lady Bea. He softened when Joanna agreed to his request that he have the honour of giving her away, and he told her how happy he was to be blessed with knowing her before it was too late.

Taking advantage of their growing rapport, Lord Stanley wanted to host a grand betrothal ball but Joanna persuaded him to moderate it to a formal dinner when Lord Strathcairn and Lady Leith arrived in town.

Joanna was not greatly taken with Max's father. When Max introduced them, the earl had offended her by subjecting her to a thorough scrutiny before saying to Max, 'You have done well for yourself, all round. She looks robust enough to give you healthy sons as long as you don't cart her off to that heathen country.'

Joanna blushed but Max replied hotly, 'I count myself fortunate that Joanna has agreed to be my wife. And we will be going to India for our honeymoon.' Further discussion was fortunately prevented by the arrival of Lady Leith.

Joanna was glad to see the kind lady, who took one look at her heightened colour and turned on the earl. 'I see you are still as objectionable as you have always been, Robert. I rue the day I ever agreed to you marrying my daughter. Come, Joanna,' she said and swept her away to the other side of the room. 'Take no notice of him, my dear. The only thing I can say in his favour is that he gave me Angus who, thank God, is not a bit like his father.'

Over her shoulder Joanna could see Max and his father in a heated but low-voiced argument. Only the social training of Lady Leith and Lady Ridgeworth saved the dinner from being a total disaster.

As they were taking their leave, Max tried to apologise for his father's rudeness but Joanna shrugged it aside. 'Fortunately I am not marrying your father.' She summoned up a smile that she hoped looked flirtatious and added, 'I much prefer you.'

'Another two days,' Max groaned, the hot look in his eyes making Joanna weak at the knees. She wished they were alone so Max could kiss her again, but Lord and Lady Ridgeworth were waiting for her by the door. 'Only two days,' she replied and tore herself away from his disturbing presence.

Joanna spent the last night of her girlhood tucked up in bed with Iris, who had arrived with her parents just that day. Reverend Armitage was to perform the ceremony and Mrs Armitage, now fully recovered, had been easily persuaded to attend the wedding of the girl she regarded as a second daughter.

'Tomorrow you will be in bed with Max,' Iris giggled. 'Do you remember how scandalised you were when Miss Waring explained what would happen? I wager you have changed your mind.'

Joanna could feel herself blushing. The rare embraces she had shared with Max had ignited a flame of desire that threatened to become an inferno had they not been constantly interrupted. Yes, she had definitely changed her opinion. 'I thought Max would fall in love with you,' she said with a sideways look to gauge Iris's response.

'Silly,' Iris laughed. 'He was so upset when he met you at the school, I thought he was going to kidnap you on the spot. And anyway, when – if – I marry, it won't be to someone who travels around the world. It will be someone who is content to stay in one place and live quietly away from the crowds.'

Joanna was reassured; she did not want her dear friend to feel rejected. She was also glad that she would be able to travel with Max and see all the wonderful things he had described in his letters.

Feeling utterly content, she said goodnight and lay staring at the ceiling, willing away the hours until morning.

Chapter 28

The next morning was so filled with people and activity that Joanna wanted to scream. For a start she was expected to have breakfast in bed, something that had never happened before and felt rather silly. Then there was the long drawn-out process of getting her prepared that seemed to warrant the attention of all the significant females of her acquaintance. Vera and Sally supervised her bath and hairstyling; Mrs Armitage, Iris and Bea were joined by Joanna's aunts to observe the final stages of her dressing by Lucy Fletcher.

Lucy's creation was a work of art. She had drawn her inspiration from classical Greek sculpture, covering the current fashion for rigid lines with a sinuous drapery of ivory coloured silk. The skirt was quite narrow with fewer petticoats than normal, and it accentuated Joanna's long legs. The soft material clung to her figure, not scandalously but in a way that drew attention to what Lucy referred to as 'her assets'. There were no frills or added decoration, and its very simplicity made Joanna rather than the dress the focus of attention.

The assembled females sighed in unison as Joanna looked into the long mirror, unable to believe her eyes. With her hair loose and wearing a simple wreath of glossy leaves and tiny cream rosebuds, she looked like a stranger.

'You look beautiful,' Iris said, her image appearing beside Joanna's in the mirror. For once Joanna did not made an unfavourable comparison. She remembered hearing it said that all brides were beautiful and put the transformation down to her dress and wedding magic. But oh, how she wished she could always look like this for Max.

***

Max sat at the front of the church staring straight ahead. He was not really nervous; Joanna was too sensible to have a last-minute change of mind. They had spent so little time together, and since their engagement there had been no opportunity for him to assure her that he loved her for herself, that his feelings had nothing to do with the Pennicott fortune. His emotions had been strengthening even before he met her physically; they had a connection that reached back into years of confidences and shared opinions.

It was difficult to discern Joanna's real feelings. She had such a down-to-earth attitude and showed little emotion after that one burst of anger at her father's will – followed by an equally strong burst of passion. From her response to his kisses it was clear she was capable of passion, but he wanted more.

He was jerked out of his reverie by a nudge in the ribs from John Armitage, who was acting as his best man. 'Something is happening,' he said quietly. 'The grand dames have arrived, so Joanna cannot be far behind.'

Max risked a look over his shoulder at the assembled congregation. It was quite large and made up of people he hardly knew, so it was reassuring to recognise his grandmother sitting in the row behind him, slightly distanced from his father. Both nodded to him with different degrees of warmth. Lord and Lady Ridgeworth were taking their places on the other side of the aisle with Mrs Armitage. He was surprised to see Miss Waring sitting with Mr Ebstone. They were deep in conversation and did not notice his glance.

The quiet music he had hardly been aware of suddenly changed to something more dramatic as Reverend Armitage walked to the front of the church. There was a rustle of movement and a sudden hush.

Max turned fully and saw Joanna. He found it difficult to breathe as she seemed to float down the aisle on a carpet of petals scattered by Cynthia. Sunlight shining through the stained-glass windows brought out the highlights in her loosened hair. Her usual purposeful stride had slowed to accommodate Lord Stanley, who was leaning heavily on her arm.

All of that faded into insignificance as he took in the reality of what he was seeing. Joanna glowed with vitality; she looked like a fertility goddess of ancient times, a statue transformed into flesh and blood. The draperies of her gown slid sinuously, a promise that they would fall away and reveal her magnificent figure. Max felt the urge to kneel at her feet in homage.

'Dearly beloved.' Reverend Armitage's voice recalled him to the time and place. Max dragged his gaze away from Joanna and tried to concentrate on the minister's words.

For her part, Joanna was equally stunned. It was a surprise to see Max dressed in his national costume. His kilt had a pale-blue background with stripes of red, black and gold. His black-velvet jacket had silver buttons and a crested silver badge pinned high on his chest. The silver was repeated in the ornate heading of his sporran and the buckles of his highly polished shoes. She just had time to take in his matching tartan socks before her eyes were drawn to his face.

He has had his hair cut, Joanna thought with some disappointment. She had been looking forward to running her fingers through the curls that usually decorated the nape of his neck. But when she looked directly into his blue eyes all else vanished. His eyes were wide open and so dark that the irises merged with the pupils in an expression Joanna interpreted as disbelief, just as she had felt when she looked in the mirror. She gazed back at him, wishing and wishing she could look this way for him forever.

'Dearly beloved,' Reverend Armitage began again, jerking Joanna's attention to the matter in hand.

She heard the words that would place her in Max's keeping for the rest of their lives. She heard Max vow to love, honour and keep her and made her own responses when prompted. There was a strange sense of unreality, as though she were watching a scene quite detached from her body.

Max's hand was warm and strong as he slid the ring onto her finger, but when he bent to kiss her she felt a wave of disappointment. The kiss was brief and cool, a mere brush of his lips against hers before Reverend Armitage invited them to follow him into the vestry. There was a murmur of conversation from the congregation as Earl Stanley and Earl Strathcairn followed. When directed, Joanna signed her name as Pennicott for the last time. Now she was Lady Robert Urquhart. Max's wife!

The sense of unreality persisted during the walk down the aisle, photographs and a shower of petals before Max handed her into the flower-bedecked carriage. Someone called to Joanna to toss her bouquet and she searched the crowd for Iris, but her friend was nowhere to be seen. With a shrug Joanna threw the flowers at random and sat down without waiting to see who caught them.

The drive to Stanley House was mercifully short, given the clatter of assorted ironware someone had tied beneath the carriage. Conversation was impossible, not that either Max or Joanna was thinking coherently enough to make a remark.

At the reception, Joanna was kissed and embraced by more people than she could remember and many she had never seen before. Max shook hands and accepted hearty slaps and nudges. It came as a great relief when they were told that it was time to change into their travelling outfits.

Iris accompanied her to a lavish bedroom where Sally waited to help her out of her wedding gown. Her excited words were an echo of what everyone else had been saying and made Joanna's head spin.

Iris sent the maid from the room and guided Joanna to the stool in front of the mirror. 'Sit down,' she commanded. 'You look ready to faint.'

That acted on Joanna like a splash of cold water. 'I have never fainted in my life!'

'You have never been married before. If it has that effect on you, I am never going to marry. I would die if hordes of people descended upon me.'

'Didn't Max look wonderful?' Joanna said with a dreamy smile. 'I did not expect to see him in a kilt.'

'From where I was standing, Max looked equally surprised by you.'

'Do you think so? Miss Fletcher's dress made me look … look... Oh, I don't know, but it was not like me.'

'You looked beautiful,' Iris repeated.

To change the subject, Joanna said, 'I am glad Miss Waring came.' She exchanged a knowing smirk with Iris, 'She looked quite young in that royal-blue costume. Mr Ebstone certainly seemed impressed!'

'Well, as Miss Waring caught your bouquet it might give him ideas.'

'Oh, no! I wanted to throw it to you but I couldn't see you in the crowd.'

'I was keeping well out of the way!'

As they talked, Iris chivvied Joanna into her travelling costume and pinned her hair into a soft coil that would not interfere with the set of her hat. 'Leave your hat for now,' she advised. 'You are in for a lot more hugs before you finally escape – with your husband!' she finished with a grin. Then the grin disappeared and her eyes filled with tears. 'I am going to miss you.' She threw her arm around Joanna's waist and buried her face against her shoulder.

Near to tears herself, Joanna returned the hug. 'I will come to see you as soon as we return, but you will be too busy being a school teacher to miss me for long.'

There was a knock on the door and the friends drew apart, both aware that they would never be so close again. 'Go on,' Iris urged. 'Max is waiting.'

There was another round of embraces and congratulations before Max and Joanna were finally alone, in a thankfully undecorated carriage, on the way to the docks.

Max flopped back in his seat opposite Joanna and ran a finger under his stiff collar. He was now more conventionally dressed but to Joanna's mind just as handsome. 'Thank goodness that is all over,' he said with a hearty puff of breath.

Even as the words left his mouth Max realised it was not the most romantic thing to say to a new bride. He looked across at Joanna, expecting to see hurt or annoyance but she answered him in the same vein. 'I now know how Iris feels – all those people staring and flattering.'

'The compliments were well deserved. You looked beautiful.'

Joanna blushed; it was so unlike Max to make personal comments. To hide her confusion she shrugged and said, 'That is just wedding magic. All brides are supposed to look beautiful.'

Max moved across to sit beside her and took her hand. 'Joanna, why do you always put yourself down?'

'Well, I am too big.' Her free hand waved vaguely in front of her body and her head as she added, 'And this,' to indicate her hair.

Max laughed and drew her into his arms. 'I thank God for it!'

197

When Joanna was released from a very thorough kiss, her eyes were shining. 'You like it – me?'

Max looked deep into her eyes. 'Joanna, I love you. You will always be beautiful to me.'

He had never used those words before, and Joanna had accepted that he only felt friendship together with a strong helping of lust. 'You really did want to marry me?' she asked in wonder. 'It was not just because…'

Max silenced her with another kiss and sat back to withdraw a folded document from his pocket. 'I have a present for you. I was going to wait for a more appropriate time but I think you should see it now.'

Joanna unfolded the paper, a copy of her father's will. She looked at Max with a frown as he urged her to read it through; it made Joanna and Max joint heirs and was dated 24th February, 1874.

'Mr Ebstone gave it to me at the reception. I was worried it would not arrive before the wedding. I told George to change his will before I left India but was not sure he would do so.'

'Thank you,' she said asked in a low voice. 'You are sure you don't mind?'

Max shook his head. 'As soon as I met you at the school, I was sure I wanted to marry you and it had nothing to do with your father.' He gave a rueful laugh. 'Is that what you have been thinking? That I was only marrying you for your inheritance?'

'Well, no – Papa had already given it to you. I just thought you were going along with his wishes.'

The carriage lurched over an uneven patch in the road and Max laughed again. 'What a time to declare myself! I will do better later.'

And he did. As they lay in the wide bed in the main cabin of the *Joanna*, Max left her in no doubt that he wanted her for herself.

Milton Keynes UK
Ingram Content Group UK Ltd.
UKHW010712050224
437294UK00018B/708